EARTH: GAME OF THE YEAR EDITION

Earth: Game of the Year Edition
Copyright © 2022 by Robert Carnevale
Maxwell Press

All rights reserved. Published by Maxwell Press. No part of this book may be reproduced or used in any manner without written permission of the copyright owner and publisher except for the use of brief quotations in a book review.

This is a work of fiction. Names, characters, places, and incidents either are the product of the author's imagination or are used fictitiously. Any resemblance to actual persons, living or dead, events, or locales is entirely coincidental.

Earth: Game of the Year Edition/Robert Carnevale–1st ed.
ISBN 978-1-7354910-0-4 (paperback)
ISBN 978-1-7354910-1-1 (ebook)

Cover by Breno Girafa
Imprint logo by Aishwarya Patwardhan

www.rcarnevale.com

EARTH: GAME OF THE YEAR EDITION

Robert Carnevale

CHAPTER 1

Bzzzt. Bzzzt. My phone's alarm clock reminds me I'm not dead yet, which really pisses me off. That little time-telling bomb by my bed needs to shut up and stop threatening me with a new day.

My body's inner systems stir to life. It's time. Wake up. Work. Eat. Sleep. Wake up. Work. Eat. Sleep. Wake up. Work. Eat. Sleep. These words aren't just the start of a bitchin' Daft Funk song—they are my life. Every day adheres to that four-step routine so rigidly that my biological clock is hardwired to make me piss at exactly 7:44 a.m. and resist the urge to jump in front of oncoming subway trains at precisely 5:25 p.m. Right now, it's time for me to complete the ten steps that stand between "wake up" and "work," starting with defusing the bomb by my bed.

Eyes fuzzy and head reeling, I whip a hand over to where said bomb should be resting on my nightstand, but my palm scrapes against the stand's wooden edge. *Fuck.* Fumbling around some more, I locate the chipped aluminum frame of my Kryocera Aqua Jive smartphone. It feels like forty bucks spent four years ago—not to be confused with my high school senior prom attire.

I kill the phone's backup alarm before it can go off thirty-six seconds from now, priming me for step two of my morning ritual wherein I take a full minute to languidly roll around in bed.

Step three: grab my Aqua Jive and cue up the music for step four. "O.H.H.A.T" by The Soup, to be precise. *Hell yeah. That's right. Oh shit. That's tight.* The fat beats and nonsensical lyrics flood my room. I flop out of bed and land on the floor, on my chest. The two twiggy soldiers I call arms assume their positions. Up. Down. Up. Down. Up. Down. My biceps may not be getting bigger, but you better believe they're getting stronger. Someone has to believe it, anyway.

Step five: put on some boxers, snatch the toothbrush, toothpaste, and room key off my dresser, then slip out of my cell—er, room—and walk down the hall. It's crowded. Human relations note to self: don't forget to wave at the impossibly sexy, hyper-masculine Scandinavian roommates who probably have cocks big enough to ski on. There's not an iota of ill will to be found on their Superman-esque faces as they smile at me with their perfect teeth and chiseled jawlines. I awkwardly half-smile at them in return, remaining cordial amid my rush to piss and brush my teeth.

Three and a half minutes later, I'm brushed, flushed, and back in my room. Inside my closet, there are eight shirts and four pairs of pants. My last laundry trip was four days ago, meaning all pants have been worn at least once. The white khakis look the least sweat-retentive, so I give 'em a sniff. Yeah, no one's going to vomit if I wear these today. I think.

No longer naked, I arrive at step six. I put my laptop in its carrying case, codenamed "Big Techy Man Purse,"—BTMP for short—and sling that sucker over my shoulder like I'm going to war.

Step seven: go to war. Go to work. I ditch my apartment complex, if it can even be called that, and grab a greasy egg sandwich from the nice Indian guy who runs the local Crunkin' Donuts. "Extra cheese, please," I tell him. I want it unhealthy. I want it perfect.

Step eight: head to the subway station. Every single slab of concrete in New York City smells like some variation of homeless person urine. I try to ignore it, like the US tries to ignore Europe. In both endeavors, success is limited. I force myself to be grateful for the ninety-two degrees Fahrenheit weather above ground, since it only gets worse beneath the pavement.

Down below, where the rats with suits and rodents with tails reside, I melt alive, watching my reflection whip past as a train pulls into the station. Wouldn't it be cool if I were a ghost and my reflection was the only way I could be seen? "Who's that moderately fit, somewhat short fella with the sexy brown eyes and stylin' facial hair?" they'd wonder. Alas, I exist and am tangible, and therefore no one thinks these things about me. God, I sound like someone from /r/niceguys.

Before I know it, I'm balls-deep in step nine. I've boarded the train and am riding it to Grand Central. There's a stunning brunette seated next to me, an absolute game-changer of a woman. You name it and she's got it: a tight blouse, big eyes, luscious lips—the whole nine yards. She glances at me. Here's my chance. *Don't blow it,* I tell myself. *Don't you dare. Don't you fucking dare*—aaaand she's already gone back to looking at her phone. I blew it.

Finally, I arrive at step ten: walk from Grand Central to work. I march across the city blocks, reach my building, and say good morning to the doorman. He doesn't respond. I take the elevator up to my floor, and within seconds a familiar set of glass office doors appears before my sweaty, tense frame.

I've arrived. I can now morph into my second form of the day: worker bee. Time to sting some fuckers and buzz myself 'til I shoot a hot load into the bathroom toilet during my lunch break.

I eyeball the office doors' security sensor and shove a hand in my pocket, fingering around for my keycard. I don't feel it. I proceed to turn my pocket inside out.

It's not there.

I check all my other pockets, then set my Big Techy Man Purse down to see if it somehow ended up in there. Twelve compartments and two Velcro pouches later, I'm still down one keycard. Past the glass doors, the receptionist is nowhere to be found. I look at the door buzzer. It's out of order.

Knock. Knock. Knock. No one's home, it seems. Maybe I'm receiving a sign from God telling me I'm not meant to be a "productive" member of society today. Maybe I should just go home while I still have a few hours of consciousness left in me, order some pizza, watch that one movie where Yennifer Lawngrin takes off her top, and—

"*How-dee, neighbor.*"

Ripping me out of my daydream like a middle-aged mom rips out coupons from the phone book, a dopey new face appears at my post beside the doors.

"Hello." I flash a split-second smile at the loud man who has materialized next to me. The act hurts my face muscles.

"I'm Jon, without the 'h.' A lotta fellas think there's one in there, but it's just not true, ha," shouts the human airhorn, laughing at his own declarative statement. Is... is this guy retarded? Why isn't he blinking? How did he get in the building?

"Nice to meet you," I blurt, even though it isn't.

"What do you do here?"

"I write. Sometimes I sit outside the front door to greet people."

"That's neat. Today's my first day here. I edit. That means I make things better, ha."

I'm baffled that the anthropomorphic opossum somehow scored a job at my place of employment, let alone an editorial position, given his inability to turn off caps lock in real life. As I stand slack-jawed in befuddlement, the look on my face likely providing the other half of the extra chromosome that exists between Jon and me, he realizes I was fucking around about the door thing.

"Oh, you're stuck? No worries," he says, slamming his very own keycard against the doors' sensor so that the glass barriers slide open.

"Thanks." I dash inside in hopes of outpacing him. Strangely, he doesn't follow me into the office lobby.

"I'm sure we'll be seeing more of each other soon," he shouts from the doorway, staring at me with those massive eyes of his as he waves goodbye.

I sure hope he's wrong. Readopting my introverted posture, I aim my eyes at the floor ahead of me and slide my hands into my pockets.

Wait. What the fuck? The tips of my fingers feel something hard and plastic—it's my keycard, resting snugly right where it should've been all along.

I spend the next two minutes splashing my face with cold water from the company kitchen sink before heading over to my quadrant of the office. Wouldn't you know, the gang's all here. Three civilians and five hostiles detected.

Civilians A through C, in order of decreasing obnoxiousness, are Stark, Amélie, and Laura. Starting with Joey Stark:

his name's basically the only neat thing about him because it's like that one superhero's, Brody Stark. He's the self-proclaimed "cool guy" of the office, the kind who'll point finger guns at you and go "bang-bang, shot ya," on a Friday afternoon right around the time you need an excuse to clock out and drink yourself into a coma. He handles product inventory.

Next up is Amélie. She has asthma, an accent, and a bad temper. She works in PR.

And then there's Laura. She's cute and personable. She codes. I like her.

As for the bad editorial hombres of the office, it's a rogues' gallery of all the usual East Coast suspects. In order of increasing threat level, the five hostiles are Pritchard, the Prog Triplets, and Tim.

Pritchard is the one who routinely claims that the hierarchical structures of crayfish society hold the secret to explaining men's dissatisfaction with life, despite my numerous protestations that crustaceans have nothing to do with it. Pritchard also has a nasty habit of rambling about how feminists who support Islam have a subconscious domination fetish. Strangely, that rant only crops up when someone in the office orders pita wraps and hummus for lunch.

The Prog Triplets are a bit more "problematic," to steal a word from their lexicon. Their names are Jamie, Alex, and Taylor. Two of them believe all men are rapists. Only one of them is female. They've been on the hunt for an elusive country-sized band of closeted Nazis for... well, I don't remember the exact date the last president was sworn in, but you get the idea.

And lastly, there's managing editor Tim Hobert. He once demanded we call him God, then backed his ass up when a Jewish guy from another department overheard him and filed a complaint with HR. Tim then claimed his order was just a joke. It wasn't.

On a perfect day, each and every one of these people, besides maybe Laura, fucks off and allows me to get my work done in peace.

"Oh. My. God. Did you see what *he* just chirped on Snitter?" Jamie says to no one in particular just a few yards away from me. Oh no. It looks like peace was too much to ask for. "The nerve of that fucker. Who does he think he is, talking down to minorities and unprivileged POCs like that?" She clutches her proverbial pearls as tightly as possible.

"I cannot believe that racist, bigoted xenophobe thinks he can get away with stuff like that," Alex squawks, in a valiant effort to out-caterwaul Jamie.

"If I could, I'd kill every single person who voted for him," Taylor coolly adds, prompting his two cohorts to smugly nod and golf clap their approval of his sentiment.

Please, God, just let me get to my desk before they can involve me. I'm feet from the fucking chair.

Pritchard tears himself away from his work to single-handedly take on the Prog Triplets. "Oh, please. The lot of you need to grow up. What the man said makes perfect sense! You Neo-Marxist troglodytes just can't fathom anything that doesn't immediately smother you with a sense of self-validation so vulgar it'd make your mothers blush."

With entropy rapidly increasing around me, I make a daring last-second dive toward my chair, desperate to avoid being sucked into my coworkers' vortex of insanity—

"What say you, Jack? Surely you agree with me," Pritchard says, his mud-coated words mucking up the path between me and office anonymity. *Sigh*.

Jamie huffs. "Why would he agree with you? He's not a fucking ableist, body-shaming asshole."

"Yeah, you fucking Nazi," Alex barks.

"What they said," Taylor calmly finishes.

"You wouldn't know what a Nazi was if one threw you headfirst into a pizza oven!" Pritchard shouts back. "Jack, what are your thoughts? Speak!"

"Yeah, Jack, what do *you* think?" The Prog Triplets say in unison.

I ease myself into my chair, sling my Big Techy Man Purse onto the ground, and open my laptop. My desk faces opposite all of them, which helps me avoid eye contact as I halfheartedly respond.

"I haven't seen the chirp yet."

"If you don't condemn it, you're part of the problem," Jamie hisses.

"Your intellectual nakedness would make Mussolini proud," Pritchard spits.

Their words hit my back like bricks: dull and hard, enough to annoy me, but not enough to cut through the armor I've developed in response to the six hundred other bricks they've already lobbed my way over the course of my employment here.

Just for kicks, I open my laptop's browser to see what the hell all the fuss is about. After logging onto Snitter and scrolling to the top of my feed, I see it: the chirp made at 9:02 a.m. by the guy running my country. It has thirty-four thousand rechirps.

Good morning, it reads.

That's why they're fighting? You've got to be kidding me.

But of course you're not, life. You're not kidding me. You never are. You just keep spawning morons who'll get riled up over anything. The most benign shit causes mass hysteria—

Then a new chirp from the leader of the free world appears, posted point-five seconds ago: *Mexicans probably refry their beans because they can't do it right the first time.*

My skin goes pale, and my pupils dilate. A storm is approaching.

I slam a hand on my desk's storage drawer, yank it open, pull out a pair of soundproof headphones, and snap them over my ears. In an instant, there is bliss.

I sense papers being thrown behind me. I feel the vibrations of screams. I smell differently scented sweats of infuriation. None of it matters, though, as "Clair de Moon" drowns out the rest of the world and takes me to a place where nothing can faze me besides the occasional unsolicited, subconsciously summoned image of a tall bridge. Ah, peace at last.

What's on the work agenda today, I wonder? I log in to my email to find out and immediately feel a piece of my soul wilt as I look at my inbox. I've been tasked with typing out five hundred nearly identical deals posts all advertising Shamazon's newest electric sprinkler. Great. I clench my jaw and let a few more soothing musical notes hit my ears before I start typing. Ten minutes later, I've successfully cleared my first deals post. Only 499 to go.

As I slog through the agonizing copywriting monotony like an American soldier traversing the rice paddies of Vietnam, a groove overcomes me—one I haven't felt in months. Why has it reappeared now? I don't know. All I know is there's a spark inside me, telling me I will survive. 498. 497. 494. 490. 480. 455. The completion pile grows larger and larger as I keep on typing, smashing each key with vigor. *Carpe diem,* I think to myself. *Carpe diem!*

"Jack, you deaf jagoff, it's time for the morning meeting." The words are spoken by none other than my editorial team's lord and savior Tim Hobert, who's shouting from the doorway of the conference room. The moment his voice overpowers my soundproof cans, the magical energy that powered me through the morning disappears. The electricity fizzles out. The fleeting sense of serenity that had somehow infiltrated me—the hollow shell of what used to be a happy, proud man—is once again nowhere to be found.

"Be there in a second," I respond, taking off my headphones.

Well over a second later, I slip into the nine-person conference room. Everyone's already there, including Stark, Amélie, and Laura. I take a seat alongside them in the back row.

"Great job last week, folks," Tim says, kicking off the meeting. "Ad revenue is up forty-three percent compared to the same time last month. That's a big get."

If I recall correctly, that's because half the staff writers were out sick the same time last month and we only produced half the amount of content. If anything, that ratio proves we've actually experienced a small net *decrease* in revenue.

"Quiet, Clancy Drew," Tim snaps, looking directly at me even though I haven't so much as opened my mouth. "Now, as I was saying: great work, everybody. Jamie, nice job on that Smashsung tablet review."

A slimy grin creeps across Jamie's face as her superiority complex kicks into overdrive.

"But try to wear less distracting clothing tomorrow."

Her smile evaporates.

"Alex and Taylor," Tim continues, focusing on his next two targets, "great team-up post on why the government's new tax policies are going to inflate phone bills."

The pair of Prog Triplets smile self-satisfactorily, but their joy is short-lived.

"Can we curb all the weird shit, though? I noticed a decrease in clicks from Midwestern readers on both your articles ever since you started inserting stuff about 'sounding' and 'bears' into your copy."

Tim takes a breath, sharpens his axe, then continues down the chopping block. "As for you, Pritchard: you nailed it with that rumor piece on Shamazon's impending worker strike. Just, uh, try not to call the workers 'the whiny, entitled proletariat' next time. I'm sure that claim has some merit, but the news photos of employees eating out of dumpsters aren't helping your case."

Pritchard scowls but doesn't say a word.

I bite my lip. Has Tim forgotten about me? Am I safe?

"And don't think I forgot about you, Jack. Don't worry, you won't have to go home tonight and jerk off all alone; I'll do the job for you right now. Decent work on last week's deals posts."

It's in the accuracy of his nightly forecast that his words' true cruelty lies. With that said, did... did he just give me a compliment?

He keeps looking at me. "I said decent work, not good. Don't think you're Will fuckin' Gates or something. Yeesh."

I still haven't opened my mouth once. Stark pats me on the shoulder. His hand reeks of cologne.

"As for you below-the-deck folks in the back..." Tim points at Laura, Amélie, and Stark. "If you do your jobs correctly, I forget you exist. Last week, I almost forgot. Keep it that way. Meeting adjourned."

Amélie mumbles something foul under her breath in French and Stark shrugs off Tim's insult, then they leave the room. Laura, however, isn't able to stride out of the meeting quite as effortlessly as her cohorts. On her way out the door, she catches my gaze. I manage a genuine, consoling smile. She returns it before slumping her shoulders, hugging her laptop, and scuttling away in defeat.

I'm pretty darn close to following suit, but just as I'm about to slip out of my chair and book it for the exit, Tim stops me.

"Hold on there, chief. We've got something to talk about."

Everyone but us has vacated the room. Before I can process what's going on and prepare my mental hazmat suit, Tim slams into one of the seats beside me.

"Do you know what today is?" he asks, his eyes locked with mine.

"Monday?"

"It's the day you stop looking like a sad sack of shit." He reaches into the back pocket of his jeans and pulls out a shiny silver smartphone, still covered in the manufacturer's screen protector.

"Is that..."

"The new Crapple 10. The latest, greatest phone in Western civilization. Not on the stands for another month. Ain't she a beaut?"

"Oh, wow. Um, I've been reading the rumor reports on it and yeah, it's a pretty phone... but what makes it better than the Crapple 9? Isn't the hardware almost identical—"

"Were you not listening to a word I just said?" Disgust drips from Tim's bourbon-drenched lips. "What makes it better than the Crapple 9? It's the 10. It's one number higher."

I never realized I was religious before now, but I feel Vishnu lending me his second pair of arms so I can double facepalm without having to openly insult my boss.

"Listen, Jack, someone's looking out for you. Sure as hell isn't me, but that's beside the point. A higher-up wants you to review the Crapple 10. It's a device that will make or break your career. You treat it right and you'll get a promotion.

Life will change for you. Senior staff writer status, cocaine, hookers—the whole shebang."

I take the phone from Tim's hand, give him a little nod, and stand up.

"Enjoy. Still can't believe someone upstairs wants you to review that gem. I even told them you think Crapples are worse than Smashsungs," Tim says, an air of wistful bitterness lazily drifting through the aural bile that is his voice.

"They are," I nonchalantly reply, sliding the conference room door open.

"Next, you're gonna tell me chemtrails aren't turning the frogs gay."

"They're not."

"Get the fuck out of my conference room."

I whip the door shut behind me and leave Tim to woefully ruminate over the gram of power he's just given me.

Once I've returned to my desk and slid into my seat, I set the new phone down. You know what? It does look pretty nice. It has a huge screen, a slick chrome finish, it's super skinny, and I'm the only one who has it. No one else is going to see it outside of their online pre-order cart for another month. Heh. That's pretty cool. Maybe the universe is actually throwing me a bone for once.

"Oh my God, the last giant panda just died in captivity," Jamie whispers loudly enough for everyone to hear. Immediately, her fellow triplets give their unsolicited takes.

"That's so sad."

"Yeah."

"What's for lunch today?"

"Burgers, I think."

"Delish!"

I die a little inside. Just as the universe giveth, the universe taketh away.

With nowhere else to turn my mental energies, I refocus on deals, deals, and more deals. I try to summon the cosmic juju that gave me the will to push forward earlier, but my call to the ether goes unanswered. 432... 431... 430... and, would you look at that, thirty minutes of my life have gone by. Joke's on you, life; taking time from me is like taking marked bills from the Federal Reserve.

Having reached a critical juncture of pure, unfiltered boredom, with my productivity at an all-day low, I prepare to throw in the towel. Thankfully, I'm distracted by a sharp vibration in my pocket. Funny, I don't recall being *that* excited by Yennifer Lawngrin's movies—oh, it's my personal phone. Not the fancy Crapple 10, but the Aqua Jive that does all the same shit for about eight hundred dollars less. And would you look at who's texting: Angela.

How's your day going? she asks.

I don't hesitate to respond. *Oddly.* Our exchanges always start in a similar fashion. She knows how it's going. She knows how it's been going. She knows how it will be going. She just pretends not to.

That's... good? Right? Odd is better than blah. How's the new city? How's the new job?

I freeze. After all, what can I tell her that she doesn't already know? *Eight million people are crammed together in the melting pot with me, and I've never felt more alone, Ange. I check my phone sixty-seven times a day and you're the only one who ever says 'hi.' My job is a stopgap. My boss wants me to drop dead just so he has something to wipe his shoes on. And maybe that'd give me more of a purpose than I have now.*

With these thoughts floating through my head, I reply: *The usual.*

It takes a few seconds for the little dots on the screen to start moving, signaling Angela's hard at work typing something. Does she have the answer? Something to explain why people work from dawn 'til dusk just to pay for a closet-sized space to live in? Why there are seven billion people alive when only a couple thousand global figureheads matter to anyone? Why the planet's dying, entire species are curling up and disappearing, and nobody cares?

She has only one thing to say: *Sorry to hear that :/*

I am too.

Why'd you text? I ask, hoping she has a news placebo for me to chew on so I don't have to resort to the Percocet in the office's medicinal cabinet. Who even put that there?

Well, that's the thing... it's not good. Do you want to talk later?

No, I shoot back. *Hit me with it.* The slow knife is always worse than the quick stab, after all. Not that I'd know; the worst knife wound I ever got was a nick on my thumb because I was too stupid to spread butter properly at the age of seven.

It's about Charley.

I realize that maybe she was right—maybe right now isn't the appropriate time or place. But now I'm spooked. So, since I can't change the time, I focus on finding a setting that's a little more accommodating. I pocket my phone, vacate my seat, take a brisk walk down the office's main hall, and slip inside the men's bathroom, claiming the handicap stall for myself since it's spacious and conceals its occupant from view. I close the toilet lid and sit on the edge. Only now do I take my phone back out.

About two weeks ago, he stopped using the litter box, and... and earlier in the week, when he and I were on the couch, I felt something—a lump. I should've told you sooner... but I know things have been rough. I didn't want to...

She stops typing for a moment. Then the bouncing dots reappear.

I got him an ultrasound. He has a "large, systemic carcinoma in his liver. The tumor is firm." The vet... she said the tumor is inoperable and chemo can't kill it.

I process just two more words before I can't read any further: "*put down.*" Breathing becomes impossible. I part my lips enough to let out a whimper, causing my tense jaw muscles to pop.

Angela types my name multiple times. When that fails to elicit a response, she tries calling. For the life of me, I can't put a finger on my phone.

After a few minutes of desperation, she gives up. *I'm sorry. I know it's the worst possible day to share such a thing, but I couldn't keep it from you any longer. You deserve to know.*

More silence passes. Her profile icon stays online as we explore the void together: the space in time where there is no feeling—only the asphyxiating objectivity of reality. And yet, the news is unreal. Absolutely, positively unreal. It can't not be.

Water drops hit my thumbs as I peer over my phone screen. The warm splashes snap me out of my daze, if only for a moment. And in that moment, I receive one last text from Angela before she goes offline.

If you want to talk later, we can. And if you want something nice after work, call me. I know it might not mean much to you now, but... happy birthday.

She's the only human being alive who remembered.

The bags under my eyes feel the hot sting of sorrow as more water trickles down my face. Every second's a fight to not let my pained, muffled noises escape the dingy stall I'm hidden in. Outside these walls, no one knows about Charley. No one cares.

Time passes, though how much of it I can't be sure. Seconds stretch on for minutes, minutes warp into hours, and hours turn into seconds. I stay here, paralyzed. Outside of my stall, there's not a person worth knowing. I know that as fact because, well, I know *them*. All of them. They'll rant about news stories, none of which have any relevance to any of their lives, and keep working while our corporation keeps making money and the sun keeps traveling overhead, and nothing will get better. Nothing ever does. Good things will just keep quietly disappearing, one at a time, until there are none left—like the last giant panda, God rest its soul.

I slowly detach from the toilet seat and brace myself against the cold tiles of the stall wall, eventually forcing my body to stand independently. Then I turn back toward the toilet, lift the lid, unzip my fly, and take a piss. It's about the only thing I can do, after all. It's the only thing I have control over.

I look down at the bowl and watch my hot, putrid stream poison the water within. As I see the waste and think about all that's wrong with everything—how we can only manufacture true joy in our minds, in our imaginations, in our movies and books and games—it hits me: What... what makes "here" real? If I can watch a movie and believe the CGI, who's to say "here" isn't fake? If I can choose to accept what's unreal, why should I have to accept what *is* real?

Though I can't prove it, in that moment—in less time than the split second it takes me to blink—I feel the burden of reality transform around me, and I swear my piss looks like a million little glimmering pixels.

CHAPTER 2

Only once my tear ducts shrivel up and I regain control of my quivering lips do I finally schlep out of the bathroom. I've forgotten to tuck my shirt back in, and there's probably toilet paper stuck to the bottom of my shoe or something, but I don't care. What does it matter? Even if I look like a complete asshole, it just means some extra abuse and derision will be slung my way today, all of which will be forgotten within twenty-four hours by the parties who doled it out. That's what tomorrow's for, after all. It's a reset—another clean slate to be beaten down by.

After a seemingly never-ending walk of shame back to my desk, I slide into my chair and prepare for more work. Deals. Deals. Deals. What's the *deal* with all these deals? Honestly, who buys all the shit I peddle, anyway? An eighty-dollar toaster with a custom slot for banana slices? A two-hundred-dollar wristwatch that does everything except tell time? A gold-fucking-plated dildo modelled after the sentient cucumber from the cartoon *Vegetable Stories*? Who. The fuck. Is buying these things?

"Well, I'll be damned—Shamazon is finally selling that tinfoil cell signal deflector armor at a twenty-percent discount!

Goodbye, mainstream media mind control. Hello, savings," Pritchard cheers behind me, serenading his own thrifty defiance of corporate America by voluntarily funding it with the very money he earns from toiling for it.

I pluck a pencil out of my desk's coffee mug and fidget with it. When is my lunch break, again? Oh. Wow. I was in that bathroom stall for a while. Looks like my lunch break came and went while I was sitting on a porcelain poop chute crying over losing the best family member I ever had. My stomach moans in dissatisfaction, reminding me that it's been hours since I ate anything. And yet, there's no time for food. I'm not allowed to get up from my seat, leave the building, and go buy a damn burrito from the food truck just across the street.

In my moment of hunger-induced agony, I hear it—the latest tantrum from the insufferable triplets, all of whom are stationed just a few feet outside my immediate haymaker-delivery range.

"Shamazon's so fucking evil," Jamie says.

I snap the pencil in my hands. "We're advertising for them," I snarl, spinning around in my chair to attack the lead hydra head.

"You're not listening! They're perpetuating socioeconomic imperialism by underpaying workers in underprivileged nations!"

"So you hate them because they're an abusive corporation that feeds off consumer laziness and complacency?"

"Yes, exactly!"

"And you realize they only have the market power they have because publications like ours keep shilling for them?"

"That's what I'm saying! It's sick! Someone needs to stop them!"

Everyone in a thirty-foot radius pauses their work to watch the unfolding shouting match.

"You know, that's great to hear, Jamie. I'm really, really glad you feel that way. Someone does need to stop them. Someone needs to stop spoon-feeding their shit to the masses. So in the interest of our shared goal: Are we going to *stop writing about them and actually stand for something, instead of selling our souls for some goddamn clicks on our stupid site?*" Spit flies out of my mouth as I savage the perky-titted piece of human detritus waxing poetic about human rights directly across from me.

The whole writing team waits for her response. Even the intern stationed way over in the corner of the office pauses his printer order to hear what comes next.

"... No," Jamie says. And yet, even though her sole word yields me a win, I don't taste the magic ingredient: shame. Shame in herself for being an oblivious tool. Shame in her work for being the facilitator of, in her own words, society's woes. Shame that her parents didn't use multiple forms of birth control.

Ugh, whatever. It's okay. I feel enough shame on her, and everyone else's, behalf to know it's time to call it in. It's my birthday, damn it, and I'm not going to spend it feeling sick to my stomach around people I hate. I can spend it the exact same way all by myself, thank you very much.

I grab my headphones, slam them inside my desk drawer, fold up my laptop, put it in its carrying case, and abandon my post, not looking back once at the band of idiots left in my wake as I exit the office.

Ten minutes later, I'm on a subway train, hitting up Angela.

I could really use that surprise now, I text. My message doesn't send. Realizing I'm underground and there's no cell reception, I quickly resend the message over Wi-Fi. She responds almost instantly.

Great. Are you on the 6 train?

Yes.

She sends me an address and tells me to get off the train in a few stops to collect my birthday gift. I don't know what it will be, but I thank her anyway.

I get off the subway and walk to the mysterious address. I must be headed toward a pretty fancy place, given the part of town I've wound up in. It's so kempt around here that I've yet to see a single roach on the sidewalks. Am I still in Manhattan?

Yes, I am. I'm reminded of that fact by the sight of a homeless man lying on his side, just across the street from where I'm walking. He's shaking... no, shivering, I think, even though it's baking hot outside. He's bundled in rags and a torn-up hoodie that's far too small for him. The parts of his clothing making contact with the sidewalk are wet, drenched in a mysterious yellow liquid that's pooling around his body. Is that—no, wait, there's a bottle of juice next to him. I think it's orange juice. Maybe. Hopefully.

After suppressing my humanity by reminding myself that it's a dog-eat-dog world, I find the strength to move past the man without offering so much as a helpful smile. It's "me" time right now. I'm going to go to the address listed on my phone and enjoy whatever's waiting for me. No homeless person is going to stand in the way of the one thing I have to look forward to.

I arrive at the address and almost smile. Almost. Angela's brought me to an éclair shop. It's the kind of place so fancy that its overhead sign spells "shop" with an extra "pe" at the end.

After entering the shoppe and looking at Angela's texted instructions, I do as I'm told and tell the girl at the register my name. She's clearly from the city, but still manages the most convincing Parisian accent I've ever heard a Brooklynite pull off.

"Jacques," she repeats, transforming me into a bonafide Frenchman for a whole second. She then disappears inside the kitchen area, leaving me to stand idly by the counter, surrounded by shelves of stupidly expensive baked goods. A few moments later, she reappears with a paper bag.

"Pour vous," she says, really laying it on thick as she hands me my treats.

"Merci," I respond, my accent just as bad as it was in my third-grade foreign language class. She politely giggles then gives me a little wave, courteously hinting for me to get lost unless I plan to buy additional food. I choose to get lost.

Filtering back onto the hard, mean streets of the Big Apple, I open up my little bag as I make my way to the subway. My haul is bountiful: it looks like Ange ordered me two absurdly gourmet éclairs. Score.

I pick one up and take a bite. Its chocolate glaze and lemon cream filling overwhelm my mouth with a sugary bliss I haven't experienced in ages. Come hither, cavities, for I have a date with dough-based joy.

As I chew my way to the halfway point of the first éclair, a thought hits me: What if I give the second pastry to that homeless fella I saw earlier? Sure, it wouldn't be doing his teeth any favors, but then again, I doubt he's been doing them any favors either. And besides, what's more important: a minor health concern, or making someone's day a bit better? I say the latter. Yeah, let's do it. Let's be the change we want to see, and all that good shit.

Coming up on the spot where I initially passed by the rag-clad man, I notice something that wasn't there before: an ambulance.

I venture closer and see the spot where the man had been. All that's left is a pool of yellow liquid.

My stomach locks up and the tastes in my mouth sour. What happened? I'd only been gone for ten minutes. What could've happened in just ten minutes? He... I was going to make his day. I was going to fix something.

I consider approaching the medic who's just closed the driver seat door of the ambulance and turned on the vehicle's engine, but for whatever reason, I can't compel myself to cross the street and get his attention. My eyes tear up for the second time today as the ambulance drives away.

The only thing left at the scene is the puddle the homeless man had been lying in as he shivered and waited to die. Is *that* what happened to him? I won't know. I didn't help when it mattered. I don't deserve to find out.

I start to walk again, though now I'm not sure where I'm headed. Devoid of feeling, I put one foot in front of the other, clutching my now-unwanted, half-eaten birthday treat in one hand while I hold the bag with the second pastry in the other.

Why am I here? I don't even get to enjoy the single day of the year that's supposed to cheer me up. I can't savor one little present without the world reminding me that it's evil and I'm evil by association. I didn't save the man. I didn't save Charley. And for the better part of twenty-one years, I haven't saved myself.

What will it take, world, for you to stop punishing me? I want it to stop. I don't want my shitty job, or my cardboard box of an apartment, or the bed I sleep in alone. I don't want any of it. I just want the big game to be over with. I hate it. I hate it so much.

That's when it strikes me: I've known the solution to my troubles all along. I've thought about it in the past, sure, but has it ever made sense? Not like it has today. The only way to escape the game is to stop playing. It's so simple. I pull out my phone and look up the last address I'll ever need, finding a subway route that'll get me there in thirty minutes or less.

It's almost over, Jack. You can still turn your birthday around. You can end the day on your own terms.

CHAPTER 3

The bus chugged through the suburban neighborhood with haste, only slowing once its driver spotted the modest two-story house marked on his drop-off route. He put his boot down and pumped the brakes, causing the yellow, rectangular box to lose all forward momentum and enter an idle hover alongside the home's driveway. A pair of boys situated behind the driver prepared to vacate their seats.

"Thanks for speeding things up today," the lankier of the two boys said, slinging the lone strap of his backpack over his shoulder before bouncing down the vehicle's boarding steps.

"Yes, thank you! And Rax, please slow down," Barry huffed. After squeezing out of his seat, the wider boy shuffled behind his string-bean schoolmate.

The door hatches of the bus slid open. "No more special requests," the driver told the pair, his tone gruff but smile visible from beneath the fringes of his big, bushy mustache.

The boys jumped off the levitating vehicle in quick succession, scurrying across the lawn in a race to see who could reach Rax's front door first. It wasn't much of a contest, really, but the faster boy gave his friend a chance at winning nonetheless.

"We're home," Rax announced as he and Barry burst through the door.

"Hi, Mrs. Teelum," Barry chimed in.

"Welcome back, you two! What's the occasion? Did something big happen at school today?" Rax's mother asked, eyeballing the two bolts of adolescent electricity who'd just zapped into her home.

"No, but Barry and I need to check something on my computer," Rax said. Without another word, the boys yanked off their shoes then shot up the stairwell leading to Rax's bedroom.

"Oh, okay... well, I'll bring up some raspberry tea for you two." The mother wandered off to the kitchen in search of the one thing she still knew for certain her son liked. *He's growing up so fast*, she thought to herself, combing the cupboards for fruity tea bags.

After clearing the stairs in record time, the boys charged inside Rax's room. They closed the door behind them, threw their backpacks on the ground, and wasted no time in gearing up for the main event.

"PC, on," Rax ordered, prompting a holographic boot-up screen to appear in the center of his room, its projection emitting from the desktop across the floor.

Barry ogled the virtual monitor spread across the air in front of his face. "I still can't convince my mom to buy me one of these."

"Well, don't rely on your mom, then, dude." Rax grabbed the wireless keyboard off his bed and set it beside his gaming chair, which he then sank into. "I could always use help leveling up burner accounts on *Galaxies of War*."

"You know I'm cagey about that kind of stuff... developers are so strict these days. What if they catch you? They'll kill those accounts. Then you won't have anything to sell."

"Eh, they won't do squat. Devs never mess with me. I'm a paying customer."

"Speaking of paying," Barry said, noticing the PC's game client had booted up, "did that hack file you bought actually work? Are you logged in yet? Can you see?"

"Just give it a second, 'kay? It's still loading," Rax replied, waving his hand through the air to move his holographic screen's cursor. "There we go... *Earth*." He pointed his index finger to check off the boxes on the game's launch menu. "Yes, I'd like to sideload it on Penguin OS. Yes, I will adhere to the end-user license agreement. Yes, I'd like to continue my saved game."

After he gave the verbal commands and ticked the boxes, *Earth* began booting his save file. Pixel by pixel, a sprawling virtual world came to life in front of the boys, filling Rax's bedroom with skyscrapers, parks, and rivers.

"The texture pop-in is kind of lame," Barry commented, wondering if the graphical issue was a byproduct of the recent developer patch Rax had been bellyaching about on the way home.

"It is what it is—wait."

"What's up? Did the hack work?"

"No." Though the game's user interface was a bit complicated, Rax could immediately tell something was wrong. His avatar was in an even worse position than yesterday. "The hack didn't do anything. It didn't fix the problem," he whined, looking at the avatar information spreadsheet in the corner of the screen. "Happiness is down fifty-three percent from yesterday, civilian playfulness is nonexistent, mental stability is dropping off a cliff, and even my account anniversary bonus didn't boost his stats. The game's RNG is screwing me!"

"Guess that hack wasn't worth the money..." Barry said from his spot atop Rax's bed, looking glumly at the numbers on his friend's screen.

"Maybe the hack didn't activate properly," Rax mumbled, grabbing his keyboard. He alt-tabbed out of the game and dug through its file directory until he arrived at the folder where he'd placed the hack's executable. He noticed a .txt file had spawned next to it—a .txt file created by the game's anti-cheat system, timestamped just sixty seconds ago. "Looks like Beluga Anti-Cheat caught me. These always-online software scans for single-player games are horseshit, man."

Rax's complaint was loud enough for his mother to hear. "Language!" she said from downstairs, prompting both boys to apologize before returning their attention to the game's files.

"What are you going to do?" Barry asked.

"If I don't get the hack running, I'm going to lose my longest-running save file's avatar. You saw his stats—something's wrong, and he's toast if I don't find a way to fix him in the next few minutes. So I'm going to force the game offline, disable the anti-cheat files, and manually activate that hack."

"But if you disable the anti-cheat, won't the developers nuke your account?"

"Not if they don't find out. I'll only use the hack offline. I'll boost my avatar with it, and the achievements I gain offline will still carry over to my public gamer profile... I think. Besides, if I lose my current avatar, I'm not going to want to play the game ever again anyway, so I have to try. All right?"

With the irreversible course of action set, Barry watched as Rax cracked his knuckles, hunched over his keyboard, and got to work.

CHAPTER 4

A railing presses against my waist as I look down at the East River. Below me, its water carries the stench of fish, salt, and pollution. I used to jog here on weekends. I used to like the bridge I stand on.

The setting sun overhead reminds me now is not the time to get sentimental or distracted. But just as I'm about to refocus, something rumbles in my pants pocket. It's my Aqua Jive—the phone's battery is dead. *At least I have the Crapple 10*, I think to myself with a chuckle, knowing I could have a magic key to the city in my pants right now and it still wouldn't change my course of action. You win, Earth. You beat me. Jack is signing off.

I reach my first leg over the railing and onto the beam that makes up the outer edge of the bridge. Beyond that strip of steel, there's nothing but air and water. The evening breeze sweeps against my ankles as I position both feet on the beam, my entire person now officially on the wrong side of the bridge's safety railing.

Far below my feet, tiny waves crash against each other. What will it feel like to hit the surface of the river at full force? Will it hurt, or will it paralyze and numb me? Will I scream when the water smashes against my body, or will I be a frozen statue, broken on contact and disposed of shortly thereafter, carried downstream without so much as a peep of protest?

I stop thinking about it. It makes no difference how the process will feel when all is said and done. I've felt enough. There's no way one last new feeling will radically alter me.

I'll miss you, Charley, I think to myself, my face motionless and expressionless as I conjure up the names that matter most to me. *I'll miss you, Ange. I'll miss you, me.*

My foot inches toward the edge. I force the tip of my shoe over the side and lean forward until a quarter of my body weight is officially dangling in midair. I keep going until I feel it—the tipping point. I'm about to fall over.

Then my phone rings. The wrong phone.

It's not my Aqua Jive, which died a few minutes ago, even though that's the only phone I have with any contacts in it. Hell, it's the only phone that anyone even has the number for.

I carefully bring my foot back onto the beam, not wanting to go for my last swim with any lingering mysteries or questions on my mind. Once I'm safely balanced, I slide out my Aqua Jive. Just as I thought, it's still dead. That means the ring must've come from the Crapple 10. But how?

I dig into my other pocket and procure the chrome handset. Its screen is lit up, claiming I have one new message. My eyebrow arches, my finger swipes, and the phone unlocks. Who could have my new number? When I was given the phone, the SIM card had just been registered. So who would know how to contact me on the device?

I look at the message on the screen, hoping for some indication of who's on the other end as well as a clue as to who they're trying to reach. There's no way in hell they're trying to get in touch with me, that's for sure.

Are you still there? the message asks. There's no sender ID or phone number shown. The text is completely anonymous.

I weigh my choices. The first option is obvious: I could respond. Alternatively, I could pocket the phone and resume today's regularly scheduled program. The message I received might just have been spam, since Crapple sells all its users' phone numbers to telemarketers and robo-texters. Yeah, that's probably what it was. Or maybe it was just a wrong number. Either way, it wasn't for me. No messages ever are.

As I go to put the phone in my rear pocket, it vibrates again. There's another new message.

Don't do it, it reads. If I was just a smidgen more stupid than I already am, I'd almost think whoever's messaging the phone is trying to convince me not to jump. That's wishful thinking, though. I know better.

Ring-ring, the phone chimes, pausing my next attempt at pocketing the device once and for all. For God's sake, can't whoever is messaging me just fuck off and let me kill myself?

The latest text from the anonymous suicide prevention hotline wannabe reads: *Look, if you jump, I can't give you your birthday present, aight?*

"Aight?" Who says "aight?"

No, Anon from the text message, not "aight," I think to myself. *I don't care about your present.*

Then, at the top of the Crapple 10's screen, I get a notification that thirty-thousand dollars have just been transferred into my PayFriend account.

Okay. Um. On second thought, maybe what's going on is aight.

Did you receive it? the anonymous texter asks.

Against my better judgment, I place my thumbs on the phone's screen. *The money?* I respond.

Anon sends me a new message. *Yes, the premium currency pack.*

I don't know what the fuck the person's talking about, but I just received enough cash to quit my job and take a few months off. And since time is the one true premium currency, I'll roll with whatever mumbo jumbo my voiceless benefactor is spouting.

I prepare to reply to Anon, though I pause when I notice a seagull flying by. It swoops low and takes a massive shit right above me. I reflexively attempt to dodge the incoming projectile. As soon as I shimmy my body outside the poop's blast radius, I realize I'm about to stumble off the steel I've been carefully balancing on. Thankfully, without dropping the phone or sending myself off the side of the bridge, I manage to rebalance myself. The seagull's blobby white excrement whips past me and slams into the cold, deep body of water below. Maybe it's time for me to move somewhere less dangerous.

After struggling to haul my ass over the railing that got me to the beam in the first place, I land back on the civilian walkway. Now safe from accidentally tumbling into the river, I resume my back-and-forth with the mysterious gift-giver.

Dude? Anon asks, following up the question with several separate messages composed solely of question marks.

Just getting into a better position, I say as I travel along the bridge in search of a bench. One crops up fairly quickly.

KK, muchacho, Anon replies.

I sit down and think about where to steer the conversation. Then it hits me: I still don't know how the person is reaching me via the Crapple 10. The whole thing feels like some weird, reversed version of that old Nigerian Prince email scam where I'm getting duped into accepting money instead of giving it up. I want answers.

All right, I'm sitting down now. You wanna tell me how you got my number?

The conversation stalls for a moment. A few seconds pass before a message hits my screen.

You wanna tell me how you got that phone?

Wait, what? What is Anon insinuating?

None of your business, I respond.

Ah, hahaha, so you don't know how you got the phone.

Who are you? I shoot back.

The question isn't who am I...

I squint at the screen, trying to wrap my brain around the ambiguous text until a new message appears beneath it.

It's "how am I." How am I going to help you? And the answer is: gladly.

CHAPTER 5

Wake up. Work. Eat. Sleep. Wake up. Work. Eat. Sleep. Wake up. Work. Eat. Sleep. These words aren't just the start of a bitchin' Daft Funk song—they are my life. Every day adheres to the four-step routine so rigidly that my biological clock is hardwired to make me piss at exactly 7:44 a.m. and resist the urge to jump in front of oncoming subway trains at precisely 5:25 p.m. Right now, it's time for me to complete the ten steps that stand between "wake up" and "work," starting with—

Ring-ring.

Actually, something tells me today's going to be different.

I reach for the Crapple 10 and check the time, then compare it against my Aqua Jive. The latter phone's alarm isn't set to go off for another three minutes.

Wakey wakey, friendo. It's Anon, sharing a good morning greeting with me via text.

I let out a yawn. *Why are you up so early? What do you want?* I send the response, yawn again, and roll out of my blanket.

Who said it's early where I am?

I'm not quite conscious enough yet for Anon's word games, so I take a note from my online dating days and ask a simple question.

Okay, buddy, enough beating around the bush. ASL?

ASL stands for age, sex, and location. Hopefully the mysterious texter who's capable of wiring thirty-thousand dollars on a whim doesn't have issues with telling me some basics about himself... or herself.

Answers 4 u, Anon replies. *Age: not your business. Sex: haha. Location: not a priority right now, Mr. FBI.*

I put on my imaginary deerstalker and do a little deductive reasoning. Anon's understanding of American English slang is good, so they must be based somewhere in the US. As for their age, I can only assume they're young, considering their response to the word "sex."

At least give me a pronoun or something, I request, lazily picking my nose as I swing my legs off the bed and onto the floor.

What? I'm a dude, dude. Shouldn't you be getting dressed?

You just gave me thirty-thousand dollars. Why would I go to work, I respond. I then set down the Crapple 10, grab my Aqua Jive, and deactivate its alarms exactly thirty-six seconds before the first of them can go off.

Standing beside my bed, I reach toward the ceiling and stretch my arms as high as they'll go. For the first time in a while, I feel relaxed. Truly relaxed. Yes, there's a real harmony in my life right n—

You're going to work. Chop chop, Anon declares, his order appearing dead-center on my Crapple's vibrating screen.

Why? I text. Anon has no say in the matter. Screw him.

I'll yank the thirty-thousand smackeroos back if you don't get your ass in some jeans right now, young man.

Pfft, yeah right. You can't do that. It's in my PayFriend account now. No take-backs.

One second later I get a notification. Fifty dollars have just been removed from my PayFriend account. What. The. Fuck.

What, I text. *Is... is my hand shaking?*

Say "what" again, I dare you. I double dare you, Anon replies, before sending a slightly less horrifying follow-up. *Just kidding :P Look, I need you to go to work as usual, k? I promise, everything will work out real good if you play nice for a bit. I'm here to help you.*

Okay, phone boy with unlimited access to my online finances. I'll play along. For now.

I get dressed, grab my toothbrushing essentials, and head for the bathroom. The morning routine is a little out of order thus far, but that's the least of my worries.

After taking a piss, I head over to the bathroom's row of sinks and turn on the one farthest from the toilets. Once my hands are washed, I pull the toothbrush and toothpaste tube out of my pocket and prepare to clean my teeth. But just as I stick the brush in my mouth, something unusual happens.

"Hey... Jack, right?" The words come from the mouth of a hunky, blonde-haired, blue-eyed Scandinavian fellow. He struts over to the sink beside me carrying a shaving kit. I recognize him; he's from the room down the hall. Except for—shit! He's never introduced himself or told me his name. And I can't admit that I don't know it...

"Oh, hey, Morgan," I respond.

Morgan? What the fuck was I thinking? That's a girl's name!

"I am surprised! I did not think you knew my name," he says, chuckling.

I narrow my eyes for a second, suspicious that there's something magical in my toothpaste. "What's, er, going on?" I try not to let foamy spit fall out of my mouth as I talk while brushing.

"The fellows and I were thinking of going to a club tomorrow night, and we have seen you around the halls lately. You do not talk much! Why don't you join us? We can all get to know each other," he says. His invitation reminds me that I live in a glorified frat house. Come for the semi-affordable rent, stay for the European clubbing invites.

On the one hand, I hate the kind of people who go clubbing and I'm not a big fan of large social events in general. On the other... something feels different today. And it's the first time Morgan's invited me to something in all the weeks I've been here even though we've seen each other in the halls at least a dozen times before. Ah, fuck it.

"Sure, I'm in." I shoot him a thumbs-up with my free hand. He gives me a thumbs-up in return and begins shaving.

Huh, so that's what socialization feels like. I'd almost forgotten.

Once my teeth feel slick, scrubbed, and ready to fend off a day's worth of junk food, I abandon the sink and head back down the hall toward my bedroom. Inside, I see there's a new message on my Crapple.

Do you even like clubs? it reads. Excuse me?

How'd you know about that? I respond. Heck, now that I think about it... how did Anon know what I was doing yesterday? Sure, maybe he has GPS info on me because of whatever weird link he has to my phone, but how did he know I was going to jump? These are a few of the questions I should've asked last night instead of passing out practically the second I got home. Shit.

I am all-seeing and all-hearing, Anon texts. *And good save with the name... you're not usually that lucky, are you?*

Clearly he's not just connected to my phone if he's referencing conversations that took place far away from it.

I peek out my bedroom window. No one's looking back at me... but that doesn't mean anything. Maybe he has a telescope somewhere. Or a drone. Or he bugged a piece of my clothing at some point. Or all three! Oh shit, is he an undercover FBI agent? Why'd he mention the FBI earlier? Was that some sort of fourth-dimensional chess move to make me think he *wasn't* with the FBI?

I don't know who the fuck you are but I didn't do anything, I frantically type. *Take your money back. Take it all. I've never even gotten detention, okay? No way in hell am I going to jail.*

After smashing the send button, I draw my window blinds shut and search my room for bugs. I lift up my bed's mattress, check under the dresser, feel the sides of my desk—no luck. And those are all the places bugs are usually planted... in spy movies...

I rip my clothes off and examine every article for pin-sized listening devices. From my dress shirt's front pocket to the inside of my boxers, there's nothing suspicious to be found.

Is—is it getting hot in here? Why is there less oxygen in my room than there was thirty seconds ago? I think I need the fetal position... I need security...

Ring-ring.

Oh fuck, now's probably the part where I find out those thirty-thousand dollars are part of a cartel's money laundering ring and I'm on the hook. With the last ounce of bravery I have left in my body, I pick up my Crapple 10 to read the latest message.

Jesus Christ, buddy, Anon says, as though I'm overreacting by rocking back and forth in the nude on my bed with the window blinds shut. Who the fuck is he to judge?

Get it together, he continues. *I can't see or hear everything you do. I just get indicators. Think of me like a guardian angel, all right? Like, I can tell you're naked right now, but I can't actually see it—a good thing for both of us, I know.*

I can't tell if his sass is alleviating the tension or making it worse. I feel lightheaded... hey, maybe I'll pass out. I'd like that right now. Especially since the Crapple 10 is ringing again.

If your phone ever gets linked to any criminal stuff, I take full responsibility, aight? I'm just someone who wants to help you out. I take all the blame and all the credit. K? Can we get the day moving again?

I take a deep breath and assess the situation. His little note about "assuming all responsibility" probably won't hold up in court, so he likely has no incentive to do right by me. However, he just watched a naked man have a panic attack and is still keen on "helping out," which ain't nothing.

...

Actually, that seems like a scary indicator of the type of guy I'm dealing with. But for now... whatever. Let's see where things go.

Don't pull any funny shit, I text.

Wouldn't dream of it.

Once we've reached a mutual understanding, I put my clothes back on, slam my laptop into my BTMP, and get on with my day.

My first stop is, as usual, Crunkin' Donuts. The line moves surprisingly quickly today and there isn't a single person who dawdles over whether they want extra caramel syrup or decaf instead of regular. At the current rate, I might actually get to work early.

When I reach the register, the gentleman behind the counter tells me I'm the hundredth customer he's had today, and as a reward, I'm receiving a fifty-dollar gift card, a free egg sandwich, and a free coffee. Whoa.

As if on cue, my Crapple 10 vibrates in my pocket and—surprise—there's a text from Anon.

There are your fifty doubloons back, matey.

All right, buddy. Maybe I don't know who you are, or how you do what you do, but I'll keep playing ball. Especially if the sandwiches keep being so, *so* good. *Mmm*. The cooks even added extra cheddar without me having to ask. Those beautiful bastards.

A few minutes later I arrive at the subway station and notice that, for the first time all summer long, its fan system is actually working. There's cold air. Everyone around me is just as baffled, but not a soul complains. The temperature is great. Maybe we won't all reek of sweat and shit by the time we get off the train.

Speaking of the train, it arrives not even a second behind schedule. I step inside one of its cars and, wouldn't you know, there's a seat available, right next to... wait, is that the girl from yesterday's ride? The one I blew my chance to talk to?

I quietly sit down next to her, not entirely sure if it's the same person. Unfortunately, Big Techy Man Purse lives up to its name and nudges her, because that is what bulky satchels do.

"Sorry," I say, inching my laptop bag away from her long, slender, pantyhose-clad legs.

"Oh, it's fine," she replies. A few seconds pass. "Hey, didn't we see each other on the train yesterday?"

Shit, here it comes. In T-minus two seconds she's going to ask why I'd been staring at her blouse on our last ride together.

She clears her throat. "Why didn't you say hello?"

Wait—she's not calling me a creep. In fact, it sounds like she wants to have a normal conversation. *Is this an invitation?* My eyes light up and a bell rings inside my head, alerting me that class has started and I can't afford to flunk the surprise retest.

"Um... I don't know. You seemed busy on your phone and I didn't want to interrupt," I stammer. Her lip curls so slightly that the motion is barely perceptible to the human eye, but I get the message: she's unimpressed. All right, Jack, let's try a new approach. "Okay, you caught me. I thought you had a nice top and a pretty face to match, and I didn't know what to say to get your attention without annoying you."

"Why not just say that?" She smiles. "I was checking you out too."

"Oh yeah? Why didn't *you* say hello, then?"

"Ha. You and I both know that's not how it works. The guy says 'hi,' and the girl either says 'get lost' or has a nice chat like the one we're having."

Internally, I grate my teeth. *Listen, lady, it doesn't have to be that way, and the only reason it is is because women like you enjoy making things difficult.* I don't say that. Instead, I keep my head in the game.

"Well, now that you've confirmed it's a nice chat, let me introduce myself: I'm Jack."

"I'm Blaire." She glances out the window. "Drat. It's about to be my stop."

As she speaks, I slip a hand inside my laptop bag's front pocket and pull out a pen.

"What's that for?" she asks.

"For you to write your phone number with so I can call you later." I give her my hand to write on. I'm milking the morning's "good vibes" for everything they're worth.

"Low on scrap paper? Clever." She scribbles her number onto my skin before standing up and handing me the pen. "Ciao, Jack."

The moment she leaves the train, I transfer her number to my Aqua Jive and Crapple 10. As I do so, people exit and board around me, and a man sits where Blaire just was—the last man I'd expect to see at the current stop, in my car.

"How-dee, neighbor."

At least he's learned to use his indoor voice. Kind of.

"Oh, uh... hi, Jon. Fancy seeing you here."

"A subway a day keeps the social anxiety away, is what I always say!"

Um, sure. Whatever floats your boat, I think to myself as the train rushes toward its next stop. I pull out my Crapple, hoping Jon will take a hint. He doesn't.

"So. How have you been lately?" he asks, eyeballing my phone.

"You know what... I've been good. Surprisingly good. Better than usual."

"That's great to hear, friend." He looks at the approaching stop and stands up.

"Wait, aren't you getting off at Grand Central with me? It'd be a hell of a walk to the office from here."

"Oh. No. Not today. I'm working remotely today," he replies, failing to make eye contact as he gets up to leave. His tone loses its amicable nature. I don't inquire further. He gets off the train as soon as the doors open, leaving me to carry on with my day.

Fifteen minutes later, I'm at my office building. For the first time in ages, the doorman greets me on my way in. And when I reach my company's lobby, I'm met with an even better surprise: the sound of silence. Have I gone deaf or is everyone actually quietly doing their work for once?

As I approach my desk, I discover that yes, in fact, my ears did not deceive me. The Prog Triplets aren't screeching about getting someone fired from their job for wrongthink on Snitter. Pritchard isn't rambling about the latest BrightBun article claiming we need more drone strikes to win the "War on Christmas." No one's saying a word; they're all just working. True bliss.

Thanks to the impossibly tranquil work environment, the day moves quickly. It feels like only seconds after I've sat down to begin churning through my pile of deals posts that Tim calls everyone in for the morning meeting. It's ten o'clock already? Nice.

Once everyone's in the room, our managing editor kicks things off. "Folks, let's get right to it. Jamie, great work on your eco-friendly electronics feature. The planet thanks you," he says.

She beams with pride. And why shouldn't she? It was a good feature with a great message and solid advice. Tim seems to agree and is about to move on, until a surprise thought bubble appears over his head.

"Also, what's the deal with that outfit? I said 'wear less revealing clothing,' not 'apply to be a nun.' Now there's no reason to call you into my office just to see you walk out."

Damn it, Tim.

"Anyway, moving on," he continues, giving his next targets a nasty look. "Alex. Taylor. Sloppy job updating that tax policy piece. Fix it. And Pritchard, about your review of the Omegi earbuds: we can't afford to keep calling every product made in China a 'communist propaganda tool.' If you want to voice those kinds of takes, go get a job in journalism."

By now, everyone's grumbling. It looks like it's my turn to get my ass put on the hot seat.

"As for you, Jack..."

He looks up from his notepad, causing us both to freeze. Tim and I realize there's a cosmic disturbance inside the room we occupy and it has to do with the fabrics draped across our chests. We're wearing the same shirt. But... but how is that possible? Mine's from France!

"Well then. If imitation is flattery, I should probably be busting my load all over the table, shouldn't I?" he says.

"Listen, Tim, we're not wearing the same shirt. It's not possible."

"You're right, it can't be the same shirt if it looks so much better on me."

Okay, asshole, the kiddy gloves are coming off.

"Check the tag," I say, looking at mine before revealing my shirt's brand to my coworkers. The materially obsessed fuckers let out a quiet, collective gasp. Looks like I'm high fashion, bitch.

"Well, mine's Mango Republic..." Tim huffs, looking at his own tag.

"Yeah, yeah, Dominican Republic, whatever you say." I lean forward in my seat, all but daring him to take a swing at me. He backs off. In that magical moment, as I hound my boss for a cheap thrill and fail to give one fuck about job security, someone chuckles. Over my shoulder, I spot Laura covering her mouth. Score one for Jack.

From there, my work hours fly by. At lunchtime, the lady manning the food truck across the street gives me free sauce with my burrito, and when I return to the office I'm told that Tim took off early for the day. Armed with good news and a greasy burrito, I plow through my remaining assignments and before I know it, it's time to punch out. How on Earth can the day get any better?

Ring-ring.

I pull out the Crapple.

Not a bad day, huh? Anon says.

I can't imagine it having been sweeter, I respond.

Well, I can. Let's turn things up a notch and try something. I'm gonna need you to get a Bluetooth earbud, pronto.

Huh. Well, why the hell not. In for a penny, in for a pound.

CHAPTER 6

"Is... is it working? Hello?" I say as I finick with the Bluetooth settings on the Crapple 10 in the middle of a public park. I'm here because Anon insisted that I set up my new earbud right away, and the park happened to be the closest place to sit down after I bought the gadget at Proud Purchase. I've chosen a secluded seat by a shady tree, so hopefully people steer clear of me while I talk to myself and try to get the damn bud to function.

"Hello?" I repeat, testing once again for audio feedback. The phone says the earbud is synced, so I don't know what the problem is. Fuck Bluetooth, man. And, while I'm on the topic, why does Bluetooth technology have such a stupid name? Ugh, whatever. It looks like I'm out of time to test my new toy; there's an incoming call on my phone's screen. The caller... it's Anon. Am I really about to answer?

For the free breakfasts, I think to myself before spending my risky tap of the day on the "accept call" button.

"Yes?" My voice is quiet. Have I just roped myself into a sting operation? Is the call being traced? I bet a SWAT team is about to leap out of the nearby bushes and beat the shit out of me. Maybe I'm being paranoid, but I don't think those squirrels by my feet are acting alone.

There's no sound for ten straight seconds. Then there's static. Is someone actually on the line? I hold my breath in anticipation until finally, at long last, words are spoken.

"Bro, what kind of hello is that?" says a semi-squeaky voice that sounds like it's about midway through puberty. What the fuck? *A child* is my secret Illuminati contact?

"Listen, kid, I'll hang up if you want." I relax my muscles, realizing I'm talking with a stalker whose balls have yet to drop. He should be easy to handle. I'll tell him I'm tracing the call and will rat him out to his parents if he doesn't leave me alone. That is, after I ask him where those thirty-thousand dollars came from... wait, maybe I don't want to talk to his parents.

"Stay on the line!" he says.

"I'll stay on the line if you give me one good reason why I'm having an anonymous call with a minor who claims to have seen me naked." I'm not getting arrested in a sting op today.

"My name is Rax and I'm fifteen. Not so anonymous anymore, yeah?"

"Rax? Sounds like a stupid forum username or something. I ain't buying it."

"Our situation's serious, man. And don't make fun of my name."

"Listen, *Rax*, I don't know why you're calling, but I'm not in the mood for games. Skip to the point."

He goes silent. For the next few seconds, all I hear are birds chirping and people bustling about. But just as soon as I think I've scared him off, Rax returns.

"Look, you might not be in the mood for games, but the fact is, you're in one."

"Yes, I get it, you've been playing games with me. Ha-ha. Funny."

"No, I mean, like, you're inside of a video game. You live in a simulation."

I have three options right now: hang up, laugh at him, or say something rude. Let's go with door number two.

"Don't laugh, Jack," he responds. "I'm telling the truth. How can I prove it to you?"

"Kid, I get it. You've got access to someone's debit card and maybe have some skills behind a computer screen, but nothing you're doing amounts to more than a few felonies. I don't buy into your zoo hypothesis schtick."

Rax sighs. Then, over the next five minutes, he disassembles my life from day one to day... well, whatever day today is. He tells me my family history, details the awful middle school secret I've never shared with anybody, and spells out my social security number as well as all my bank information. Either he's a demon with a bad sense of humor, or he's telling the truth.

"How do you know all of that?" I ask, trying to steady my hands and keep my voice down.

"It's all on your lore page, man."

I pause for a second and, between deep breaths, try to recall some concepts from my gaming days. If he's bullshitting me, maybe I can call his bluff.

"So... it's a game, yeah? Is it one of those third-person games, or..."

"More of an isometric, top-down angle by default, but yeah, I can zoom in and see the fine details if need be. For example, there's a woman about thirty steps north of you who's putting something in her purse. Is that a pinecone?"

I look ahead and see the exact woman he's talking about.

"Yes, it's a pinecone," I respond, fumbling over my words as I try not to pass out.

"Keep watching. A bird's about to fly over her and drop a present. She'll be within earshot of you when it happens, so you can warn her if you want."

I keep my eyes laser-focused on the bizarre old lady in the secretary suit who's shoving pinecones in her purse and scuttling toward me. Just as Rax foretold, a pigeon appears overhead.

"Ma'am, move over!"

Thankfully, she realizes I'm talking to her and hops to the side. At that moment, the bird unloads its ordnance and a fat glob falls from the sky, smashing onto the spot on the walkway where her feet were just a second ago.

She doesn't notice the shit missile she just dodged, so all I receive in exchange for my warning is an annoyed glare as she shuffles away. I take a moment to feel embarrassed before returning to my call with the owner of planet Earth.

I stammer a bit and say a few random, disconnected words, but can't seem to form a sentence. Everything that's happened over the past twenty-four hours has been miraculous, and, well, "it's a video game" seems like a convenient answer, but I can't deny it. Rax's story adds up.

Unexpectedly, the kid sympathizes with me.

"Listen, man... I'm just as surprised as you are. I didn't expect our little phone call experiment of mine to work... I thought I was just having artificial arguments with scripted code..."

I lock up. Am I scripted? Is everything I do predetermined? It sounds like *he* doesn't have control over me, but that "the game"—if that's what the world really is—does.

"Is... is my life already set? Am I just a character?" I mumble, feeling my face tense up. Are my eyes actually getting watery or do zeroes and ones just feel wet to me?

"No, man. Don't be like that," he says. "You're in the world's first truly dynamic game. Nothing's predetermined. Sure, there are likelihoods and statistical variables coded in, but nothing's set in stone. Why do you think I went to all the effort to talk to you?"

"Why did you, Rax? If my world is just a game, and your world is real, why bother screwing around with me?"

The fifteen-year-old in charge of my life tries to formulate a decent response. It's an impossible task, but based on his babbling, it sounds like he's taking a swing at it anyway.

"Look, the game is a huge deal and I love it. My mom says I'm addicted to it, but, like, she reads stupid romance novels all day and I don't judge—"

"Rax."

"Okay, okay. Basically, you're my longest-running save file, and the rarest achievements in the game are only unlockable past a certain score, which we're finally at. So from here on out, if I keep boosting your score, I earn achievements to decorate my player profile with. And, like, bragging rights come with that. Duh."

Bragging rights. Jesus, that's all I am. *Bragging. Rights.*

"But I can't do any of that without you living a healthy, full life! Your score—my score—*our* score," he clarifies, "is dependent on you being a success and not copping out and killing yourself. So I thought that maybe, if you'd be up for it, I could help you out by making your life better, and you could help me out by... well, first of all, promising not to kill yourself. And secondly, by enjoying life! I can give you good stuff, man.

Why not make the most of it?" He pauses. "Why aren't you speaking, dude? My voice is getting tired."

I'm... I'm not sure what to say. Frankly, I kind of do want to kill myself, now more than ever. Is my life just some bundle of pixels that exist solely for a kid's amusement? Is that all I am? A virtual clown born to help "real" people get high scores?

It looks like my hyperventilating is distressing a nearby mother and daughter going for a walk. But why should I give a fuck what their reaction is; they're just pixels too, right?

"Jack, buddy, I know a lot must be going on in your head," Rax says, as though he can even vaguely imagine what I'm going through. "But here's the thing: I get it, man. Now that I've heard your voice—I get it. I'm not some asshole who's here to pull the plug after he's had his fun—"

In the background, a woman, early-middle-age and motherly in tone, shouts at Rax to watch his language. He shouts back an apology before continuing.

"I... I don't think anyone else even has the ability to communicate directly with their avatar. And, honestly, it changes things, man. Do I want to do well in the game? Sure. But... so do you, because it's your life. Isn't that a joke, in your world? 'The game of life,' or something like that?"

He's right, it's a phrase people use here on Earth. Now I realize it's just some sick joke coded in by a pack of really, really shitty game devs. I'm not going to share these thoughts with Rax, though; the kid's trying his best to ease me into my new reality. I may as well hear the rest of his spiel.

"The point is, what I'm trying to say is, um... oh, right. Why not let me help you out?"

"Gimme a few minutes to digest, kid."

I get up, stretch my legs, slide the Crapple 10 in my pocket, and mosey around the park. I see a lovely rose bush and lean in until my nose is just a few inches away from its flowers' petals. *So what if it's all code*, I think to myself. It still brings me happiness, and that happiness is real enough to me. Besides, "code" is just a term—even if I'm digital code, the kid has to be made up of some sort of genetic code, right? Who's to say he's not trapped in a zoo too?

As I walk around and look at the green grass, the trees towering high into the big blue sky, the children giggling and chasing each other, and the scores of adults goofing around, I feel so many different emotions, each one exactly as strong as it's always been. Just because the building blocks of my reality aren't what I thought they were doesn't mean that everything I see, hear, taste, smell, and feel is invalidated. No, I think... I think I had a good day today, and that Rax is right. I could use some help making the most of what I have. Yesterday was not okay, and I'm not going to let it happen again.

"Kid." I hope he's still on the line.

"Yeah?"

"You promise to never nuke my save file? Not even after I'm gone?"

"Of course, man," he responds, as earnestly as I've ever heard a fifteen-year-old sound. "If that's what it takes to make you feel good, I'll keep that promise. Besides, time operates much faster in your world than it does out here, so it won't be hard for me to keep an eye on the file until an asteroid hits Earth or something."

While that answer isn't totally reassuring, the kid said the important stuff, so I'll let the "asteroid" bit slide.

"Okay then, Rax... if that's your real name... I'm in."

It sounds like he's making a poor attempt at muffling his end of the line, because his voice gets fuzzy for a second as he lets out an audible cheer of victory. But what's he muffling? A phone? A headset? What does he look like?

"Out of curiosity, are you human? And how are you communicating with me?"

"A fancy mic, muchacho. And yeah, I'm human. Art imitates life, and all that."

I prod a bit to get more information out of him. After all, every detail he shares is groundbreaking news.

"What did you mean, time moves faster where you are?" I ask.

"A day and night for you is one turn for me."

"Wow. Must be some pretty long turns, no?"

"It's dynamic. Like, when I interact with you directly, the game slows down so I can micromanage and chat in real time. But when we're not interacting, things speed up on my end so it's not as much of a grind. Now, my turn to ask a question."

"Shoot."

"Can you explain some stuff? Like, what was up with that pronoun question earlier? I don't think I understood what you were asking..."

"I wanted to know if you were a man or woman. Or, I guess in your case, boy or girl."

"Like, male or female? I get that my voice is kinda high," he says, clearly embarrassed, "but I, uh, I hope it's easy to tell."

"No—that's not what I meant. Are you confused because you're fifteen or are we dealing with a game thing? The deal is, sex and gender are two different—"

"Ah, shoot. I'm gonna stop you right there; I forgot about those changes."

"Changes?"

"Yeah, they came with the..." he lowers his voice, likely so his mom can't hear his next word, "...shitty *2012: End of the World After-Party* expansion pack. It totally overhauled all of the game's systems and unbalanced the meta. I don't know why the game devs do it; it just divides the community and pisses everyone off. The vanilla game was fine."

"Wait, what?"

"Double-definition words like race and ethnicity, sex and gender, racism and prejudice—all those words that split out of nowhere around 2013 so half could be 'social constructs' are just the devs playing with in-game language rules to stir up society's algorithm. Turns out, the result is a lot of angry, confused people."

The gears spinning in my head kick into overdrive as the scope of the revelation reveals itself to me.

"Uh... what else did the devs mess around with? Have you guys ever elected a reality TV show host to run your government?"

"Like I said, dude, the devs really hurt the realism of the game. They just started changing the rules and stuff for laughs, I guess, 'cause ever since that expansion pack, things have been going further off the rails with each new in-game year."

The madness that's eating society alive on Snitter, the weirdos that dominate my office, the state of the union, the lack of any good movies after *The Avenging Squad* and *The Dark Night Falls*... I knew something changed after 2012. There's a reason society fell apart.

"Huh. What else is just 'part of the game'?"

"Okay, so, like, you know when you use the subway?"

"Yeah?"

"Loading time. Same with planes, trains, boats, and all that stuff."

"Wait a sec, kid. Why can't I alert people that we're in a game? I think I've got enough proof. I could get everyone to calm down. I could fix the society algorithm, or whatever you called it."

"I wouldn't do that, broseph. My guess is that because of their programming, at best, they'll probably disregard you and think you're crazy. At worst, you might corrupt their system files, and... well, I'm not exactly sure what'll happen, but it won't be good."

"But... but *I* know I'm in a game. How come I'm not corrupted?"

Rax takes a good chunk of time to explain that because I'm the avatar, I have different system limitations than all the "NPCs"—non-playable characters—around me. Therefore, I'm the only character he can hack. He then explains the hack and the modifications he's made to the game's files.

"So that's why I got my new phone..."

"Yep."

"If you can hack me... why not just make me God? Laundry list of stuff I want, in no particular order: lightning hands, the ability to fly, and invisibility powers would be great, thanks."

He laughs. "Nah, man, it ain't like that. The game's code is pretty delicate. If I go too wild with hack mods, there'll be compatibility issues, and I don't think we wanna find out what happens if the game crashes."

Yeah, I suppose he's right—I'd rather not find out. We'll save that idea for a particularly rainy day.

"All right then, mister game-and-watch. If you can't make me God but you can help me out, where should we go from here?"

He ponders the question for a couple seconds. "How about we start grinding out those achievements by boosting your stats a bit?"

I like the sound of that.

CHAPTER 7

"Give me a refresher: How, exactly, are we going to boost my stats with a shopping spree? Your shorthand explanation didn't really spell out the details," I say as I walk down Forty-second Street, heading toward Times Square.

"I told you, we're gonna buy you some clothes and you're gonna sleep better after," Rax responds, his voice confident and words nonsensical.

"For a master hacker, I don't think you understand how the..." I hesitate for a moment, before forcing myself to spit it out. "The, um... game, works. Clothes don't affect sleep here. Certain drugs and some foods do, but nobody's ever conked out because of the perfect pair of pajamas."

He muffles his mic to speak to someone who's not me. The voice that responds is pretty similar to his, but just a bit... wider? I'm not sure how to describe it. It's airier. It is most definitely *not* his mother, that's for sure. Then I hear a sharp wheezing noise.

"You guys have vacuum cleaners in the... er, out there?" I ask. My comment manages to lure Rax back.

"What? Oh, no, that's not a—that's my friend Barry."

"The hell, kid? I didn't sign on for a co-op game. Can he hear us right now?"

"Um... yeah."

My earbud echoes with the garbled greeting of a new teenage boy. He sounds exactly like what I imagine someone named "Barry" would sound like.

"Can he repeat that?" I ask.

"Get closer so it'll pick up your voice," Rax orders. I hear the clinking, clanking sound of someone manhandling a microphone.

"Um, uh, hello? Hi?" Barry says, his voice wavering as awkwardly as mine did back in my high school years. Just thinking about that time period makes my skin crawl. I soften up a bit, losing the chip on my shoulder. I wonder if the kids I'm speaking with go to school.

"Hi, Barry."

It sounds like the mic falls and hits some stuff. Static blasts my ear. Once that noise dies down, I hear Barry's voice say something along the lines of "Oh crap, it just talked to me." Instantly, the fallen chip returns to its resting spot atop my shoulder.

"Listen, doughboy," I say, not needing to see him to know he's packing a Crunkin' Donuts variety platter above the belt, "I'm a 'he.' All right? Not an 'it.' Check your fucking pronouns."

"Barry! He already told us pronouns are a big thing where he's from. Show some respect, man." Rax continues to scold his friend for a bit before telling him to go back to watching the game from the bed. "Sorry about that, Jack." He reclaims the mic, returning things to normal. Well, as normal as—yeah.

"Just don't hot mic me again."

"Okay. Can I at least give him an idea of what you're saying?"

My eyes roll into the back of my head searching for empathy that's no longer there.

"Sure," I grumble as I arrive at my destination.

The sun starts its daily descent overhead, drenching the colossal glass-walled department store in shimmering orange light. Even from the outside, it's easy to see the place is filled with tacky clothing and even tackier people, as is always the case whenever I happen to walk past it on my way to the movie theater down the street. Kind of wishing I was there right now, honestly.

"We're getting you a suit."

"Why?" I let out a sigh as I step inside the heavily air-conditioned, ice-cold interior of the biggest clothes-shopping hotspot New York City has to offer.

"Get to the men's section and I'll explain," Rax says. In the background, keys clack—he's typing something. As if on cue, he apologizes for the noise. "Just looking up a quick tip guide."

I step onto an escalator bound for the second floor. Since I've left my dignity at the shopping outlet's front doors for safekeeping, that leaves just me and my BTMP to explore the thickest part of the consumerist jungle together.

Rax's voice is barely audible over his typing. "You really can't stand clothing stores, can you?"

"Was it the smile that gave it away?" I reply, not bothering to adjust my scowl. If he wants a fun avatar to look at, he should have me go someplace fun.

"Ha-ha. Funny," he says, poorly impersonating my voice. "See what I did there? Get it? Little reference, because you said that earlier, and—"

"Yeah, kid, I get it. Anyway, clothing stores suck. It's just a bunch of people paying money for designer shoes that'll get muddy and ruined the next day, and people fussing about 'fashion,' as if that means anything. Seriously, it's baking hot outside! Why are we even wearing clothes? I'll go naked. I'm not ashamed of my body."

"If it makes you feel any better, I'm not a fan of the *High Fashion* DLC either."

"DLC?" The term's familiar, but I'd rather get a definition straight from the geek's mouth.

"Downloadable content—extra levels, missions, and stuff that releases after the main game is already out. I'm pretty sure the devs released the current DLC we're discussing just so kids would have more reasons to buy loot boxes and waste money gambling for cosmetic items."

My desire to sock these damn game devs in their throats grows stronger with every new bit of info I hear about them and their activities. Not that I'll get the chance; they probably aren't susceptible to getting their windpipes smashed by code. Besides, I have other things on my plate right now, such as picking out a suit. I arrive at the men's floor and am confronted by row after row of dress shoes, blazers, and gold watches that cost dangerously close to what I make in a year.

I notice the herd's thinned out. Gone are the wannabe fashionistas and poor souls restricted to perusing the unisex and off-brand clothing selections of the first floor. I'm now in the designer section, where only the upper crust can get their monocles polished.

"Lot of pricks up here," I say under my breath, looking around at the douchebags I share the second floor with.

"Don't pay attention to them, man. Just get the goods and get out. You're looking for a... Tucci-branded suit. Yeah, I think that's the one with the XP modifier."

"XP?"

He stops typing.

"Time for that explanation, I guess," Rax starts. "Look, my family's not rich—"

Barry grouses in the background, but Rax ignores him.

"I do okay, but I'm not loaded, so I can't afford a 'premium' account. That means you, my avatar, get less cool stuff. You level up slower, get less experience—XP—from activities, and the RNG for your 'luck' stat is worse. RNG stands for random number generator, b-t-w."

"Did you just say 'b-t-w' out loud?" I scan aisles for the Tucci collection. What's the point of different brands if all these suits look identical?

"That's not the point," he replies, his words tangled in self-conscious awkwardness. "The hack I installed inserts premium perks into our basic account, so it'll make leveling your stats up a lot easier. And the more you level up, the better your overall well-being score gets. That's why I asked about your mood—saw your number take a slight dip when you stepped into the store."

That's not invasive at all, I think to myself. However, in the interest of getting out of here as quickly as possible, I don't interject.

"We've got a few different stat categories that count toward your well-being score. Sex, money, luck, health, and... well, some weird fifth metric that the whole playerbase is pretty confused about and the devs won't comment on," he tells me. "But let's not worry about that one for now, yeah?"

Let's not worry. Pfft. Rax keeps blabbing as I trudge over to the Tucci section, which I locate by stalking a couple of Wall Street clowns who've just finished stocking up on hundred-dollar socks. Do those jerks really make that much money?... Yeah, probably. I think I remember reading a feature a few days ago about banker bonuses reaching new heights, right above that one story about kids in Africa not having clean water.

"... It was a rookie error, I admit it. I shouldn't have put every last one of your basic perks into the 'health' category."

I snap out of autopilot the second Rax says that.

"Wait, you're telling me *you* are the reason I haven't had sex in months and can't get a job that doesn't make me want to shoot myself?" I keep my voice low, not wanting to make a scene in a place where I'm worth less than the floor tile I'm standing on.

"Whoa there, buddy. It's not like I didn't help you at all—if it weren't for my choices, you'd probably have diabetes or something. Be grateful."

The kid's beyond lucky my hands are trapped in a game, where I can't smack the insolence out of him.

"Besides, the premium perk I put into your money stat already talked you off a bridge, and the one I put into luck is having great effects so far. Admit it: We're making progress, yeah?"

"I guess." I scratch my chin. "So what's the suit for—oh. Are you serious?"

"As serious as can be, my guy."

"But how's a suit going to..."

"It's a limited-time event suit, so it's going to give you a temporary passive confidence bonus for all sex-related activities. Pretty sure that bonus stacks with your luck perk, too."

I chuckle as the fifteen-year-old kid spells out how he's going to help me get sex and a good night's sleep by dressing me up like an absolute tool. Whatever you say, lil buddy; whatever you say. I find the Tucci suit and tie that match my measurements and go to the fitting room to try them on, not expecting much in the way of magic results.

Then I actually try them on. Facing the mirror, I think I see what Rax was getting at. I look like a hundred bucks. Scratch that, a thousand bucks. Scratch that—am I dyslexic or are there really that many zeroes attached to the getup I'm wearing?

"Don't worry about it, man," Rax says. "The hack is going to keep your PayFriend account pleasantly plump. The suit won't make a dent in the long run. Or in the short run, really. Heck, why not buy a better pair of dress shoes while we're here?"

I straighten my new tie. "Not a bad idea, kid."

A little over an hour later, I'm back home at the apartment, decked out in a suit that costs more than the box I live in.

"Rax, you mind making an anonymous donation to help get me out of the hole here?" I ask, setting my BTMP on the ground before tossing the bag I have my day clothes stored in onto the bed.

"What hole—oh, yeah. The apartment. We can work on that in a bit, once the hack's perk dispenser cooldown timer gets a bit lower. Like I said before, compatibility, crashes, yada yada. Don't want to overload the game's internal calculators and destabilize anything."

"That's fine. So now that I'm home, what's the next step?"

"There's a concert going on in Central Park. You're not too far, so let's get over there and boost some stats."

The game defines concerts as sex-related activities? That doesn't add up... wait.

"What genre of music?"

"Umm... looks like EDM."

Ah. Guess I'm going to need a little extra cologne to combat the inevitable smells of alcohol, sweat, and repressed daddy issues.

I go to the bathroom to give myself some final touch-ups. Inside, I spot Morgan. He, too, looks sharper than usual. I wonder what the occasion could be.

"Hey, man! Slick suit. Going out?" he asks.

"Yeah, I am, in fact," I say, my voice a little higher than usual. "You?"

"Definitely. There's a concert going on in Central Park. Did you know?"

Oh. Oh, my.

"That, um, happens to be where I'm going, too."

"What a beautiful coincidence! Care to go with me? I am looking to 'pick up some chicks,' as they say here in America, ha-ha. The rest of the guys are busy tonight, but if you—"

"Yeah, let's do it," I say, politely cutting him off. My night's sex prospects just dropped off a cliff.

"Great, great." He pats me on the shoulder.

We finish cleaning ourselves up for the night ahead. After we've exited the bathroom and are about to split up to put things away in our respective rooms, Morgan stops me.

"Jack, one suggestion."

"Yeah?"

"Drop the tie. Trust me," he says, giving me two thumbs-up as he continues onward to his room.

"For sure, I—I forgot I had it on," I mutter. I then slip inside my room, rip off my tie, and whip out the Crapple.

What is happening? I text Rax.

Y u no use earbud? he responds.

Not here.

I still have the Bluetooth earbud in place for later tonight, but the walls in my apartment building are thin, and right now I do not want to risk alienating a pack of borderline-superhuman Viking descendants.

Ivar the Boneless is going to the same concert as me and just made us a unit, I explain. After a long pause, Rax gets back to me with some bullshit game statistics and a line about how I shouldn't sweat it. Sure, fifteen-year-old kid. I won't sweat the fact that I'm now in direct competition with a European demigod.

Knock-knock.

Speak of the devil.

"Are you ready to go?" Morgan asks from the other side of the door. Looks like I'm out of time and options.

"Yep." I'm as ready as I'm going to be. I take one last look in the mirror and put my game face on.

Twenty minutes later, Morgan and I enter Central Park. It's a warm, steamy night. Light pollution masks the stars in the sky. Loud music echoes through the tree-laden walkways in front of us. We're not far from our target: amid the park's usual smell of dog walkers, their respective dogs, and the natural scent of flora, I catch gusts of marijuana smoke wafting our way.

"Wow, your boss sounds like quite the fucker," Morgan says, fresh off my answer to his inquiry about what I do for work.

"He sure is." We share a brief laugh.

Our conversation peters out as we finish our stroll through the park and arrive at the main event. It's everything I expected. Neon lights blast all over the place, guys with the sides of their heads shaved press buttons on a stage, and the surrounding crowd jumps up and down like there are fire ants biting their toes. Thick wubs dominate my ears and my mind goes blank. What am I here for, again?

"Look over there, by the bar—right next to the torch with the purple flames," Morgan says, refocusing my attention on our mission. Our mission is wearing a skimpy crop top, torn-up short-shorts, and she has a tattoo of a dart hitting a bullseye right on the bottom of her ass. I won't deny that she's stunning from head to toe, but something tells me she might not be as tastefully subtle as I'm hoping for.

"Damn," I say, unsure if any other thought of mine would be appropriate.

"For sure! I am going to introduce myself." He then struts over to the perky blonde who's already busy playfully swatting off guys left and right, leaving me to my own devices. Taking one more quick glance at her bullseye tattoo, I decide to ping Rax.

"Kid, how do you know I'm not going to wind up with HIV by the end of tonight?"

"Dude, don't psych yourself out. I put all your original perk points into health, remember?"

I'm not sure I believe anything the kid says, but just the idea of having some special protection against waking up with crabs helps put the rational side of my mind at ease.

"Ah, right. Thanks."

"Oh, now you're grateful," he sneers, before gloating about his gamer instincts being on-point or some shit. With every word he speaks, a thought grows clearer and clearer in my mind: I need a drink.

I head over to the end of the bar opposite where Morgan is. Since the guys with the stupid haircuts on the main stage just fired up their next playlist, most people have gravitated back to the mosh pit, meaning the line for drinks is short and sweet. In fact, there's only one girl ahead of me, and it looks like she's about to be served.

"Thanks," she says to the bartender as she's handed her drink.

Now that it's my turn to order, I remember one crucial detail: I don't know drink names. Like, any of them. Upon further reflection, I don't even really like drinking in general. Hell, I'm pretty sure the biggest reason I stopped talking to one of my best pals a few months back is because of how pathetically, cripplingly addicted to alcohol he became straight out of college.

With all that garbage swirling through my head, I do the only thing a man of my infinite wit can do when faced with unfamiliar and dangerous territory.

"I'll have what she's having." I point a thumb at the girl who has yet to move more than a foot away from where I stand.

"That's not a very manly choice," the girl comments, spinning around and lifting her glass to show me the drink I've just unwittingly ordered.

"The drink doesn't make the man." I don't even process the words before they've flown out of my mouth and slipped directly into her ears.

"Is that so?"

The bartender slides a drink across the counter at me. "Sir," she says, deliberately pronouncing the word with uncertainty in her voice.

The bartender's jab makes the girl laugh and somehow fails to emasculate me. I chalk that up as two points in my favor and proceed to press the advantage. Holding onto my confidence like a tennis player holds onto his racquet, I take another swing at impressing the belle beside me.

"It is so, yeah. In fact, I heard it's the suit."

"Not buying it." Her tone plummets right alongside my confidence. I have a single moment to save my sinking ship before it's too late. Think, Jack, think.

...

Think!

"Tell her *you'll* buy it—another round of drinks," Rax whispers in my ear, his voice coming to the rescue just in time.

"Well, I'll buy it," I blurt, as smoothly as someone who's being fed dating lines can. "That is, another round of drinks. If you're in?"

She takes a sip from her glass then looks at me. "You think you can buy my attention?"

Her eyes lock with mine. She looks like she wants to tell me to fuck off. We spend one more moment staring each other down before I break the link, throw my head back, and down my drink in a single gulp.

"I think I can try," I reply, raising an eyebrow ever-so-slightly. While she remains perplexed by the finely suited, socially awkward goober across from her, I take the liberty of ordering another round of drinks. "Let's start over."

"Sure." She flicks her wavy brown hair over her bare, pale shoulder.

I'm going to need to bring my A game for things to go anywhere tonight. And it seems my A game agrees, since he hits me up via the earbud before I can open my mouth again.

"Ask her if she came to the concert for the music," Rax says. I follow his instructions as the bartender slides the next round of drinks our way. I smoothly swipe both off the counter and hand one to the girl as she gives her answer.

"Actually, I came because I was bored and my sister says I need to get out of the house more." She laughs and takes a gulp of her drink. I think she's loosening up. And... unless I usually feel so weightless and funny... I think I might be loosening up too. How much alcohol is in these things?

"And what about you?" she asks. "Why did you show up here, in your fancy suit?"

"I go where I think fun will be found, and a friend convinced me this concert would be a good place to find some. I think he might've been right," I say, looking her in the eyes as I churn out line after line of ridiculously cheesy nonsense. And yet, she's not distancing herself—in fact, she's getting closer. How is this shit working? I don't even know her name!

"Don't stop," Rax says. "Let's roll out the heavy hitters."

By the time a few more drinks have come and gone, my voice has dropped a full octave and the girl has repositioned herself within inches of me. As much as I want to credit myself for the entirety of my masterful performance in debonair douchebaggery, I can't ignore how much Rax is helping—the kid's working magic up there in the digital sky.

"You're in the home stretch, man! Let her keep talking and I think you've got it!" he advises, cuing me to lean against the bar and let the lovely lady steer the ship to the finish line. She continues telling me about all sorts of shit I barely even process, and I respond with nothing but nods, laughs, and dashing smiles. Turns out, the key to winning the game isn't to go all-in or cop out entirely—the trick's to just barely participate.

"You know, you're a really good listener." She puts her hand on mine. "And talker too. I think... I think the concert's gotten boring, yeah? Wanna do something else?"

"Like what?" I ask, taking a gulp from my umpteenth glass of mystery alcohol.

"Maybe we could go back to my place?..."

There's a big ol' mischievous smirk on my face. "And what would make that more exciting than the concert?"

She pauses, then bites her lip and flicks my shirt's cuff link with her finger. "Well, let me go find my sister, and maybe you'll find out."

She turns and walks away from me, looking over her shoulder to mouth "one minute." Then she gives a little wave and disappears into the sea of people beyond the bar.

Dude.

"We fucking *nailed* it," I say to Rax the second the girl is out of earshot.

"My man, what did I tell you." He's cool as a cucumber. But just as he's about to keep bragging, a voice in the background steals his attention.

"Rax?" I say.

"Sorry about that. Barry... he, uh, feels bad for annoying you earlier and wants a chance to make it up."

"Barry?"

"H-hi, Mr. Jack, sir. Sorry for earlier," Rax's friend says.

"It's fine, blueberry. We're fine." I rub my eyes to make sure they're still working as I wait for my supermodel-status drinking buddy to sashay those long legs of hers back to me.

"If it's okay with you... can I try playing? I think I can be as good as Rax."

Rax makes a "pfft" noise in the background but doesn't interrupt. I think I'm with my guy on that one; it definitely sounds like a bad idea. But, eh, what the hell. Everybody gets one.

"Sure, chief. Take the wheel." I'm too full of mirth to risk being brought down by having to reject Rax's buddy. It's not like that fella can screw things up so far into the night anyway. Brown-haired and beautiful has just returned and she's not alone—wait. Oh shit.

"Meet my sister," says the girl I've been talking to all night, formally introducing me to the blonde bombshell I'd seen earlier—the one with the bullseye tattoo on her ass.

Holy shit. I try my darndest to keep my eyes away from the tattoo snaking around the inner edge of the sister's thigh.

"So, you want to get going to our place?" Blondie asks, winking at me as she runs her fingers down the side of her sister's exposed midriff.

"I, um, yeah—"

"Order another drink," Barry interjects, his voice lacking the confidence of his buddy's. Still, he said he knew what he was doing. I oblige.

"Yeah. Just let me order us one more round before we go," I tell the girls.

Both express mock-disappointment before reverting to buzzed gaiety. While I signal the bartender, Blondie whispers something in her sister's ear which is then relayed to me.

"My sister is wondering if..." embarrassed, the brunette puts a hand over her eyes before delivering the whole message, "if you have a 9-iron for golfing."

The girls then burst into a fit of giggles while staring at me, hungry for an answer. Before I can whip out my response, Barry chimes in.

"Tell them you don't want to brag, but you're more of a basketball guy."

I say what I'm told and both girls' giggles die down as they give half-smiles of confusion. Shit, things aren't going right. Barry...

The next round of drinks arrive quickly enough to save me. I faintly hear Barry and Rax having some sort of discussion, though the mic is muffled.

"Isn't that a woman's drink?" Blondie asks.

"The drink doesn't make the man, he says," her sister replies with a grin. Phew. As long as they keep each other occupied, I can't fuck things up.

Or so I think. Just as we're about to finish our glasses and hit the road, a new challenger approaches.

"Jack! Friend, I've been looking for you," Morgan says, appearing beside me. Shit.

"Oh, um, hey, man. How's your night been?" I gesture to the girls. "Ladies, meet my friend Morgan."

"You don't have to tell me who he is," Blondie replies, pointing at my hulking comrade. "He and I were just getting to know each other before sis stole me away." She gives her sister a light smack on the bum as punishment. The latter lets out a soft moan.

"Aren't they beautiful?" Morgan asks, putting a hand on my shoulder.

"Sure are." I pray to the game devs that an orbital laser strike evaporates Morgan before he can ruin the night for me.

"Hey," the brunette sister says, sliding her hand out of her sister's pocket to point a finger at us. "You two wouldn't want to join in on the fun together, would you?"

"Say 'the more the merrier' to them," Barry instructs, sounding confused by his own orders. In full-on panic mode, without thinking, I reflexively spew out the words that've been fed to me. Instantly, I want to die. Both girls' eyes grow wide with delight as my gut threatens to regurgitate all the liquid trash I've been downing for the past few hours.

"Barry, get off the mic!" Rax hisses before commandeering it from the other boy. "Hey, man, I'm here. Sorry about that. Quick, tell them you need to talk to Morgan for a sec."

"Hey, ladies," I say. "Mind if we consult for just a moment?" I point at Morgan and the two girls nod. Once he and I have stepped a few feet away, I get down to brass tacks.

"Morgan, look, I've had too much to drink." I rub my forehead. "I didn't mean to say that, back there—I get it, neither of us are into that, and it ain't happening—"

"Brother! I would not take offense if you had meant it." Is... is he encouraging me?

"Say you really didn't mean it and you're worried you're both going to lose the girls because of it," Rax orders. I follow his command and convince Morgan to recalibrate his hopes for our quartet's trajectory.

"I understand! No worries. I will convince the blonde one that tonight is not the right night for such an activity." Morgan smiles and pats me on the back. He returns to the girls while I stay behind to chat with Rax mano a mano.

"Dude, kick Barry out right-the-fuck now," I say, struggling to hold back vomit as drunken anxiety overtakes my body.

"Listen, man—"

"Do it! And fix this mess!"

"I'm trying, all right? These branching dialogue options are really confusing!"

"Figure it out!" I whisper as I move toward Morgan, who has already begun dissolving our group's union.

"... he and I don't think it's a good idea," Morgan says, addressing the ladies. "If we are distracted with each other, that leaves us less time for you."

The girls pout.

"So that's a 'no,' then?" Blondie asks. Her sister eyeballs me.

"I would never say such a thing! Not a chance," he responds, whisking her off her feet after she dares him to make a move.

"Say 'you two have fun,'" Rax instructs. I take the hint and do as I'm told. Morgan tosses the giggling blonde over his shoulder and the two depart, happy as can be. Now it's back down to just me and the frustrated lady I've spent all night trying to woo.

"If you didn't want to, why not just say so?..." she asks. Before I can screw myself over even further, Rax swoops in and feeds me a line, which I swiftly execute.

"I wanted to, it's just... Morgan. He was being polite, but it felt like I was pressuring him and I didn't want to put him in an awkward spot," I lie, working to rebuild rapport at Mach 5.

"Oh. That's... considerate." A small smile forms on her face.

"Dude, you've got it. Save the day and invite that girl from the subway. It'll work! Trust me," says the teenager in my ear.

"Besides, I think there's another way we can still have the night we were hoping for," I tell the lone sister, pulling out my phone.

"Is that the Crapple 10?" she asks, looking down at her Crapple 8 with a hint of shame.

"Yep." I draw her attention to the first contact in the phone's directory. "Check it out. I've got a friend who would probably be game to join us."

"Oh?"

"Yeah, and I think she'd be your type."

The girl reads my eyes and, apparently happy with what she finds, grabs my wrist. It's time to ditch the park.

An hour later, Rax's prophecy is fulfilled and me, the brunette I never learned the name of, and Blaire, the eye candy from the subway, are back at the latter lady's apartment. The night moves at superspeed, and as I spend my time in heaven swimming through sheets, exploring the scents of expensive perfumes, and hearing sounds so carnal they'd make teenage-me need a tissue, I come to a conclusion: I can get used to my new life. I can *definitely* get used to my new life.

CHAPTER 8

My eyelids flutter open, tickled by rays of sunlight. Hello, world. How are you today? And speaking of "hello"s... the bed doesn't smell like lilacs anymore. Where are the girls?

I roll around, searching for traces of the sexy duo until I realize: these aren't Blaire's sheets. I'm not in her apartment either.

Why do the sheets smell like me? Why is the room so small? And why am I currently cuddling a bag of sweaty, day-old work clothes—

Oh, I'm back at *my* apartment. How the heck did I wind up here? What time is it?

My Aqua Jive's alarm goes off, reminding me that even though I had a long night, I'm not off the hook from going to work. For the first time ever, that thought doesn't immediately bring my spirits down. In fact, if everything goes as smoothly as yesterday, I bet work will be swell.

How am I in such good condition after a night of hard drinking? I feel like a million bucks. Did... did I imagine last night? Was I just trapped in some weird, adult-only dream? I grab my Crapple, curious to find out if Rax knows why I'm not getting torn apart by a freight train of a headache right now. Before I can send a text his way, a message notification catches my attention. It's from a contact I don't remember adding.

The new contact's name is "Misty." Hmm. I'm going to venture a guess that's the name of the sister that wound up with this mister at Blaire's place last night. And speaking of Blaire, it looks like I've got a new message from the subway girl herself. There's an attachment. Let me just give that picture file a quick download and open it up—

Oh, my. That's explicit.

Reflexively, I save the image to my SD card. *I know what I'm going to be doing during my first workday bathroom break.* Then, instead of keeping the picture out to buzzsaw the morning wood with, I refocus on Rax. Even if he has a weird name and a lame friend, that kid is my ace in the hole.

Good morning! I text. *Quick question: am I supposed to be immune to hangovers?*

A few seconds later, he replies.

Did I mention how smart I was for putting all those points into your health?

All right, kid, that's enough of that. I toss my phone to the side, stretch my arms out, give myself a good scratch on the ass, then flop out of bed, ready to start my day. First stop: the dresser. Exactly how bad do my clothes smell now that they're three days overdue for a wash?

One sniff later and I'm pleasantly surprised. Not too bad! Not too bad at all. I think I can make a pair of jeans and a plaid shirt work for today. Yeah, if I roll up the sleeves and don't tuck anything in, I can still look cool and smell almost as good. I just have to remember to lay the deodorant on thick and maybe do a spritz of cologne.

Satisfied with my clothing situation, I grab my toothbrush and travel to the bathroom, wherein I once again bump into Morgan. He stands in front of the mirror brushing his teeth. I notice bags under his eyes, and that his free hand is wrist-deep in his boxers, furiously scratching at some itch just beyond my line of sight.

"Hey, man, how was your night?" I ask, approaching the sink beside him as I prepare to clean my pearly whites.

"It was not good. You 'dodged a big bullet,' as they say—I think she had some sort of disease. My cock's been burning all morning," he replies, scratching even more aggressively at his member while speaking to me.

"That sucks, man. I assume that means no club for you tonight?"

"No way," he shoots back, causing me to pause my brushing. "I've recovered from worse; we're still going. I'll be healthy again in no time. No worries."

Um... let's hope so, for the sake of whatever poor girl you meet tonight, I think to myself, trying not to dwell on his genitals. I finish brushing and take a quick piss. Shortly thereafter, I dip out of the bathroom and book it back to my room. I grab my Crapple and hit up Rax.

Morgan got hit with an STD from that one sister Barry cost me, I text. Cue more gloating from the teenage overseer.

Did I meeeeeentioooon how smart I was for putting all those points into your health?

Eh, pretty sure dodging that bullet falls under "luck," buddy, I respond, referencing the stat category I could've benefited from way earlier in life had Rax not been so tunnel-visioned with his perk point distribution. After all, health points can't protect you from STDs if you're not having the "S" part in the first place.

The stats are probably stacking. Either way, you're welcome. And keep on crushing it; our score's finally climbing again, he says, before telling me to get going or I'll be late for work. Looking at the time and realizing he's right, I kick my morning ops into high gear and am out the door no more than five minutes later.

The second I hit the street, I beeline for Crunkin' Donuts. The sandwich I order is delicious as usual. I then hustle to the subway station. Its air conditioners are still working. People still smell nice. My train arrives right on time, the car I get in isn't too crowded, and I score a seat. Nice.

It's smooth sailing all the way to my office. When I get there, for the second day in a row, everyone's actually minding their own business and working. The Prog Triplets, Pritchard, you name it—they're all mute. Is a quiet office the new norm? Will there finally be peace in my time?

Just as I'm about to prematurely thank my lucky stars, Tim calls my team in for an early meeting. That can't be good. The only time Tim arrives at the same hour as the grunts, aka *us*, is when he's pissed. Can't wait to find out what's got his knickers in a knot.

I take my seat alongside the rest of the editorial team as Stark, Amélie, and Laura fill in the back row. Once we're all situated, Tim marches to the front of the conference room and slams his notepad on the long table. He's wearing his full-on "I'm the boss" outfit today, complete with suspenders, a tie clip, and... is that a cigar in his hand?

"We've got a situation, ladies and gentlemen," he says.

"T-Tim? Excuse me, but you're excluding some genders—" Alex pipes up, unable to control being a pain in the ass even in the face of Tim's rage. The consequences are dealt swiftly.

"I'll exclude whomever I damn well please!" He picks up his notepad just to slam it on the table again. "In fact: Alex, get out."

"But I—"

"*Out!*" he shouts, forcing Alex to exit the room like a scared gerbil. The rest of us sit still as statues.

Tim pulls out a lighter and fires up his cigar. He lifts it to his lips, takes a drag, then releases a big, fat puff of smoke. A fit of coughs erupt from the back of the room. Amélie. Oh no.

"Monsieur Hobert, you know I have asthma!" Amélie hisses between coughs, her face reddening from a lethal mixture of asphyxiation and rage.

Tim gestures for her to get lost. "Blame your parents for bad genes."

"I will be filing a complaint!" Amélie gets up to leave. "You are not allowed to be smoking indoors like zis!"

Stark helps her ditch the smoky meeting. "Put that cigar out in your eye, Tim," he says before exiting the conference room with Amélie, patting her back as they go.

I can't believe what I just heard. Neither can Tim.

"That right there is why we're having a meeting." Tim pounds a fist against our poor long table. "It's come to my attention there's a lack of respect in our office."

The remaining five of us look at each other, confused. Tim shoves his cigar back in his mouth, scanning the room to see who'll figure out his cryptic bullshit first. When none of us bite, he narrows his eyes and points a finger at us.

"A lack of respect for authority."

He starts walking around the table, moving past our chairs. He puts his cigar within a few inches of each of our necks, close enough for us to feel the heat. HR's going to have a field day later in the afternoon as long as Tim keeps acting the way he's acting.

"You might not understand why I operate the way I do, but it's good for you. It's great for me, and it's good for you. I run our team like a well-oiled steamboat, and I'm not going to have some ungrateful mutineers with scurvy poison my crew."

It's an awful analogy, but the man with the suspenders keeps going.

"So today, I'm giving everyone a set of unique assignments. Hopefully these teach you something about loyalty and make you think twice about picking a fight with your betters. Anyone who fails to complete these assignments gets fired." He returns to the front of the table and picks up his notepad. "First off, Pritchard, you'll be writing a feature on why communism is good for the future of tech, because I'm sick of you alienating unionized corporations. Even if they are greedy bastards."

Pritchard double takes, then storms out of the conference room while ranting to himself about hierarchical dominance gone wrong or some shit like that.

"As for you two," Tim says, pointing at the remaining two-thirds of the Prog Triplets, "I want a group op-ed written up about how microaggressions are essential to healthy workplace bonding. And get your third musketeer on the case too."

"That's outrageous!" Jamie protests.

"Not as outrageous as you were last Thursday night. Why do you think I'm wearing suspenders? Now, both of you, get out!"

Jamie and Taylor slink out of the meeting room as quickly as their tiny feet will allow, and mere seconds later I see they're already on their phones posting some nasty, passive-aggressive work-related chirps on Snitter.

I glance at Laura. She's looking back at me. Now it's just the two of us against a raging maniac armed with a lit cigar and a penchant for workplace cruelty.

"Laura!" Tim barks, eager to mow down one of the final survivors in the meeting room. "You're on double duty today. First up: whenever Stark brings Emily—or whatever the hell her name is—back from the hospital, tell them they're both fired. And, in the meantime, you're working with Jack here on a project."

Laura's eyes widen, but she's unable to open her mouth to respond. She's normally a pretty confident, capable woman, but in the presence of Tim, she just locks up. I don't think she can handle him. Though, to her credit, I don't think any of us can. Except me, that is. Yeah, I think I can afford to lose my job. Rax has my back, and, well, I have my back too. Time to clock out with dignity.

"Tim, cut the tough guy act." I stand up, unwilling to watch him abuse Laura. Hell, I should've stood up to the guy minutes ago and smacked that cigar out of his hand before he could put Amélie in a coughing fit.

"What the hell did you—"

"You know what I said. And here's something else you should know: I'm not doing your bullshit assignment or putting up with your bullshit attitude. So, as a wiser guy than me already said, you can shove that cigar right in your eye socket, because we're done here. I'm going to file a complaint with HR, then I'm going home."

Tim gives me the craziest stare I've ever seen, then breaks into a grin. A big, big grin. It quickly turns into a full-on smile and, before I know it, the man's burst into hysterical, unhinged laughter. Then, as quickly as the laughter started, it stops, and his face loses all its humor. Looking into my eyes with stone-cold seriousness, he lays down the law of the land.

"No, Jack, that's not what you're going to do today. You're going to sit down, take your orders, and complete the damn assignment I give to you and Laura."

"And why would I do that?"

"Because if you don't, I'll fire Laura. Right here, right now."

I freeze. Laura is in full-on panic mode, internally melting as her job goes from totally secure to hanging by a thread—a thread held by two hot-headed assholes.

"What makes you think you can get away with firing her for something I do?" I ask.

"I can get away with it because it's easier for me to file a pink slip than it is for HR to undo one," he fires back, calling my bluff. "At-will employment's a bitch, ain't it?"

I back off, realizing he's got me by the balls. I slowly sit back down in my chair.

"Good man, Jack. Way to look out for your colleagues," he says with a smirk. "Now, about that assignment. A company's pissed that they sent us a review unit we never published a review for. However, I explicitly remember proofreading our review and putting it in the edit queue. It's not in my work email's outbox, though."

He reveals a small manila folder hidden underneath his fat notepad and shoves it toward Laura and me.

"That's the info regarding the product. The review must be lost somewhere in our database, so you," he says, pointing at me, "and you," pointing at Laura, "go find it."

"Who reviewed it?" I ask.

"The intern."

"Why don't we have it on the cloud?"

"He wrote it offline before we got him hooked up to the office's Wi-Fi. The only spare copy was on an external hard drive that got fried thanks to a damn coffee spill," Tim growls, taking another puff of his cigar. It's absolutely astonishing the fire alarm hasn't gone off yet; the smoke haze in the room is getting thicker than the shit magicians use for vanishing tricks.

"Why not ask the intern if he stored it anywhere else?" I say, trying not to cough.

"Can't. Already fired him. I won't have idiots spilling coffee and keeping their jobs in my office. Now find. That. Review!"

After delivering his final order, Tim grabs his things and hastily exits the room, but not before poking a head back in for one last jab.

"Oh, and both of you: that shirt wasn't made in the Dominican Republic. It was made in Taiwan." He then slams the door shut behind him and cackles all the way down the hall, leaving us to exit the second-hand smoke box in our own time.

I grab the dossier Tim gave us, whip out of my chair, and squad up with Laura, who's still paralyzed at the back of the room, unsure if she'll have a job by the end of today. I help her out of her seat and we exit through the back door of the meeting room.

"At least we know what the fuss is about." My tone is grim. I can't believe that clown is putting everyone in a pressure cooker just because he picked—and lost—a fight with me over a fucking button-down the other day.

"Yeah," Laura says. Her mind is clearly on other matters.

"Laura, you're not going to lose your job, all right? We'll finish the wild goose chase and then make sure Tim Hobert never torments another employee again."

"You can't guarantee that," she counters, her lip trembling as she fights the urge to cry. She's not wrong. I can't guarantee anything. But, based on my luck stats, I'm betting there's a damn good chance I don't need to.

"Look," I say, pulling out my Crapple 10. I quickly open my PayFriend account to see how much is left, before showing Laura. "I'll bet you every last penny in my account that you keep your job."

She calms down just a bit and looks me in the eyes. At first, she seems to think I'm joking, but after she realizes I'm not fucking around, her expression softens and she tells me to put my phone away.

"Jack, we barely know each other." She gives me a weak smile and takes the manila folder from my hand. "I don't want your money. But I appreciate the gesture. Let's get to work."

"Let's."

At that moment, the fire alarm goes off. I look back at the conference room—seems like I forgot to shut the door on my way out and the smoke from Tim's little Cuban surprise leaked out onto the rest of the floor.

One building-wide evacuation and two crowded elevator trips later, Laura and I finally make it back inside the office. Our first order of business is scouting out a location to work from, since it's not like we can use the computers at our desks. Our team's corner of the office is so toxic right now, both in terms of air quality and the mood of the people occupying the space, that the area is basically no man's land. All of the site engineers and other non-editorial personnel have distanced their desks from us as much as possible in order to let Pritchard and the Prog Triplets go wild, and Tim's certainly not making the grounds any friendlier.

So, since neither Laura nor I are in the mood for additional conflicts, we abandon our normal workstations and take refuge in the cramped research room on the other end of the office. It has a computer, printer, and a small snack area with a coffee maker, so I think we'll be fine.

I pull up chairs for us as Laura drops the manila folder beside the computer. "Where should we start?"

"At the beginning?" she says, already looking fatigued.

We take a few minutes to examine the dossier Tim gave us. It tells us what the gadget is, who sent it to us, shipping info, the date we have to return the unit by—we've got all of the details we could ever need. All that's missing is the review.

Now that we've thoroughly versed ourselves in the necessary background info, we fire up the research room's desktop and get ready to data dig. Laura enters her site administrator credentials so we can poke around bits of the CMS that I, as part of the editorial team, might not have access to, and soon enough the two of us are looking at a massive catalog of all the company's proprietary documentation. The issue is, said documentation isn't easy to skim through.

After fruitlessly exploring a ton of folders that seemed like they'd be hiding unpublished copy, Laura and I decide it's time to bite the bullet and search through every product review alphabetically, in order to see if our target is saved as a draft somewhere. As we scan through a particularly dense batch of indexed reviews, Laura tears off a bit of paper from one of the sheets inside our dossier. I take over scrolling duties while she does her weird papercraft thing. I can't blame her for wanting a momentary distraction; the shit we're scanning is drier than an Arizona summer.

"Your job is usually more interesting than what we're doing right now, correct?" My eyes glaze over at the sight of a few hundred more product review listings. Laura flicks a small paper football at me in response. She then retakes control of the mouse.

"No, but, for real," I say through a yawn as I watch her skim through the next batch of article titles, "how are you not unconscious right now?"

"Because, smart guy, my job's on the line," she responds, frowning. Her expression is directed at the monitor.

"I told you I'd bet all the money in my account that things work out." I cover my mouth in a poor attempt to hide a second yawn.

"Why are you so keen on throwing money at me?" Laura stops her work and looks at me. Weird question, but I guess my offer isn't very normal either.

"I just don't think you deserve to be shit out of luck whenever Timbo decides to put your job's fate in someone else's hands. Yeah?"

"Sure, that's nice and all, but don't we basically make the same amount? I don't know about you, but I definitely don't have spare pennies to flaunt."

Shoot. I can't exactly explain to her that I've got a teenage boy laundering me money from the cyber ether, so...

"Laura, I'm going to be real with you." I gesture for her to lean in closely. Once she's within a few inches of me, I whisper my secret.

"I'm a drug trafficker, all right? Massive stacks of cocaine in my closet. My contacts call me El Jacko. But you can't tell anyone." I point a finger gun at my temple before pulling the trigger and tilting my head sideways. She looks at me for a few seconds without saying a word. Then she rolls her eyes.

"You're weird," she says, starting to laugh. "You're really weird."

"I'm *also* great at hoarding cash and bad at making big financial decisions, so if you want me to walk down to Tim's office and take a piss on his desk, my offer still stands."

She laughs some more, resting a hand on my shoulder.

"I'll keep that in mind," she replies, chortling a bit as she returns to scrolling duty. From there, things get better. We loosen up and start to have some fun together, what with the weight of Laura potentially losing her job not hanging over us quite as heavily. The paper football makes its return and we get some healthy small talk going, learning about each other's interests. Suddenly, our doomed-to-fail cooperative assignment doesn't seem so bad.

That sentiment remains true even when we get back into the thick of work, wherein absolutely no progress is made. After a staggering round of yawns from both of us, Laura suggests we use our secret weapon.

"Coffee?" she asks. "I didn't get much sleep last night."

"Neither did I," I reply, getting up from my seat to go visit the snack area.

I brew a pot of liquid energy while Laura keeps digging through files. We share ideas about where the lost review might've ended up. As we down our first—then second, then third—round of hyper-caffeinated beverages, potential locations of the lost review start occurring to me faster. Did we check the article-in-edit queue's backlog? What about all the sent and received messages in the editors' shared inbox? Why don't we do a scan of Tim's work email to see every message he's sent that's reached the queue?

"Hey, should I get my laptop from my desk? Maybe that'd speed up the process, y'know, if we're both searching," I say as my legs start to jitter from all the caffeine. Laura grabs my arm, just as hyped up on speedy bean juice as I am.

"It's not worth the risk. You could get shot," she replies, prompting us both to giggle a little.

"Pretty sure Pritchard has a concealed carry license, so maybe you're right. Anyway, how are we not seeing a draft under Tim's name? If he sent it like he says he did, we'd see it under 'Tim Hobert' for sure."

Laura squints at the screen and rubs her temples.

I take control of the keyboard. "Let's try a new search. Tim, space, is, space, a, space, dick."

I press "enter" and Laura and I go back to laughing until, just as my silly search finishes loading, Tim appears at the entrance to the research room.

"Am I interrupting anything, ladies?" he asks, staring at me. His devilish smile broadcasts that he's here for pleasure, not work.

"Yes, sir," I say, not missing a beat. I'm taking the fight to him. "We're busy finding the lost review. Speaking of which, wouldn't it be faster just to rewrite the thing?"

"Heh, yeah," he replies. "Anyway, Jack, in my office. Now."

With that, he disappears. I look at Laura. All the joy has drained from her face.

"I'll be fine." I grab my coffee and head for the door. "Don't stop the party while I'm gone."

Sixty seconds later, I'm in Tim's office.

"Have a seat." Tim points at the chair in front of his desk.

I plop down and make myself comfy.

"Listen close, Jack. I know you're in here against your will. But remember, without my benevolence, you wouldn't be here at all. That's what I want to talk to you about: your virtually nonexistent level of personal commitment to me and the company."

What the fuck? Does he know how many thousands of immaculate, edit-proof deals posts I've made for him and the company? Does he understand how mind-numbing my job is, and how willingly I sacrifice my gray matter in order to do it well?

You know what, fuck it. I'm not in the mood for his shit. I'm having some coffee. He can talk to the back of a paper cup.

Without a second's hesitation, I lift the cup toward my lips and start to take a sip.

"What are you doing?"

"I'm drinking coffee, Tim."

"No, you're disrespecting me again," he says, tugging on his suspenders. "Need I remind you Laura Holland's job rests on your shoulders? So, I'm going to ask one more time: What are you doing?"

Realizing my potentially costly mistake, I stop mid-sip.

"I am listening intently to your insights on my behavior. While also having coffee."

"No, Jack, that's not what I see. I see a caffeine junkie who can't go more than a minute without a fix. Here I am," he says, his voice rising as he flails his hands around like hairy windmills, "trying to enlighten you as to why I am so constantly disappointed with your performance. And what are you doing? *'Having coffee.'*"

He does his best to imitate my tone while also sounding like a gigantic asshole. On one of those counts, he succeeds with flying colors.

"Where the hell do you get off doing that in front of my face? Un-fucking-believable. First it'll be taking a small sip of coffee in the middle of me lecturing you, then it'll be expecting me to film you dipping your balls in pineapple juice from the comfort of *your* desk. I give you an inch, you'll take a mile."

I find it odd that he's emphasizing the bit about the desk of all things, but I don't interrupt.

"I bet you want me to just shrug it off like it's no big deal, right? You want me to let your bullshit just slip under the radar so that you can continue living the life of leisure your job affords you. The life *I* afford you. Is that what you want?"

All right, time for plan B. I lean forward and set my coffee cup on Tim's desk, hoping that by relieving myself of the drink, the hysterical madman and I can reach some sort of momentary truce.

"No. No. No. Jack, that right there is exactly the problem. You think you can disrespect me then fix everything by placing a damn cup on my desk. What, do you think I want a sip? You think I'm jealous of your glorious coffee?"

He lifts the cup like he's a claw machine at an arcade, then rotates ninety degrees and drops it into the trash can beside his desk.

"That's what I think of your coffee, Jack."

"Tim," I say, speaking up for the first time in what feels like hours, "You're blowing things out of proportion. I took a sip of a drink. As I reflect, yes, maybe it was poorly timed. But you're being completely irrational."

Tim's face turns redder than a tomato as he activates ultra-pissed boss mode. Before I can get another word in, he launches into what has to be his most vicious tirade of the month, one primed to surpass the fiery rant he'd let loose upon Jamie last week when she forgot to wear the pantyhose he likes so much on casual Friday.

"You don't know when to stop, do you, Jack? You'll just mouth off to anyone who doesn't tolerate your atrocious behavior, won't you? God, you are so lucky that I was in a forgiving mood today, otherwise you'd be out there right now searching for a cardboard box to rent after I fired you and got you evicted from whatever shitty little apartment you live in."

I mean, he's not wrong. My apartment is pretty shi—

"And then!"

Aaand he's even interrupting my thoughts.

"And then, if I ever saw you in that box on my way to work, I'd turn around, buy a cup of coffee, come back, and pour it all over your little cardboard shanty so you'd have to live in a soggy mess. Although, that probably wouldn't faze you since you'd be too busy getting off from the smell."

I stare at him, dead-eyed and emotionless.

"Disgusting, Jack. You're disgusting," he says. "Damn it, you've flustered me to the point where I can't even remember why I called you in here. Maybe I wanted to remind you who's in charge. Maybe I just wanted to see you squirm. Or maybe I actually can't remember because my damn wife hasn't gotten me those vitamin B-6 supplements from the pharmacy I'm not allowed in anymore.

"Anyway, I don't remember. But when it comes back to me, just know that you'll be right back in that chair—without your little beverage of the day. And then we can talk about the previous issue along with your newfound penchant for caffeinated substance abuse. Now get the fuck out of my office."

I resist the urge to kill my boss with a stapler and schlep back to the research room.

"Jack, you have to see what I found," Laura says as I walk through the doorway. No "How did it go?" or "Are you okay?" She just makes it all about her—

"I got proof that you-know-who's been committing fraud."

Holy shit.

"We're not talking about that review anymore, are we," I say, bolting into my seat.

"Nope. You know that search you did, right before you left?"

"Yeah?"

"And do you remember what Tim's middle name is?"

"Um... Richard?"

"Which can be shortened to..."

"Dick!" we shout, before realizing our mistake and lowering our voices. The research room's door might claim to be soundproof, but it's not like we want to put that to the test.

"So when you searched 'Tim is a dick,' it brought up a weird string of emails in the CMS's spam folder. All the messages were from..."

The email address on the screen reads "TimBDick@achoo.com."

"He didn't send the review from his work email. That's why we couldn't find it. He sent it via his personal account and it got filtered into a spam folder!" She's giddy as can be.

"He has another initial?" I ask, pointing to the "B."

"I... I don't think the 'B' is an initial." She makes a grossed-out expression before diving back into the good news. "Anyway, here's the thing: He didn't just use that account to send the review. Turns out, he's been using it to send fake invoices."

"What?"

"He's been ordering things with his own personal info, then claiming them as 'business expenses' so the accounts people will reimburse him. Thing is, none of what he buys ever reaches the office or gets used for work. Look at these."

She points at a cluster of receipts on the screen. It doesn't take long to figure out that she's right. What do an electric back scratcher, turbo foot massager, and 84-inch flat screen TV all have in common? They're all things the office has never seen yet somehow got billed for. That's thousands of dollars' worth of tech billed in just the past month, and there are emails going all the way back to last year.

"You know how Joey," she says, referencing the individual whose sole job it is to manage office product inventory, "has been begging for an 84-inch flat screen for our office? If that TV had ever been intended to come here, he would've been the first to know. Same with a ton of other stuff in these emails."

"But what if—"

"But what if these were items Tim wrote about on his work-from-home days, hence the home shipping address? That's not it, either—no write-ups exist anywhere in the CMS for any of these products. And besides, each invoice explicitly states the product was bought for in-office testing and review."

Jesus. So Tim's actually been scamming the company the whole time, and we've got all the proof we could ever need. Is... is my phone vibrating in my pocket, or am I getting excited?

"Jack, our discovery is huge. So huge. What do we do with it? Should we go to HR?"

A lightning bolt strikes me.

"No," I say, "Not just HR; they're not enough. We have to start bigger. I've got the editor-in-chief's email address. We'll go straight to her."

"Won't she be annoyed we're bothering her while she's doing business in Tokyo?"

"I wager she'll be more annoyed if we keep letting Tim embezzle company funds."

Many, many minutes later, after screenshotting and compiling every last bit of evidence we need, Laura and I prepare to hit the send button on our epic exposé. We have everything: fraudulent invoices, a record of every item to have ever passed through our office's doors, as well as a lengthy synopsis of what Tim put everyone through today.

"Are you sure about sharing everything?" Laura asks, letting fear of shaking the hornet's nest chip away at her confidence.

"Sure enough to bet my PayFriend account on it." With that declaration made, I proudly hit the send button. "Now, let's file some HR complaints, yeah?"

Laura and I spend the next hour of our lives whipping up the most thorough complaint emails the office has ever seen, and by the time we're done taking turns on the computer, I can already smell Tim roasting in hell.

After Laura sends her complaint, we swap back to my account to see if Human Resources has acknowledged my support ticket yet. Turns out, they have. The message they've sent reads like the usual bullshit, complete with a "we'll respond within a few business days if action is taken." But at the very bottom there's a new line—something that's not part of the standard form letter fare: "We apologize if it takes us longer than usual to update you; we've had a spike in tickets today."

It sounds like everyone else has had enough of Tim's shit as well. Oh, what a lovely day. I mean, he can't fire us if we all filed complaints... right?

Laura taps me on the shoulder. "Look!"

There's a new message in my inbox. Holy shit, it's a response from the EIC. But how? If she's in Tokyo, that means it's... oof. Guess she's an early riser?

Laura reaches to take the mouse away from me. I beat her to the punch and open the email just as my coworker is about to tackle me out of my chair. In an instant, we're rendered immobile by the words on the screen.

"Thank you for bringing this matter to my attention," Laura says, reading the email aloud. "I will handle it."

But that's not what sets Laura over the edge. What does the trick is the next line of the email, which boldly declares: *And as for the threats leveraged against multiple staff members' jobs today, ignore them. Timothy has no authority to make such remarks until I've assessed the state of the editorial team's management.*

What a fancy way to say that Laura's job is safe and Tim is about to get his hair lit on fire.

"Yes!" Laura squeals, tackling me with a hug. I can tell she's over the moon about not having to file for unemployment benefits. After a few seconds of squeezing me to the point of suffocation, she lets go. Not that I minded; she smells nice and has soft hair.

"I can't believe we did it," she says, still reeling. "If... if it weren't for that one stupid search of yours..." She laughs. "I just can't believe how lucky you got. And you were so willing to just bet your account. It's like you really did know that everything would be fine..."

I tug at my shirt collar. God, I really shouldn't say...

"I, um, it wasn't just me," I blurt. "You're the one who did all the research and hard work while Tim was digging my grave in his office."

"Sure, yeah. *I'm* the one who saved the day. Thanks for nothing, junior."

I give her a playful shove.

"But really... I think we made a good team today," Laura confesses with a smile. The earnestness of her happiness and appreciation shines through like a beam of sunshine on a cloudy day. She's so pleasant to be around and so easy to understand. Plus, she has cute dimples. Should I?... No...

Not wanting to ruin the moment, I grab the manila folder that kicked off today's events and stand up. My actions catch her off guard, but she adjusts moods quickly. Business before pleasure, after all. We have a lost review to turn in.

CHAPTER 9

I point a finger gun at the mirror, take a shot, then blow the smoke off my imaginary firearm's muzzle. It's so easy to imagine how cool I'd look if I got into a fight with my suit on. It'd be like a scene out of an action movie or novel where the hero has to go undercover to a ritzy social event or cultural festival and then, smack-dab in the middle of it all, gets involved in some sort of showdown. Ha, yeah. That'd be awesome. Too bad I don't know shit about fighting and have no plans to do anything remotely as cool as that. Still, the suit looks great on me.

Midway through admiring myself more thoroughly than any other person likely ever will, I hear my phone vibrate. Not the trusty Aqua Jive, of course; The Crapple 10. Whoever could be calling me at six o'clock at night?

"Howdy," I say, popping in my inconspicuous Bluetooth earbud. I don't even entertain the possibility that the caller is either of the ladies from last night. I know who calls at six: the boy who's just scarfed down dinner so he can get to playing video games. Unless—wait. I actually have no idea what time it is in his world. Scratch all of that. Maybe it isn't him. Shit,

I hope it's not Blaire. That picture she sent me certainly wasn't earned by a guy who says "howdy."

"Wearing the suit again? See, it's already paying for itself," a chirpy teenager says, signaling that it's safe for me to let my guard down. I ain't dealing with a lady, just a boy with a voice as high as one.

"Yeah, kid. It's turning out to be a solid investment," I concede. "Mind topping me up so I can make more investments?"

"I got you, fam, I got you. Hitting your account with a deposit right now."

"Great. And thanks again for all the perk points; they're coming in handy. Anyway, what're you calling about?"

"Nothing much. Uh, Barry left because he felt bad about almost messing you up last turn, so, I'm, uh, I'm playing alone now. I just wanted to say hi."

Should I inquire about Barry? I grit my teeth and recall last night, wherein I almost got an STD in a mixed orgy thanks to a socially awkward teenager with a God remote, and decide it's better to let sleeping dogs lie. I think I'll let Rax figure out his friendship issues on his own.

"Mm," I say, commiserating with my teenage lifeline. "I gotcha, pal. Well, thanks for checking in. I'll hit you up if things get weird. Otherwise, enjoy watching my score! Or, uh, achievements. Whatever it is you're after."

"Huh? Oh, right, the achievements. Yeah, um, thanks. I guess I'll go now."

I shoot a thumbs-up toward the corner of my room's ceiling where I imagine his invisible, all-seeing camera is hovering, then return to checking out myself and my slick-as-hell suit—

A phone buzzes to life—now it's the Aqua Jive that's crying for attention. Who could be trying to reach me?

I pick up the handset, see the contact name, and feel a little pang of guilt. I haven't spoken to Angela in days. I don't think I thanked her for the éclairs, either—fuck, and I never told her about the incident.

I answer before the call can go to voicemail.

"Ange!"

"Didn't you get my texts? You haven't responded in days! I've been worried sick."

Did I get any of her texts? I don't think I did...

My inbox tells a different story. There are dozens of unread messages. Shit.

"My phone's been having some issues." I smack myself on the forehead with my free hand. "I'm sorry. I should've emailed you."

"Seriously, Jack, what's going on? Are you in another rough patch? Are you still processing Charley?"

She takes the wind out of my sails with that remark. Suddenly I'm too woozy to stand, so me and my precious suit sit down on my shitty, cheap mattress.

"I've... I've been trying my best not to think about that, honestly."

"Shoot, I'm sorry. I didn't mean to upset you."

"It's fine," I respond weakly, rubbing the bridge of my nose.

"Would it help if we changed topics? We can talk about anything. Want to talk about the news?"

"Sure."

"Okay, um—oh, never mind..."

"Why?" I lie down on my bed and look at the pasty white ceiling. I've never really liked my room. Not even for a day.

"Because the first three stories that appeared on my feed are just going to make things worse."

"Try me."

"CMM is reporting a mall bombing in Chicago, a mob on Snitter is defending a lady who was arrested for getting her husband killed due to a false rape allegation, and, uh, there's a viral photo circulating of a kid who died of starvation while cuddled up next to a puppy."

"Slow news day," I say, getting hit with the first unsolicited, subconsciously summoned bridge fantasy I've had in a whopping three days. I continue to analyze my ceiling. I think I actually hate my room.

"I'm sorry I'm not making things better. I swear I'm trying to help."

I know she's trying. But how can she succeed? The only person who *can* help isn't even from my world, and there's a damn good reason for that.

"I'm sorry, Jack. I'll go—"

"I'm just happy to hear your voice. And before I forget, thank you for the birthday gift. It was the best surprise I've gotten in a long time."

I mean every word.

"Well, it's good to hear your voice too. Promise you won't leave me hanging again?"

"Promise."

"All right, well, I can tell your mind is probably on other things right now, so I'll let you get back to it... thanks for talking to me. Let me know if I can do anything for you from all the way over here."

"I will. Have a good night, Ange. Talk to you soon." I end the call, but Ange's words haunt me. The news... my "rough patch"... Charley, that fuzzy little angel... what a mess. I feel tears welling up. Jesus, Jack, come on. You're going out with the guys tonight. To a club, no less. Get it together.

I shove my face in my pillow until I'm sure the pillowcase has absorbed any would-be tears and then go straighten myself up again. No use dwelling on the rearview mirror. The only way forward is through.

As I fix my hair and get back into shape for a night on the town, my phone rings. Really? I'm popular all of a sudden?

It's my Aqua Jive making noise, which throws me off. Besides Angela, who'd call at the current hour—

Oh, fuck. I think I recognize the number on the screen.

"Tim?" I say, praying it's just someone with a wrong number on the other end.

"Jack, Jack, Jack..." a voice whispers. Shit.

"What do you need, Tim? It's late."

"Call me..." he starts, interrupting himself with a burp, "boss."

"Tim, do you have a real reason for calling, or should I hang up right now—"

"*Boss*," he insists. "Make me the big boss again, Jack-Jack. Please, just, uh, for fun. I need it. Just say it. Just once."

Christ, I can smell the bourbon from here. Well, if it helps end the call sooner...

"Yes, *boss*?"

"I'm not your boss anymore, you lousy sack of shit! And I'm not drunk, either!" he shouts, his voice doing its darndest to rupture my eardrum. I pull the phone away to recover while he keeps his surprise offensive going. "*You're* drunk! Got it? And while you're at it, get this: I got put on administrative leave. It's bullshit."

He softens up again.

"I... I can't believe the scandal that got me," he says, sounding like he's on the verge of tears. "I spent years dumping money into an attorney that specializes in sexual harassment lawsuits, and it was all for nothing."

That's one hell of a weird way to fish for sympathy.

"Look, Tim, unless you have something serious to say, I have a place to be."

"You don't think I know it was you, Jack?"

His tone might've just turned ice-cold, but I'm not freezing. Not tonight. "No, I don't think you do," I reply. A few seconds of silence pass.

"Well, shit, you're right," he says, hiccuping between each word as his voice loses its vindictive edge. "But, uh, while you're here... you think the moon landing was faked, right? Right? My bitch of a wife thinks it was real and I want someone to tell her what's what besides me, for a change—"

"Goodbye, Tim. Don't call my number again."

"Bah, you're no help. Get the fuck out of my living room."

"It's 7 p.m. and I'm not at your house—"

He hangs up before the word "house" leaves my mouth.

I go back to ogling myself in the mirror, doing my best to replicate the little touches that made me look like a million bucks last night. I undo two buttons on the ol' dress shirt, slick a rogue strand of hair over the side of my forehead to illustrate that I'm a bit dangerous and unpredictable, and spray cologne all over myself so I smell like sex—but only the kind with good smells, like in movies. I think I'm good to go.

I look at my Crapple 10 and realize I could save myself the trouble of going out with the guys tonight for a mere chance at scoring big if I just pick up the phone and hit up one of my two new friends from yesterday. But something deep inside me, right at the corner of mommy issues and a deep-seated inferiority complex, tells me that option won't cut it. Sorry, Blaire and Misty, but I'm not done using my newfound amazingness to score as many perfect tens in as few nights as possible. Where there's dignity to be discarded and skirts to be chased, I'll be there, decked out like a goddamn superhero starring in their very own video game.

"Hey, you ready?" Morgan says, knocking on my door.

I press my earbud in, grab my phones, keys, and wallet, and take one last look at my smug mug in the mirror. "Yeah."

Ten minutes later, the boys and I close in on the subway station set to take us to whatever place Morgan thinks is a good barrel for us to catch some fish in. I'd ask where the hell we're going, but honestly, it doesn't matter. It's going to have overpriced booze, ladies who lack self-respect, and a bald guy who never went to college checking my ID. In that sense, tonight's not just about the destination. It's about connecting with the crew I'm traveling alongside.

Much to my surprise, the guys from our apartment that Morgan's invited aren't just the Scandinavian warriors I thought they were. They're also entertaining people. And they come in a few different flavors, to boot. There's Mathias, who's basically an equally hunky, brown-haired version of Morgan. Beside him is Sven, who's lanky and a bit closer to normal human proportions but still not close enough for me to relate to. And lastly, there's Tyrell, the one black guy in our crew. Normally I wouldn't dwell on such a detail, but he likes to bring it up ad nauseam, claiming that it's "amusing" how fixated Americans are on race. I guess his gimmick is kind of funny, in an ironic way. Plus, he's the only one of these guys who's close to my height and general proportions, so I'm inclined to like him a bit more than the human menhirs he and I are squadded with.

"Thank God you decided to join us," Tyrell says. "I was getting tired of being the, how you say, 'dwarf.'"

"No problem," I reply, flicking the bird his way. The other guys laugh.

"Jack, I've been meaning to inquire: Have you seen *Papa Mia*?" Mathias asks, prompting all the guys to groan.

"No... have you?"

"Why, it's funny you should ask—"

"Don't you do it!" Sven says as we descend the subway stairwell, getting blasted with waves of displaced air. Looks like the train's here.

"Papa Mia, here we go agaiiiiin!"

Mathias' impromptu performance causes the other guys to plug their ears once they've swiped their metro cards and made it past the turnstiles. Everyone around our little posse looks at the hulking European man singing chick-flick musical numbers. Surprisingly enough, I don't feel self-conscious for being associated with him. In fact, it feels nice. As I step foot on the subway train alongside my band of Vikings, I can't help but think tonight might actually be decent.

"Shut up, Mat," Sven orders, giving the bigger man a jab that gets him to stop singing and start snickering. Meanwhile, Morgan reminds me about his genitals.

"Jack! I almost forgot. Good news about that thing earlier from earlier: the burning stopped about two hours ago."

I give him the "okay" hand gesture, not sure if I can really congratulate the guy given what he's planning to do with that fire stick tonight. But, hey, not my problem. He's not my problem. The other guys aren't my problem. No one is. As a wise teenager once told me, I'm here for no other reason than to enjoy myself. That's the plan.

Unfortunately, the plan—along with my mood—sours a bit when I spot a hooker giving a one-armed homeless man a blowjob at the back of the train car. None of the other guys in my group notice, and the few other people in our car are seated far enough away from the unsavory duo in question to not be affected by their activities, but... yuck. The scene just looks gross. The hobo clutches a wad of grimy, dirt-covered cash in the only hand he has, and that's all the woman's eyes focus on as her head bobs up and down. I know I should look away, but I can't. Because, as sick as the sight makes me... am I really any different? Throwing money around to get a fancy suit, buying drinks, and indulging in meaningless small talk in exchange for... hell, the only difference between the hobo and me is that I'm not dumb enough to prioritize a warm mouth over rent money. What an idiot. Maybe he deserves to be homeless.

No, I shouldn't think that. That's awful. I'm awful. Everything's awful. I... I blame society.

"Hey, man, you okay?" Tyrell asks. I snap out of my daze.

"Uh, yeah, fine. Just thinking about something."

"It's our stop. Time to hunt down snow bunnies! That, er, is the correct English, yes?"

"Yeah, that's correct," I say, giving him a pat on the back. I slip out of the car with the rest of the guys, getting just a bit ahead of Tyrell so he can't see my face.

After a few minutes of navigating midtown Manhattan's muggy midsummer streets, the five of us step onto a particularly active city block. I squint to see what all the fuss is about. In the distance, I spot a neon-lit doorway gradually gobbling up the huge queue of people cluttering our block's sidewalk.

"Are we there?" I ask.

"Yes! I know a guy who knows the DJ. We should be on the list," Morgan says. Though I wonder how the heck he has connections here when he's, like, five months from being fresh off the boat, I don't question him. If Odinson says something's the case, I'll roll with it.

We skip the riffraff and go right to the bouncer. The way he flexes his biceps gives me uncomfortable high school flashbacks. Thankfully, the bulk of my posse are close to his stature and don't flinch when he sneers at us. In fact, my guys don't react to the bald bozo's attitude at all. They're completely oblivious to his social cues. Are we about to get our asses beat?

Morgan waves. The bouncer growls. I gulp.

"Hello, party for Morgan," my pal says. The gatekeeper checks his clipboard. A second passes. He then unhooks the rope blocking off the entrance and waves us in. I start breathing again.

The five of us step forward and shuffle down a flight of stairs leading underground. Seconds later, the evening sun that'd been heating up my back disappears, replaced by neon-blue lights and jet-black walls. Fog clouds the air. I look around and see cushy lounges, a bar, a stage with "musicians" who press soundboards once or twice a minute, and a dance floor packed tightly enough for me to feel claustrophobic just looking at it.

"Sven, Mat, let's go greet our boy," Morgan says, pointing to a guy wearing a glow-in-the-dark cat helmet situated beside the DJ across the floor from us. "Ty, Jack, you two think you'll be good for a few minutes?"

"We'll be fine," Tyrell replies. I nod, despite the bad vibes overtaking me.

"Then we divide and conquer!" Mathias says, proceeding to beat his chest and make gorilla noises. He and the other two giants lumber off to meet their pal, leaving Ty and me to figure out where we should start the night.

My Scandinavian wingman doesn't waste a moment. "How about some drinks to get us in the mood?"

"Sure."

We mosey over to the bar and I do exactly what I did last night, ordering one of whatever the person nearest me is having. I'm handed a glass of something clear as crystal. It smells like straight alcohol. I'm guessing it's vodka.

"Bottoms up!" Ty says, clinking glasses with me before downing his drink in one gulp. Um, challenge accepted, I guess.

We do another round shortly after that one. I pick up the tab to buy myself some cool-guy brownie points with Ty. He thanks me and declares it's time for the main event.

"Who should I keep an eye out for?" I ask, in case he has a type.

"I'm looking for strange tail." He winks and bumps me with his elbow. What the fuck does that mean?

"*The Hunt for Red November*, six o'clock," he says, pointing at a curvy redhead near the dance floor. I'm surprised he knows that flick.

"Listen, what's our story?" I ask as we approach the crimson viper and her equally busty friend. "If they pull any cross-reference shit on us, we gotta know some stuff about each other. What kinda movies you like, favorite sports, your educational background, et cetera."

"Oh, right. Um, I like action movies like *The Speedy and the Sinister*, I play a lot of basketball, and I have a degree that here in America would translate to, um, a master's in international banking law."

"C'mon, gimme something else; I need something with flavor."

"Uh... I had a threesome with my sister's best friend and her sister once," he says, his words slurring a bit. He almost trips but catches himself.

"Okay, first of all, you're not telling anyone that. And secondly, how the hell did two glasses mess you up so bad?"

Just as I start having second thoughts about letting the guy make a fool of himself in public, the redhead and her plus-one catch wind of us. Too late to back out; the game's begun.

"Are you two boys here for us?" they say in unison, both reeking of alcohol.

"Ladies!" Tyrell replies a bit too loudly. "My friend and I have been meaning to come over and introduce ourselves."

"Hello to you too. What a nice voice," the redhead says with a pronounced Bronx accent. "Where you boys from? Is that accent Scottish?"

Jesus.

"No, ha-ha, it's Swedish," he says. "I'm from Sweden."

"How ex-aw-tic." She giggles with her partner. "Well, I'm Shauna, and she's Daphne."

"And who are we speaking to?" Daphne asks, filling in while her fire-haired friend takes a sip of her almost-depleted drink.

Before I have a chance to open my mouth, Tyrell jumps in. "I'm Tyrell." He tears his eyes away from Shauna's cleavage to look at me and remember my first name. "And my friend is, er, Jack!"

"Why's your friend so silent?" she prods.

"I don't have a fun accent." It's the best thing I can whip up under the circumstances. Tyrell's hung me out to dry and is back to drooling over Shauna, and Daphne's giving me the most uninterested look on the planet, likely wondering why I'm even here. *Well, fuck you, Daphne; I don't know why I'm here either.*

"That's a little rude," Shauna says, quickly bouncing back to focusing on the boozed and amused European guy beside me. They yammer on for a few minutes and eventually Daphne joins them, meaning I only speak when Tyrell drags me back into the conversation because he doesn't want his unsociable wingman to stop making him look so good by comparison. And for whatever reason, I choose to swallow my pride and put up with it—to a point.

"Ty, you sound, like, so smart. Not lying, when I first looked at you, I thought you were gonna be, like, a dumb basketball player or something," Shauna says.

"Me? No, no. No basketball. Not a fan. I prefer tennis."

Unbelievable.

"Oooh, fancy. You do a lotta stuff like that up in Swedeland? You still in school up there?"

"Why, yes, actually, I'm here for a fellowship, but back home I'm in school—"

"Wait, wait, don't tell her." Daphne claps her hands. "Shauna here is smart too; she's a psychic. It's her side job. She can predict anything. Try her!"

"Yeah, let me predict your major. They have those in Europe, right? I can figure it out. Just look into my eyes..." Shauna says.

Are you fucking kidding me? Am I really sticking around to watch this idiocy play out?

"Are you a... liberal arts major?" she guesses.

"Amazing!" Tyrell cheers. "I can't believe you guessed it on the first try."

"We have so much in common!" Shauna tugs him close to Daphne and herself. "Believe it or not, I'm a liberal arts major too." Then, she lowers her voice. "I major in erotic performance art. Ever seen a girl paint a canvas seafoam green with nothing but her tits?"

That's it. I'm out of here.

"I don't feel so good. I'm gonna sit down," I say, walking away from them as I speak, knowing not one pair of ears is listening. I spot a relatively empty lounge area where a few other tired souls are hiding out and head there, away from the masses and shitty music.

I arrive at a big black couch. Though it looks comfy enough, there's a weird stain on the right cushion. I thank my lucky stars that there aren't any nearby black lights and sit my ass down on the left cushion.

I sink deep into the couch and look at the distant dance floor, hoping to spot the guys I came with. Maybe one of them is getting petered out by the club and would be willing to head home with me. Going solo would be a social faux pas, but perhaps I could parlay someone else's exhaustion into my escape plan.

I spot the Euro boys and realize there's not a chance any of them are calling it quits anytime soon. I'm definitely the weakest link here; the rest of them are having fun and getting more and more drunk, doing shit in public I can't even imagine doing in private. I shouldn't have come here. Coming here was a mistake.

And yet, I can't leave. As I look down at my legs, which are splayed out across the couch in the most antisocial way possible, preventing anyone from sitting anywhere near me, I notice a bulge in my pocket. I forgot, I brought my phones. Since the company here isn't any good, maybe I can call someone.

But who? I have no friends.

Well... almost no friends.

I pull out my Aqua Jive and dial the one number I know I can trust to try to lift my spirits.

Ring. Ring. Ring.

Ring.

"Hello?"

Thank God.

"Ange, help."

"What's wrong? What's all that noise in the background?"

"My roommates convinced me to go to a club."

"Do they know *anything* about you?"

"They're gonna, Ange, if I don't clean up my act." I eyeball the rest of my crew as they dance the night away. I silently pray that a fire starts so everyone's forced to evacuate and the night can be over with.

"Why'd you agree to go in the first place?" she asks.

"I... look, I've been feeling different lately," I reply, tiptoeing around the video game elephant in the room, "and... I don't know. I wanted to be sociable."

"And?" She's not buying my shit for one second.

"And maybe meet someone or something, I don't know." I roll my eyes.

"Well, that's good for you. Why'd you call me, if you're busy looking for—"

"C'mon, Ange, don't be like that. I'm fucking dying over here. You know how I get. Remember when you used to care when I got like that? 'Cause I remember. I want that Angela."

A moment of silence passes. And then another moment. Fuck, she's about to hang up on me, isn't she?

"Jack—"

"Yes?"

"Listen, you only get uppity when you pay too much attention to things. Why would you do that to yourself?"

"Sorry for having five senses."

"Seriously."

"I can't help it; shit's been everywhere tonight. I saw a hobo getting head from a hooker on the subway, and—"

"Ewwww."

"That's what *I* thought! And then one of the guys I was with turned out to be a tool, and the girls are all dumb as a bag of bricks here, and—"

"Stop. I get it, I get it. It's a normal day."

She's right... I don't feel bad. I feel normal. The awful feeling I'm feeling *is* my normal. And that's bad. Fuck.

"Look, I'm not comfortable giving you advice on the subject, but... well, you're there for the girls, I assume?" she asks.

"Unless you know any guys with C cups."

"You really want to go down that road—"

"No, no, fuck, I didn't mean—forget I said that. Just gimme advice."

The conversation pauses as she winds up a little lecture for me.

"Have you considered, and it's a wild suggestion, so be warned, but have you considered just looking for the good in the people around you? You only get super bummed when you feel rejected, meaning you probably already alienated someone. Maybe you'll get better results if you change your tone."

"Really putting that psychology degree to use tonight, Ange."

"You're the drunk boy who called me asking for advice."

I scratch my chin and let out a small burp. It was only two drinks... right? Did I forget about some? Either way, she has a point.

"Are we good here? I have to make dinner and get my bike to the shop before it closes," she says, sounding the teensiest bit impatient.

"Ange," I spit out, getting a little dizzy as I follow the moving blue lights on the ceiling with my eyes, "why can't everyone be like you?"

"Ha, haven't heard that in a while."

"No, I mean it..."

"Hey," she says, softening up a bit, "Most people aren't like me. But all the riffraff is worth it for the one in a million who are. So you better remember that and treat me to dinner the next time we meet up."

"Deal. Thanks," I whisper.

She somehow hears me over the music and people screaming in the background.

"You're welcome. Goodnight, Jack." She then hangs up on me.

Well, shit. Now it's just me and my thoughts again... as well as Angela's advice. Time to get positive. Activating optimism generators in three... two... one.

Output: minimal. I can make that work. Time to look for the good in people. Is there good in that girl by the bar wearing the tiny tube top? Well, I can't tell, but I'm pretty sure if that tube top keeps squeezing the way it is, something good's bound to pop out.

I smack myself. *Bad Jack, don't let the alcohol talk.* I definitely made a trip to the bar that I'm not remembering. Maybe several. Anyway, I have to keep looking for "the good." Um... oh, hey, it's Morgan. I can probably think of something good about him! Like, good thing he just grabbed the cat helmet from his friend and vomited inside it; it'd be a real shame to stain the nice floors here.

Damn it, that's not what Ange meant by being positive. Why can't I turn off the—wait, what's that sound? Is that sniffling? Whimpering?

I turn to my side and see a girl scrunched against the other end of the couch, packed into the only space I'm not hogging. Her face is buried in her hands and otherwise hidden by her dense, frizzy hair. Um... how long has she been there?

"Um, hey," I say, sitting upright. I tap her on the shoulder. "Is there anything I can help you with?"

She reveals her face and I see why she was trying so hard to hide it. Her mascara is smeared, and her eyes are puffy from excessive crying. That's certainly not a good look for a place like where we are.

"What? No," she replies between heavy breaths, brushing my hand away. "I don't need anything."

"Well, do you *want* anything? I'm a stranger, y'know. You can get stuff off your chest with me and we can just forget it ever happened afterward."

"Why do you care?" She sounds annoyed.

"Because I don't like seeing people cry," I say flatly, losing my soft edge for a second. "And because I've had a bad night as well. I get it."

She looks at me for a second, then wipes her eyes dry. "You have a minute? I just really need to tell someone... about..." before she can get her next words out, the floodgates reopen, and she goes right back to crying. Oh boy.

"I've got all the time in the world since my dummy friends are going to be here all night," I reply, gently patting her on the back. Eventually, she gets a grip and looks up again, ready to tell her story. It all started earlier today when an ice cream truck drove over a kid's toe, which led to her helping the kid to the hospital, where she ran into her ex-boyfriend who's a nurse there. It somehow came up that he's engaged, and that he did the special balloon thing with his fiancée that only she and him used to do. That got her worked up, so she went to hang out with her girlfriends to cool off, but it came out that one of them was sleeping with Todd, her roommate who she's had a crush on since he moved in. Then, when she and a few of the gals came to the club about an hour ago, it turns out Todd was here and flat-out rejected her when she told him how she felt. Fucking Todd.

"Screw Todd. He can sleep on a friend's couch tonight," I say.

"That'd be nice," she replies, laughing as she wipes more tears from her cheeks. "But he pays rent too. He isn't going anywhere."

"I'd offer you a place to crash, then, but I live in a room that's about the size of a cardboard box." Just thinking about my housing situation brings a small frown to my face.

"It's fine." She smiles. "You've already done more than enough."

I smile back. How could anyone be mean to her? She looks so innocent and full of life and joy when she's not crying.

"Hey," she says, noticing how I'm looking at her. "I... I don't think I should drink more tonight. But... want to go grab a snack down the street? I need fresh air."

My tummy gurgles.

"That'd be great," I reply, pornographically fantasizing about some greasy-as-fuck French fries covered in enough salt to kill a man. "You wanna go right now?"

"Sure."

I get on my feet and take her hand when she asks for help getting off the couch.

"I never got your name, by the way," she says.

"Oh. I—"

I feel a buzz in my pocket, and it ain't the pocket with the Aqua Jive.

"I'm so sorry—I need to take that," I say. "It's probably work. Two minutes?"

She doesn't make eye contact but smiles and nods, effectively telling me to fuck off. Ugh. I shuffle away from her and, once I'm out of earshot, accept the call.

"Kid, now isn't a great time. What do you need?"

"Your stats fell off a cliff a few seconds ago, my guy. Sex, money, luck, health, all of those are good, but that fifth mystery bar is tanking points across the board. What gives? How you feeling?"

That is why he's calling? Fuck my points, man.

"Looks like even with hacks I can't cheat life, huh," I reply, tapping my foot. "Funny how that works. Now can you go away and let me get back to doing what I was doing?"

"Whoa, man, what's with the attitude? I was just trying to look out for you."

"You were looking out for your high score. Now end the call."

"What the," Rax starts, lowering his voice so his mommy can't hear him use a big boy word, "hell is your problem? I give you everything and now you're ignoring me?"

"It's my right to not be in the mood to chat with some needy kid, *kid*," I snap, probably a bit too rudely for my own good.

"First off, I'm fifteen, dick, and second, maybe it's not your right. You're my game character, after all," he says. That entitled little son of a bitch.

"Oh yeah? So, what, you're going to force me to like you? You know how pathetic that sounds? How about, instead of harassing some pixels on your screen, you go and fix things up with Barry? You know, your real-life friend who you scared away over a video game?"

Neither of us speak a word after I let loose that last line, even though the call stays connected. I take a few deep breaths as I wait for him to say something, but he doesn't. Seconds of silence pass, and keep passing, until I can't take it anymore.

"Rax, man, you know I didn't mean to be so harsh. Please say something—"

The sharp crack of gunfire cuts me off. Like everyone else in the lounge area, I duck behind the nearest piece of cover—in my case, a table—and wait for what happens next.

I hear screams and hundreds of footsteps as people race for the stairwell entrance and emergency exit, both of which I can see from my current position. More gunshots sound off and two well-placed bullets land right above each doorway, freezing everyone in their tracks.

"If anyone tries to leave, they die!" a man shouts from somewhere near the dance floor. His voice is wild and aggressive; he sounds unstable. Not that that matters—if the speaker is the guy who fired those shots, then he still has enough of his marbles intact to aim well.

"Everyone, shut up! Juliet, stay right where you are!" the man continues, silencing the room. "And you," he says, addressing someone I can't see, "you don't move either."

"Me?" a familiar voice asks. It's Morgan.

"Shut up!" the crazy man screams, firing off two rounds.

Shit. *Shit.*

Against my better instincts, I move toward the danger, abandoning my safe table far away from the gunman. Staying crouched, I scuttle behind chair legs and club decor, weaving between clumps of whispering, worried people. I stop at a chest-high wall dividing a row of seats from the first neon-blue tile of the dance floor. From here, I peek out and get a better look at who's causing the commotion.

"I said don't move!" a tall man with disheveled hair shouts, firing a shot at a person trying to push open an emergency exit door. Immediately, the gunman's bullet makes contact with something, the person who'd been pressing the door falls down, and the people near the would-be escapee scream.

"Rax, buddy, get back on the line!" I hiss. The call's still live, so why the fuck won't he say anything? "I swear to God, if you don't get back on right now, I'll go out there and get myself shot just to spite you!"

Am I actually willing to do that? Probably not. But time's running out and if I don't do something soon, Morgan and that girl are toast. I don't see anyone else taking action.

"Rax, please!" I think back to what Angela said about looking for the good in everyone. "They might just be code to you, but they're real people to me, and they're scared. I need you!"

Silence.

Then a microphone crackle.

"Not the worst apology," the smarmy little fucker replies.

"Stop joking!" I whisper as the gunman advances toward Morgan and the girl, who are now the only people still trapped on the dance floor.

"What the fuck were you doing with Juliet?" the armed wacko says. "Juliet, you cheating, lying whore!"

"Hey, fucker!" Mathias and Sven shout from the sidelines, trying to buy their friend time to do something. The risk doesn't pay off; the crazy guy just shoots at their feet and scares them back.

"I—I'm so sorry, Steven," Juliet says as every inch of her body shakes uncontrollably. "It, it wasn't like that—"

The man fires a few warning shots into the ceiling before returning his aim to my roommate and the girl beside him.

"Rax, help me stop him, *now*," I say.

"You need to hide and wait for the cops! I'm serious. If that rando takes you out, it's game over, man. You're in a permadeath game. No respawns!"

"Rax, help me stop him or I'm going to die trying anyway."

"Okay, okay. Fine," he concedes, his words quick and stressed.

"Tell me how to get close to the guy without being seen."

"Right. Um... he'll see you if you step on the dance floor from where you currently are. I think he's about to rotate a little with the hostages, so his back will be facing you for a second. Dive behind the cover to your left when that happens."

I do as I'm told and clear the gap as soon as my opening appears. The gunman's still too far away for me to safely rush and tackle him, though.

"Is it safe to keep moving left?" I ask, unable to see over the top of my cover and gauge the psycho's cone of vision. I have to make it past the dance floor's transparent glass edge guards to reach the next entrance, but I don't know if it's safe.

Rax's silence kicks my anxiety into high gear. No one else is stepping up to deal with the threat, and the clock's ticking. "Faster, man!" I whisper.

"I'm going! I'm going. The camera is stuck on a texture. Gimme a sec!"

"We don't have a sec—"

"Move, now! It's clear!"

I whip past the sheets of glass and end up at the edge of the dance floor right as the gunman, who's now within a few yards of me, starts to turn his back again.

"You don't think I saw you and that Eurotrash together? You don't think I saw what you two were doing?" Steven the Lethal Lover shouts, still waving around that damn firearm.

"What the fuck!" Morgan blurts, his heavily accented proclamation only angering his captor further.

"That's it, give me one more reason to pop your fucking cap." The string bean shooter aims his gun once more, and something tells me he's not going to wait around much longer to finish what he started.

"Is the coast clear?" I ask, getting ready to whip out from behind cover and enter the floor.

"You get one shot, man," Rax says. "Good luck."

"Just say when."

"Wait for it. Wait for it. . ."

I take a deep breath.

"Now."

I ditch my cover and dash across the neon dance floor, lighting up tiles with each step I take in my rush for the gunman. He must hear me, because he spins around damn fast. As I close in on him, I realize he's too tall for me to waist-tackle, so I do the only thing I can think of and jump, hoping my downward momentum can knock him over. He points his gun at me.

"Jack!" Morgan yells.

The gunman fires. The crackle is deafening. I land my hands on him and we both go down.

The gun falls out of his hand. I see it happen in real time, meaning I must still be alive. I roll off the top of him and, the second I'm clear, Morgan, Mathias, and Sven come bolting over to restrain the club shooter, with Mathias throwing in a few punches to make sure he's docile. I think I see Tyrell drunkenly stumbling around somewhere in the sea of people rushing forward to help us, but I'm not sure. I don't really care. All that matters is that the nightmare's over. I stopped it. Er, we stopped it.

"Thanks," I say, hoping my partner can still hear me.

"No problem," Rax and Mathias reply at the same time.

Morgan helps me get back on my feet. "Thank you, man."

I dust off my suit. As I brush against the shoulder pad, I feel a single strand of shredded fabric. I give it a quick sniff. It smells burnt. Holy shit, that's where the bullet grazed me.

Morgan, with his eyes glued to my clothing, comes to the same conclusion.

"Holy shit! You are the luckiest man alive! That cannot be possible," he says, holding his head in disbelief. That's when other people start to take notice, squinting at my shoulder pad to verify that yes, in fact, the bullet that was fired my way came that close to injuring me.

"You lucky son of a bitch." "So brave. You're incredible." "You could've died!" They all keep talking, and talking, and talking about me. And somewhere, deep down, I think I like it.

Twenty minutes later, the club is entirely evacuated and I'm outside with everybody else, being checked by medics and the police. The one guy who tried to escape via the emergency exit apparently took a bullet to his ring finger, but beyond him, no one was hurt.

When I'm done being questioned by the cops, the Scandinavian squad tries to get me to join them so they can congratulate me some more, but I tell them to wait a minute. Because, as much as I appreciate their gratitude, the truth is that someone else deserves a lot of thanks right now too.

"Hey," I say, stepping away from the evacuees, ambulances, and police cars so my earbud can pick up my voice.

"That was close," Rax replies. He's awfully quiet. And even though the action is over, he doesn't sound relieved.

"Are you kidding? We killed it back there."

"Yeah, and more importantly, you didn't *get* killed."

"I know, I know," I say. "The save file lives to fight another day."

"That's not what I meant, man. I... it's not just about the score or the achievements. What you did... I dunno. I was scared. I didn't wanna see you go."

Aw, the little fella likes me again. Hopefully his camera isn't zoomed in enough to see the smile on my face.

"I'm not going anywhere, so stick around. You saw it yourself: we make a good team."

"Thanks... I think we do too." He softens up. "And, um, I'll try to be more considerate about things, going forward."

"You and me both, kid," I say, ending the call. I look over my shoulder at the street full of emergency vehicles and scared people. I no longer need to be afraid of the world like they are. The only thing I need is to be grateful for what I've been given.

Well, grateful and sure that I don't fuck up and waste it.

CHAPTER 10

Ooh boy, what a night. *Yawwwn*. I like my bed. I don't want to leave my bed. Doubly so because the sun's not yet high enough in the sky to blind me through the window and force me out. Which makes me wonder: Why am I even awake right now? My alarm definitely didn't go off; it's way too early—

Bzzzt. My Aqua Jive vibrates on my nightstand. *Bzzzt*. Who could it be at such an odd hour?

Turns out, it's everyone. Just about every person who has my number, including people I haven't spoken to in years, has sent a message my way: old acquaintances, rivals, former coworkers and friends, and even an ex-girlfriend. There are so many texts that my crotchety, ancient phone lags just trying to count them all, as if to tell me it's too damn old to handle me being popular. Well, sorry, friend, but today is my big day.

... Why is it my big day, though?

I read the messages as they come in.

Just read about what happened in the morning paper.
Are you okay?
Is that seriously you in the news?

There are dozens of messages like these. Some ask how I survived, others question why I put my life on the line in the first place, a few say they're impressed by my bravery, and one even tells me they no longer think I'm a piece of shit. I... I feel loved.

Then reality sets in. None of these people actually give one fuck about me. They just heard that I became a hero overnight and wanted to pretend like they had some sort of legitimate connection to me. Can't say I blame them; they're only human, after all. Hell, up until a few days ago, so was I.

One string of texts sticks out like a sore thumb. It isn't from all the posers and ill-intentioned former colleagues half-heartedly reaching out for a shot at acknowledgment. It's from the person who told me to look for the good in people, a piece of advice I've already failed to act on even though I've been presented with hundreds of opportunities to do so within the first five minutes of my day.

Maybe... maybe some of these people are legitimately concerned about me. *There, Ange, are you happy? I did it. I gave them the benefit of the doubt.*

I imagine her ridiculing me. "No, Jack, if you believed they had good intentions, you'd also reply to them. It's called being polite." Fiiiiiine, I'll do that. Later. For now, I just want to see what you texted me about.

The first part of her text-essay reads as expected: *What the fuck happened?! You took on a gunman?? What the fuck??? It says he fired a shot at you. A shot?! Why did you not call me?!!?!?!?!?!1!!?!*

She then goes on about how I'm cocky, self-endangering, and an idiot, before eventually complimenting me—once—for saving peoples' lives. Toward the end of her messages, she says something about incoming retaliation for me not picking up her calls. What calls?

I look at the top of my screen. Ange dialed me six times in the past hour.

... Well, I sure as hell missed those. So, what's the retaliation going to be? Probably some cupcakes or movie tickets, knowing her. Ha.

I'm coming over.

That's what her next sentence reads. No cheeky "you've been bad" gift or joking threat. She's being straight. *I'm coming over. And don't even think about telling me not to. I bought the plane tickets already. I arrive Friday night.*

I know two absolute truths about Angela. The first is that she'll never invite her mom's cousins to any family gathering she's in charge of, and the second is that she doesn't take "no" for an answer. I craft my reply text accordingly.

What time am I picking you up from the airport?

Next item on my agenda: bathroom, since I feel my loins churning and know it's that time of the morning.

When I enter, surprise-surprise, Morgan's there. It's a bit early for him, though, isn't it?

"My man!" Morgan says, waving at me.

"Hey." I wave back at him then disappear into a stall to unload a pint of hot lemonade. Once the tank's empty and I'm done having one of those weird little post-pee shivers, I pull my boxers up and head to the row of sinks. Morgan's still there, shaving his barely perceptible stubble.

"Early day?" I ask.

"Yeah, my boss is being difficult." He puts down his razor and looks at me. "Hey, about last night—thanks again, brother; I can't tell you how grateful I am."

"You would've done the same for me," I reply, walking away from the sink.

"I hope so. Now get out of here before the other guys show up and you never get to leave," he says with a laugh. He's right. I need to use my unexpected window of early morning free time for more important things than chitter-chatter. Namely, I need to use it to do laundry.

I get back to my room, toss all my clothes in a bag—except for the set that smells tolerable enough to wear to work—and head to the dry cleaner down the block. Gotta get these things freshened up before they start smelling too funky.

"Hey, Mr. Chen," I say, walking through the front door of the cleaners.

"Hey, you!" he replies, friendly as ever, failing to remember my name even though I've been to his business once a week since the day I got here.

Then he pauses, and his tone changes. "Oh, *you*! I read about you in paper. You can have free dry clean today." He beckons for me to hand over my laundry.

"That's kind, but you don't have to do that," I say, using my free hand to reach for my wallet. He sticks out a palm and waves it.

"No. No payment. Maybe next time," he commands, giving me a little bow before snatching my bag of clothes.

Well, all right, Mr. Chen. If you say so.

I buy breakfast and head home, since I still need to grab my BTMP, Aqua Jive, and almighty Crapple 10 before I can book it for work. As I walk back through the apartment complex's front doors, I can't help but wonder when the last vestiges of my formerly shitty life—the cramped, dingy living space and menial day job—will disappear. According to Rax, I can't quit my job or move yet because juicing up my life too quickly with hacks will cause compatibility issues or something. So as far as I can tell, I just have to sit tight and keep waiting for things to gradually get better since they're out of my control. Even though I'm basically the chosen one. Lame.

I slip inside my room and grab my shit, then dart back out and hit the subway. The air conditioning, the train being on time, and the fact there's always somehow an empty seat waiting for me in whichever car I enter—it's all lost its charm. Who cares if I don't have to sweat like an Olympian anymore just to get to work? By now, I want a private pumpkin carriage to take me to my job.

Alas, I don't get my wish. I get off the train and walk to my office without fanfare, besides the random waves, salutes, and hugs I get from strangers who recognize me from the morning paper. All right, I guess that counts as fanfare. But beyond that, it's just another morning.

Unsurprisingly, I get a good deal of praise from my colleagues when I arrive at work, though the seemingly well-intentioned congratulations quickly turn into the exact kind of horseshit debates that I hate the place for.

"I can't believe you even came in today, like, after what happened last night. That situation is exactly why we need stricter gun control," Jamie tells me, not realizing that all she needed to do was say "hello" and be quiet in order for me to have a pleasant morning.

"Oh, please. You know Jack would've had an easier time saving everyone if he had a gun of his own to put that madman down with," Pritchard says, abandoning his work now that he has an excuse to debate someone over shit that has no business being argued about in our office.

"Are you fucking stupid, Pritchard? If no one had guns, last night literally wouldn't have happened."

"The attacker would've just used a knife instead! Should we ban all of those too, Jamie? Want to learn how to butter your toast with a spoon?"

"The second amendment is a relic of centuries-old toxic masculinity that encourages men to resort to violence. Besides, it was written to defend musket ownership, not handguns," Taylor says, his face blank but tone smug. "You won't topple the government with your stupid hunting rifle."

Alex vigorously nods in agreement, which irks Taylor. Alex then apologizes for not offering a trigger warning before such an intense physical motion.

"Perhaps it is a relic," Pritchard replies. "Maybe we should update it so it protects firearms that actually *can* defend our civil liberties. Everyone deserves an assault rifle. A rocket launcher, even!"

It's like the minds behind each half of the debate have just enough brain cells to power fifty percent of a light bulb, but instead of uniting to hit one-hundred percent, they just keep trying to short-circuit each other. Can't these clowns go back to congratulating me and being silent?

"Listen, Pritchard," Jamie roars. "I don't want to hear one more word about your phallic-shaped rocket launchers, so shut it. And as long as Alex and I are splitting interim managing editor duties, that's an order."

My work email is a second away from loading when I hear that ungodly comment. No. It can't be. Please, simulation, say it ain't so.

My email loads and I see the cursed message from our EIC naming the two interim managing editors. Jamie wasn't kidding: she and Alex are, in fact, the new sheriffs in town, due to their tied seniority. Maybe I can perform some witch ritual to summon Tim back, if I act quickly—wait, that gives me an idea.

I need a ton of fuckin' luck points, pronto, I text Rax. He doesn't respond, so I send him another text. Still nothing. I proceed to pester him with messages that range from emotional blackmail to uncalled-for comments about his mother, as well as apologies for said comments and desperate pleas for help, but absolutely nothing I send earns a reply.

Seeing as my watchful guardian isn't living up to his title, I grit my teeth and prepare for a hellish day. But somehow, it never comes. Since Jamie and Alex are so enamored with their new titles, they actually pretend like they're good leaders who won't abuse their power. Of course, it's only day one of the new totalitarian regime, so there's still a lot of time for things to get ugly. However, I'll give Tweedle Dee and Tweedle Dum the benefit of the doubt since, on their first day in charge, they leave me alone from clock-in to clock-out and don't harangue me about my mildly flirty break room exchanges with Laura.

I power down my brain as the first rays of evening sunshine smack across my laptop screen. It's time to leave the office, grab dinner, and get home. I'm feeling pizza, maybe from that nearby Italian place that douses all their garlic knots in a liter of liquid butter. I can smell the bubbling mozzarella and pools of salty grease from here. *Mmm*. Thank God—er, Rax—for those health perks, 'cause I'm betting them all against a cheesy heart attack tonight.

On my way out of the office, I bump into the below-the-deck crew. Against all odds, Amélie was back at work today. I see her leaving the office alongside Stark and Laura. I know I almost took a bullet last night, but at least that was on my own time; that poor woman had to deal with our former boss deliberately giving her an on-the-clock asthma attack. Shouldn't she be at home filing a lawsuit?

"Guys," I say, squadding up with them as they head for the elevator.

"Ah, Jack, I've been meaning to see you," Amélie replies. "I saw you on ze news. Great job on not dying! And *ten-Q*," she continues in her impossibly thick accent, "for handling ze Tim situation avec Laura. Good riddance."

"Yeah," Stark adds. "Thanks a ton for that. Not sure if it's 'cause he's getting sued or something, but it looks like that son of a bitch is going to have to fork over all the toys he was billing the company for, meaning we're finally getting that flat screen. Huzzah!"

What a couple of dorks. I'm happy for them, though, and glad I could help.

"Shoot, I forgot my smart pen at my desk," Stark says as we arrive at the elevator's opening doors. "I'm gonna double back and grab it."

"I will join." Amélie pats her pal on the back and the two peel away from Laura and me.

"Guess it's just us," Laura says.

"Finally," I reply with mock exasperation, following her into the elevator. The mood's different than it was yesterday, or even earlier today when she and I were munching on granola bars and sipping godawful sparkling water.

"Must be pretty exhausting being called a superhero all day long."

"You'd be surprised."

"Nice ego. That notwithstanding, I wanted to say... I don't know why, but I like seeing you around."

The elevator doors shut, locking us in a tiny, pleasantly claustrophobic cube with each other. Like magnets, we gravitate closer, driven by forces I don't think either of us fully understand. Then there's a buzz in my pants.

I slip out my Crapple 10 and see I have a new text from Rax. *Hey, sorry, was busy, just logged in and saw your messages. Dude, you wouldn't believe how many achievements we unlocked last night!!*

I pocket the phone, ignoring the rest of Rax's message.

"Was that someone important?" Laura asks.

"That? Oh, no. Well, sort of. Like... a seven out of ten on the importance scale. But I don't need to take it."

"Might as well," Laura says, pointing to the elevator's glowing declaration that we've made it to the ground floor. Before an awkward pause can settle in, she resumes talking. "Maybe we should do something some other time."

The elevator doors open.

"Maybe we should."

We join the crowd of people leaving the elevators around us.

"Keep up the heroics," she says, slipping into the stream of worker bees headed toward the lobby doors opposite the ones I'm aiming for.

Someone's shoulder hits me as I look back to see her disappear.

"Yeah, Jack, keep up the heroics," a man says.

I know that voice. I twist around and grab the arm of the guy who just brusquely bumped into me.

"Hey, you, the hell was that about?"

The man turns toward me. We lock eyes. His face twitches and hands jitter.

"Didn't, er, see you there, friend," he says, clenching his jaw the second he's done speaking.

"Didn't see me there? That's funny, *Jon*. It is Jon, right? For someone who claims to work here, I haven't seen you much at all. You wanna tell me what your deal is? Why you're skulking around?"

Another wave of people comes hustling out of a newly landed batch of elevators, flooding the floor once again. Jon shakes off my hand and disappears into the sea of bodies.

"Hey, wait up!" I shout over the rabble, jostling against people to try to keep up with him. But it's too late; he's vanished beyond the dozens of moving heads and suits blocking my vision. By the time I follow his trail out my building's front doors, I've lost him entirely.

"Shit."

I look down the sidewalks and across the street but can't spot any signs of Jon. I reach into my pocket, pull out my earbud, and pop it in.

"Rax, you there?"

"Heck yeah, my bromo sapien. What's up?"

"Listen," I say. I walk toward the subway, looking over my shoulder as I do so. "Some nut is stalking me, saying he works at my office. Did you see the guy? He was hassling me a second ago."

"Yeah, I saw someone interacting with you on my screen, but—"

"Do you know where he went?"

"I got no clue," Rax admits. "I wasn't paying close attention to a rando."

I speed up my power walk. "Shit! There's no way you can find him now?"

"Not if I don't know what I'm looking for." He sounds a little bothered. "Look, dude, there are bugs and glitches in every game; he's probably just an NPC acting up a little."

Rax's theory isn't very reassuring. If every stalker is just a buggy NPC, then the devs responsible for my hellhole of a planet are even worse at their jobs than I thought.

"Hey," Rax says, likely in response to seeing me speed up even more as I try not to break into a full-on panicked run for the subway station. "Don't be scared, okay? You've got me right here."

"I didn't a few hours ago!"

"Well, you do now. Nobody's gonna mess with you, ah-kay? I'm watching more closely. Anything funny shows up, I'll let you know and you'll see it coming a mile away. You're good."

When a video-game-addicted teenager tells you he'll protect you from sketchy people in one of the most dangerous, overpopulated cities in the world, you *know* you're in trouble. So, game, make no mistake: I know—and I'm on to you.

CHAPTER 11

"I'm telling you, brochacho, it was a bug. Move on," Rax says.

I exit the subway station and am instantly, mercilessly hammered by ray after ray of blistering hot sunlight. My ears are so sweaty that I'm surprised my earbud hasn't fallen out. God, it's sweltering outside. How come no one else is sweating?

I look over my shoulder to see how everyone else is handling the warmth. It turns out they're all doing fine. Just like the last thirty times I checked.

It doesn't add up. I've bumped into that creep thrice, now, and still have no clue what the hell his deal is. Thanks to him, I haven't been able to enjoy a moment of the past twenty-something hours. Yesterday, after the subway ride home from work, I rushed so recklessly to grab my dry cleaning that I almost got hit by a car. I ordered Chinese just so I wouldn't have to go outside for dinner. I slept for less than three hours because I swore I kept hearing voices outside the window across from my bed. And now, on my way to work, I'm eyeballing every stranger I walk by, feeling as though each and every one of them is carrying a garrote wire, just waiting for the right second to catch me while my back's turned.

"Kid, you don't know that. Is there even a New York City where you're from? People don't play around here... if someone has it out for me, that's bad news," I respond, hustling at Mach 5 toward my office.

"Dude, you took on a gunman at point-blank the other day and survived getting shot at. Why are you spooked over a glitch?"

"Because you couldn't figure out who the glitch was, or why it's harassing me!"

"It's been one turn, dude; I'm working on it. Go easy on me. And stop worrying so much, it's messing with your points." He lowers his voice. "Pussy." He hangs up.

Yeah, maybe the kid's right. *Get it together, Jack, get it together.* I give myself a slap on the cheek and then a harder one when the first fails to snap me out of my funk. I regain control over my breathing just in time for work. No weirdos in the lobby—a good start. I step in the elevator and no one suspicious joins me, meaning I'm almost at my desk and in the clear. Whew. Okay. I can do it. My little Big Brother has my back; he's watching everything I do and seeing everything I see. But... but what if Jon can do that too?

The elevator chimes, its doors open, and I bolt out. Amélie and Stark appear alongside me, exiting from a neighboring elevator.

"Hey, have either of you met a new guy named Jon? Ghost white skin, about yea tall, probably on the spectrum?" I ask, bombarding my colleagues with questions as I make stupid hand motions to illustrate Jon's proportions.

"No," Amélie answers. "And it seems you are ze one who is white as a ghost." She pulls out her ID card and opens the office door for us.

I shuffle inside and ditch those two goobers; they're no help. After a quick pit stop at the kitchen sink to splash cold water on my face, I dry myself off with a napkin and travel to my desk. I slide into my chair and survey the surroundings. My heartbeat settles down. Nothing's wrong here. Nothing's out of the ordinary. I'm back at work, doing the good ol' nine-to-five grind. Life's boring. Life's dull. And that's a good thing.

Yeah, as long as I can block Rax and that creep out of my mind for a few minutes, things should be fine.

"Hey," Pritchard says, spinning around in his chair to face me.

Pritchard! Of course! Why didn't I think to ask him? If there's some nutcase pretending to be an employee around here, he'll know. Or he'll have a theory, at least. Wait... conspiracy theories... should I call... no, I'm not that desperate. Yet.

"Do you know anyone named Jon? Claims to be a remote editor?"

"No. Can't say I do."

"But if he's an editor, shouldn't everyone know him? Maybe I should email the EIC. Yeah, yeah, she'll know. She'll know," I say, vigorously nodding in agreement with myself.

"Well, I was going to ask if you'd heard the news, but you seem preoccupied," Pritchard replies, squinting. I can't tell if he's annoyed or suspicious that I'm pranking him. Surely I'm not the only one who could've met Jon, right? Is the game wiping people's memories to mess with me? Am I going insane?

Wait. Am I?

"No! No, I'm fine," I say, realizing how wide my eyes are, feeling them strain to stay alert and squirrel-like. Jesus, I think the side of my mouth is twitching. "It's a long story. I don't want to bore you with it."

"Good, because we don't have time to dawdle on small talk and pleasantries. We have bigger fish to fry."

"Aren't you vegan?"

"Only because of whatever the government's putting in national meat supplies. But that's not important!" He scoots his chair closer to me and leans in. "You really don't know about what happened yesterday, after you left?"

"Can't say I keep up with the office gossip, no."

"Then allow me to inform you." He turns his head to look down the hall at Alex, who's standing at the printer, well out of earshot. "Alex and Jamie, they've gotten in a row."

A row? When did my office become *Downton Alley*?

"Yesterday, Jamie and Alex had a video conference with the EIC in Tokyo to discuss interim managing editor duties."

"And?"

"And by the time the meeting ended, it was after 9 p.m. Everyone from every department had left."

"So why were you still here?" I scratch my chin and look at Alex, who's still far away. In a time of such vast uncertainty, the last thing I want is to lose my lame job because of "locker room talk."

"I wasn't," he replies.

"Then how do you know what you know?"

"Let me ask you: Do you know our building security manager's favorite assorted pastry combo?"

What the fuck? Did he just admit to what I think he just admitted to? Is he even going to address the irony of him, of all people—the tinfoil hat man himself—using security devices to spy on people? Oh, what am I saying. Of course he's not.

"I didn't think so," he says, misinterpreting my silence by a mile. "Anyway, as I was *saying*, it was just them. And things got a bit heated during the conference call, so afterward, Alex stormed out and left the office."

"Which leaves us with Jamie…" I mumble. Speaking of Jamie, where is she? I haven't seen her today. I look around but can't find the lead head of the Prog Triplet hydra anywhere.

"Quite. And at precisely 9:17 p.m., Jamie, all by herself in our big office, thought she could get away with perusing some lewd online videography."

"Porn?" I ask, not grokking the significance of what Pritchard is laying down for me.

"Yes, but not just any pornography," he says, lowering his voice so much that I almost consider texting Rax to ask if my game can have subtitles enabled.

I snap out of my mental digression when Pritchard leans in to whisper in my ear. I feel the warmth of his breath and catch its scent too. It smells like mint and iron. It makes me uncomfortable.

"Heteronormative pornography."

"That's ninety-five percent of porn," I counter, getting antsy about the prospect of Alex returning from the printer.

"Not just any heteronormative pornography! The kind with men peeing on women while calling them filthy harlots! Don't you see? When no one's around, when her Snitter followers and real-life lackeys aren't there to judge her, she indulges in her darkest male domination fantasies! She wants to be degraded. It's exactly as I predicted—"

"Listen, Pritchard, I'm gonna cut you off right there. Glad your psychology experiment panned out, but, frankly, it's none of my—or your, for that matter—business—"

"That's not even the best part!" He puts a hand on my shoulder to stop me from swiveling my chair away. "The best part is that Alex apparently forgot some files and came back to the office around ten minutes into Jamie's little online excursion."

Oh boy.

"Alex caught her in the act and they had *quite* the argument. Now one of them hasn't even shown up to work. If you want to talk about strange things related to our office, I think my story takes the proverbial cake. What was yours? Something about a fellow named Josh?"

"I'm gonna get back to work." I give Pritchard a curt nod before spinning back toward my desk to start my day's worth of worthless deals posts. But no sooner do I tear myself away from the conversation than Jamie comes shuffling into the office, face hidden behind tactically held folders. She heads straight to her desk just as Alex returns from the printer. Neither of them so much as looks at the other.

"Morning meeting in five minutes," Jamie says quietly, darting to the conference room without another peep. Flames have risen in Alex's eyes, signaling hellfire is soon to rain— and, would you look at that, I forgot my umbrella. Maybe it's not too late for me to tap out and take a sick day.

Pritchard notices me packing my laptop and grabs my arm.

"Don't you even think about it," he says. I give him the biggest "fuck off" look my face can muster, but he doesn't flinch. "Don't leave me with... them."

He stealthily tilts his head in the direction of the emotionless Taylor and agitated Alex. There's genuine fear in his eyes. Truth be told, I don't think I care what happens to him or any of them. But, then again, these people are part of my job and life, at least for now. I should probably stay in the loop on current events. Besides, as long as I'm in here, I can't be stalked. Right?

"Fine," I respond.

Four minutes later, everyone's in the conference room. Laura, Amélie, and Stark hide in the back seats, while

Pritchard, Taylor, and I fill the front ones like the editorial sacrificial lambs that we are. Standing in front of us are Alex and Jamie, who actively refuse to make eye contact with each other.

"All right, everyone," Jamie begins, keeping her eyes on her notepad. "There are a couple of things to be addressed—"

"Everyone, we need to talk about something," Alex declares, glaring at Jamie. Class is officially in session.

"Alex, I don't think it's the time or the place—"

"Well I don't care what you think. Everyone, I have news to share regarding my co-managing editor." Alex's eyes narrow. "Some problematic news. Last night, I left important folders at the office. And when I returned to get them—"

Jamie swings a hand over Alex's mouth before the latter can spill the beans.

"You don't want to do that here," Jamie says through gritted teeth as she keeps her hand over her colleague's mouth. "Strong women are mightiest together, remember?"

Alex breaks free of Jamie's hold. "Not today. Everyone, the cis-hetero woman beside me watches porn!"

The cricket chirps in the room would be audible if it weren't for a poorly muffled gasp from Taylor.

"And not only that," Alex continues, "but fetish porn. The kind reserved for—"

Everyone in the room practically chokes on their own saliva as Jamie tackles Alex to the floor. I twist around and see Amélie and Stark abandoning their seats, rushing toward the meeting room's doors while shouting something about getting security. Laura remains stationary and perplexed. Pritchard takes his phone out and starts recording the altercation, his eyes wide with shock, fear, and a dash of glee. Taylor pushes his seat far, far away from the front of the meeting table.

Jamie pins Alex down and covers her cohort's mouth once more, but her opponent shouts through the gaps between fingers.

"—bigots! Jamie likes urination! Domination! She's normalizing patriarchal structures!"

Alex escapes Jamie's hold and stands up, grabbing the pen beside Jamie's notepad on the conference room table.

"Don't take another step, you heteronormative bitch," Alex warns, watching Jamie get up and bare her claw-like nails.

"Take another step," Pritchard says from the sidelines. I follow Taylor's lead and back my seat up a bit. Alex's weaponized pen thrusts in Jamie's direction a few times, warning her not to come closer. Jamie, now red in the face, ignores the pokes and continues to circle Alex. By the time Jamie's back is to us, she's closed the gap with her fellow co-editor and goes in for a swipe. Alex's pen then launches like a dart in an attempt to take out Jamie's eye but misses its mark and shoots across the conference room table instead. I snatch it out of the air. Holding the pen in place where I caught it, I turn to Laura, who's busy letting out a frightened "eek." She closes her mouth the moment the pen stops rocketing toward the spot right between her eyes.

Meanwhile, at the front of the room, Jamie's landed one hell of a blow on Alex, whose cheek is bleeding from four parallel claw marks.

"I'll make sure every office in the city knows what kind of self-hating feminist you are," Alex growls.

"Not if you're dead!" Jamie shouts, diving forward and knocking Alex to the ground again, just in time for Amélie and Stark to return with a few of the building's security staff in tow. The large men in black polos make quick work of restraining both of our co-managing editors, though the two keep shouting and reaching for each other all the way through the office as they're dragged—er, "escorted"—out of the building. Looks like it's time for an early lunch!

Fast-forwarding a bit, lunch is great. I haven't had a quesadilla that cheesy in months.

I return to the office from my midday break a little later than usual, not too worried about clock-in times since there's no managing editor to harangue me about tardiness. Three down in one week. The company's getting better by the day.

Speaking of the company, it seems that while I was gone, every single neighboring department on our floor shuffled their desks as far away as possible from my team's corner... again. Dozens of fellow company employees I've never spoken to ogle me as I return to the bullpen to tackle the aftermath of the morning meeting. Not that there's much left to tackle; if I don't count the non-editorial trio, the only people left are Taylor, Pritchard, and me. Since those two clowns have gone mute and are reading stuff on their computers, I decide to follow suit.

I log back onto my laptop and, wouldn't you know it, there's a notification telling me I have a new email from the EIC. I wonder what that could be about.

Dear colleagues, it's come to my attention that there have been a series of serious issues in our editorial department. Both interim managing editors have been let go. I am authorizing Pritchard, the most senior current member of the editorial team, to be the new managing editor, until I return from Tokyo late next week.

Just as I thought the tides were turning! Fuck. On second thought, though, Pritchard is still better than Jamie and Alex. Yeah, the news is good news. I'll round up and say the glass is half full.

I take a deep breath and reach for the drawer holding my headphones, but I'm interrupted midway.

"Jack," Pritchard says, having sneakily swiveled his chair around to ambush me, "we must talk."

"What for, Mr. Fourth Managing Editor of the Week?"

"That's just it, I can't do it," he says. "Why do you think we've gone through so many in such a short amount of time?"

"Because everyone who works here has some sort of crippling social condition that stops them from acting like normal, healthy people?"

"No! Because power corrupts and *absolute* power corrupts *absolutely*."

"Oh."

"I won't do it, Jack. I won't do it. I've seen enough good men and women, and whatever the hell Alex was, fall at the hands of Marxist greed, lusting for power." He raises a trembling fist into the air as though to mourn the loss of his comrades.

"Why are you telling me these things?" I ask. My eyes glaze over in anticipation of a lengthy diatribe against the communist ideology, the recently disbanded Prog Triplets, and GMO-enhanced whole milk.

"Because I want you to take the position in my steed."

What?

"Are you fucking around? Can you even do that?"

"By the power vested in me, I declare that I can! Jack, I must relinquish my position. I do not trust myself to remain pure of spirit and mind. The only person who I believe can withstand the soul-corrupting touch of the title of managing editor is, after careful examination, you. The way you've constantly held your tongue during office squabbles in order to appear impartial—even when you knew I was right and clearly silently sided with me—as well as the way you stood up to Tim during his darkest hour, and protected that one woman from his unjust wrath, have proven to me that you are worthy of the mantle. What say you?"

If I reject his offer, his title will default to the next person on the seniority totem. I look at him, then at Taylor, who's busy taking a dumb, open-mouthed selfie for his Snitter account. No, I can't let Taylor be in charge—I have a moral obligation to my office to not let that happen.

"Sure, I'm in."

Pritchard shakes my hand and thanks me for my service, officially rendering me the newest interim managing editor.

What should I do with my newfound power? Should I inject some dignity into the office and lay down the new law of the land?

Actually... I'm thinking pizza party. Yeah, a pizza party on Monday sounds good. I'll pay for it myself so there's no recreation budget red tape to worry about, and I'll invite all of the other departments too. It'll help our team make friends with everyone else, since that should've happened a long time ago. And besides, it sounds nice. Let's have some fun at work, damn it.

I start drafting the office-wide email blast and get as far as the opening greeting when my Aqua Jive vibrates. I've learned my lesson about ignoring messages on that thing and am not eager to see another angry text from Ange or something—wait, it's Friday. Ange!

You better be at the airport when I land!

Looks like I need to gear up for next week's pizza party, then for Ange—'cause whether I like it or not, I've got plans tonight.

CHAPTER 12

"You're sure no one followed me here?"

"Yes, dude. You're fine."

"Just keep any psychos off my back, especially while Ange is in town. Promise me you won't let anything happen while she's around," I say, tapping my foot as I sit in the waiting area of the airport.

"You got it, chief."

"Thanks."

I check the time on my phone and wonder what's the holdup. The arrival board said her flight was coming in on schedule...

"So, uh, can I ask what your plan is here, with her? I get that you two aren't, like... but then, what are you—"

"Talk to you later, buddy." I hang up on Rax. Angela enters through the sliding doors on the other side of the room. I leave my seat and move toward the crowd of travelers she's mixed in with. Much like myself, she isn't tall, so there's no telling if she's spotted me past the shoulders and heads of everyone in front of her.

"Angela," I shout. As if on cue, the sea of strangers parts and reveals her in full. Just by looking at her, it's like I've traveled back in time, to when things made sense—to when things were good. She stands a few yards away. At that distance, she could drop her suitcase handle, come rushing forward, and tackle me. She doesn't. Instead, she calmly walks over and leaves a respectful amount of personal space between us. I extend a hand.

"What are you doing?" she asks.

"I'm, uh—it's a handshake—"

"Come here," she says, letting go of her suitcase handle to pull me in for a big hug. I reciprocate.

With my head over her shoulder and hands wrapped around her back, I admire the woman who's flown so far just to make the current moment possible. Besides being a bit tanner than I remember, she's identical to when I last saw her. The same chocolate-brown hair and eyes. The same light scent of ginger and lotus. And when she pulls away from the hug, I see the same shiny smile, stretching cheek to cheek to assure me things are okay. But deep down, I know they're not. Her visit is a crutch, not a cure. That's why it's just a visit—temporary.

"It's great to see you again—" She's interrupted by a ringing sound emanating from her pocket. "Do you mind if I take care of that?..."

"Go for it," I say, feeling a vibration in my own pocket. Two twenty-somethings focusing on their phones only seconds after meeting up to spend time together. What a surprise.

I pull out my Crapple 10 and see new messages from Rax.

You all good there, pard'ner? Your stats just took a major dive, fifth mystery category 'specially. Score's dropping a bit. What gives?

My impulse is to bite his head off, but I stop myself. *Look for the good in people.* I can't slip back into being that sad son of a bitch on the bridge, especially with Ange here.

Is that your way of telling me you're worried about my well-being? The real thing, I mean. Not the score, I text.

Yes ofc I am, okay? We're tight. It's just weird to say it like that. Besides, high score and achievements are very important as well. Easier to talk in terms of that. We're close to the top; a little longer at our current gain rate and we'll be kings. Gotta be careful.

Why do you care so much about scores and achievements, anyway? I ask.

Why do people compete in sports, or spelling bees, or nerd crap like chess club, he replies. *Dumb question. Shouldn't you be busy with busty?*

Watch it, I fire back. I look up from my phone at Ange. Why *aren't* I busy interacting with her? It's a good question—and the answer lies with whomever is texting her right now. Should I ask? No, it's not my place.

She notices I've stopped looking at my phone and lets a second pass before pocketing hers, affording me time to change my expression and save face. Not that it matters; I know she saw the look I was giving off. Stupid, stupid Jack. Get a grip.

"You good to go?" she asks. I slip my Crapple 10 in my pocket and give her a nod.

Ten minutes later, we're in a taxi headed for the big city. Ange's luggage is in the trunk and she and I are in the back seat.

"You know, TSA wasn't *that* bad—for once," she says.

"Have you seen the way you're dressed? They probably went easy because they thought you were an American with a sunburn."

She gives me the bird and says something in her native language, which I still don't know more than four words in.

I laugh. After pretending to pout for a few seconds, she laughs too. It's just like old times.

A little under half an hour since leaving the airport, we arrive at our destination: a street with some good restaurants that I think would make for a respectable reunion dinner. Did it occur to me that maybe Ange would want to check into a hotel or drop off her luggage first? No. Is she pissed at me? Of course not. Am I embarrassed? Marginally.

"You know why it's called luggage?" she asks as she unloads her suitcase from the trunk of the taxi.

"No, why?"

"Because your ass is lugging it around since you didn't drop me off at my hotel."

I grab the suitcase handle and give the taxi driver a wave with my free hand, prompting him to burn rubber out of the hipster-y neighborhood. If it weren't for the food, I wouldn't step foot near here, either. Speaking of which...

"I was thinking we could go for dinner," I say.

"Where?"

"There's a killer mac 'n cheese place a block or two from here."

She sticks her tongue in her cheek and ponders.

"You know, I remember there being a great Chinese place around here too," she says, squinting down the street.

"I, uh, actually had Chinese last night," I reply.

"It's exclusively vegetarian."

"So was my food last night."

"I mean you wouldn't be stuck ordering lo mein."

"Who says I did?"

"All right, friendo. Do they serve mac 'n cheese at my hotel?"

I look at her. She returns my stare.

"Lead the way to the Chinese place."

Ten minutes later we're seated next to a gong and drinking herbal tea. It tastes like piss.

. . .

I'm lying to myself. It tastes fine and is doing wonders for my throat.

"So," she says, taking a sip from her cup. "What's going on?"

"I'm drinking tea. With you. Here." I take a big swig of my mystic herbal fluid, knowing I'll eventually have to lower the cup and make eye contact. She waits until our line of sight is unobstructed.

"Cut it out, Jack. You dodged it at the airport. And on the taxi. And on the way here. What the hell is going on with you?"

Is it getting hot in here? For the prices the restaurant charges, one would think they could afford air conditioning—

"Hello?" she says.

I've drifted off and am staring at the carpet. Maybe... maybe I should text Rax. I don't know what'll happen if I— wait, I don't think he knows, either...

"You haven't been answering my calls or texts for days at a time. You never do that. And now you're in the news! Just talk to me. That's all I'm asking for."

"It's... just been a weird week. Did I tell you I got promoted?"

She stares blankly at me. Our waiter appears with food. He drops it off and she continues to stare at me, until eventually, without a word, we both start eating. She's ordered some sort of vegetable stir fry. I have soy chicken in soy sauce.

The only sounds at our table are chewing and eating noises. Ange slurps up saucy string beans almost loudly enough to drown out my own gratuitously squishy chomps as I scarf soy nuggets. Everything sounds so goddamned *moist*.

"*All right*," I say a bit too loudly, lowering my voice the second I notice a group of old Asian men peeking at me from a few tables behind the gong. "You asked on the phone a few days ago if I was in another rough patch. Well, I was. I've been doing some stupid stuff. But I cleaned up, okay? I handled everything."

She puts down her chopsticks. Her eyes move from her plate to me.

"And..." I start, juggling the words in my mind, "I think I might've made a new friend."

"You want to tell me about them?"

I put down my fork and take a deep breath.

"Yes. Yes, I think I do."

And so I tell her about the fellow who came into my life on Monday, took me to the park on Tuesday, helped me save lives on Wednesday, let me enjoy myself on Thursday, and gave me the tools to score the promotion I didn't even know I wanted just earlier today.

"Wow, he sounds... pretty special," Ange says, her face oscillating between happiness and—though she tries to hide it—frustration. Jealousy.

"He is, but I don't phrase it like that. I wouldn't want to make things weird and scare him away. You know what I mean?" I say before sucking up a wet, slippery noodle from the side dish of lo mein I ordered.

"I, uh, wow. Scare him away? I'm... I'm so happy for you!" she says, a bit flummoxed but filled with outward enthusiasm. "Where'd you say you met him, again?"

I pause.

"I didn't."

"Oh." Her cheeks redden. Jeez, that got awkward fast. Think, Jack, think...

"But, uh, since you asked: the bridge," I blurt. "Down by the river. Ten minutes from here. You know the one?"

"Oh, the—"

Our waiter interrupts us and drops off the check. Without hesitation, I grab it.

"Whoa there," Angela says as I whip out a few bills from my wallet. "You don't have to do that. I can handle myself."

"I've got spare cash for a change, Ange. I know neither of us are rich. Let me handle it."

She puts up a fight and grows increasingly suspicious of me, so much so that eventually I cave and have us go Dutch. She knows something is up and can smell it on my breath. Well, that and nuggets.

"How about a movie?" I ask after we leave the restaurant. I'm struggling to think up ways to shut up both of us for as many hours as possible. "There's a theater around the corner, I think."

She squints.

"I really should get to my hotel soon... check-in, and all that."

"Oh, yeah, you're totally right. I forgot. I'll get us a cab."

The moment I raise my arm to hail a taxi, she pulls it down.

"I changed my mind. I think we have enough time for a movie. Let's do a movie." Ange's words are quick, squirrelly, and strange. Yet I know better than to question her and start a fight. So, without protest, I grab her suitcase and we get moving.

Shortly thereafter, we arrive outside the cinema. Posters for all the films currently showing line the building's walls.

One immediately catches my eye, but I do the gentlemanly thing and field Ange's preferences first. "What kind of mood are you in?"

"Hmm, I don't know..."

"How about *Guardians: Everlasting Conflict*? I heard it's got, like, over fifteen superhero franchises in it—"

"No," she says, moving past the colorful sci-fi epic's artwork without a second thought. "I want something cute and fluffy."

"I thought you said you didn't know what mood you were in?"

"That was five seconds ago." She walks toward a poster featuring roses, a guy with his shirt off, and a woman in a wedding gown. "I think I want to see... that one."

Damn it. She's chosen the only film I absolutely do *not* want to sit through. And, upon closer inspection of the poster, I grow even less interested: the dopey looking rom-com she's eyeballing stars Gerad Pittler and Yennifer Lawngrin. The issue is, I'm pretty sure in a recent interview Yennifer said she's no longer taking on roles with nudity involved. *Sigh.* I don't pay for her acting, Hollywood!

"Really, Ange? Really?"

"I travel so far to see you, and you don't even want to see a movie with me..."

"I didn't ask you to come," I say, eyeballing the cringeworthy poster. Big mistake. She gives me the puppy eyes and starts quivering her lip. It's not a warning, it's a threat.

"Don't you fucking d—"

She lets out a single whimper.

"All right, okay, fine. We'll see *Lovers' Games*," I hiss, grabbing her arm and pulling her inside the cinema where infinitely less people can see her theatrics. Not that it matters; she's already dropped the act and has a huge grin on her face.

For a minute, all seems good. Then we get to the ticket counter.

"Sir, you can't bring that suitcase inside."

Shit, that didn't even occur to me.

"What if we choose an aisle seat? You want to see the contents or something? It's just clothes and, I dunno, a hairdryer. Stuff like that," I reply, hoping the dork with the bow tie will just let us buy our damn tickets and move on with our lives.

"I'm sorry, sir, but suitcases are against policy."

"Look," I scan his shirt for a name tag, "Adam. I get it, it's unusual. Weird, even. But the lady just got off a long flight and she wants me to take her to a movie. Go easy on me, yeah?" I put on a charming smile, but even that doesn't sway the movie theater employee who's wearing two damn earrings and an "I <3 anime" bracelet. I cool the good-cop routine. "Buddy, what do you think is in here? A fucking bomb or something—"

"Hey." Angela puts a hand on my shoulder. "There's no need for that."

"Listen to your girl," Adam says. I shoot him a glare and Ange and I leave the line.

"I guess you get your wish after all," she mumbles, looking mildly disappointed.

I clench my jaw. I can't believe I'm about to cash in some chips for such a trivial thing, but...

"Gimme a sec." I slip out my Crapple 10.

Rax. I need another luck point and I need that clown at the counter to take a hike.

Within the time it takes me to inhale, a response hits my screen.

You got it, bro. The hack's cooldown clock just reset, so it's perfect timing. Btw, your good vibes are off the chart and that fifth mystery stat is really powering up for some reason. Big score boosts! We gonna be achievement kings in days!!! Keep it up!1!

I roll my eyes and pocket the phone.

"Who was that?" Angela asks.

"It, uh, was the guy," I say. "Forgot I needed to cancel my Friday night plans with him."

"Oh, you should've said something! We don't have to do—"

"No, it's fine." I take her hand and walk us back to the counter where that gatekeeping dweeb is stationed. "I'm getting us into the movie."

Adam's eyes narrow. He cracks his tiny knuckles, clearly believing an unstoppable force is about to meet an immovable object. He's sorely mistaken. No NPC is immovable in my game.

"Here's what's going to happen in the next two minutes, Adam. You're going to accept my money, print our tickets, and let us watch that damn rom-com or so help me God, you're going to write up today as the worst day of your life."

"Oh yeah? How do you figure that?"

"Call it a bet. I'm a lucky guy." The cool line lingers in the air for a few seconds, but no miracle materializes to legitimize my threat. Adam smirks.

"Sir, I think I see a customer behind you. Do you mind moving aside—"

"Nope! Nope. Count it. You're in a world of trouble in three... two..." I count, my face remaining confident even as my balls go into hiding, "one."

Then... crickets.

"Sir, I really need you to leave the line. If you don't, I'll have to get my manager—"

"Shhhh. You hear that?" I lean over the counter toward him. "That's your demise. In three... two..."

"That's it, I'm getting my manager—"

"Threetwoone!" I blurt as the theater doors burst open behind me, revealing a seething-hot, ultra-pissed middle-aged woman.

"Adam Sanford Lebowitz! You get your ass on the other side of that counter right now!" the plump frump shouts, shaking her fist in the air as she closes the gap between herself and the pants-shittingly-scared goober withholding my tickets.

"B-Betty, I, um, what are you—" he stammers while attempting to slip out from behind the counter.

"Don't call me that, you little shit! Show some respect to your mother!" She waddles toward her son, sticks out a hand, and grabs him by the ear. Had she yanked just a centimeter lower, one of those dumb earrings of his would've torn off and created a bloody mess. Hell, that still might happen. Not that I want to be around when it does; I have enough blood to deal with—I'm about to watch a movie in a room full of women on their periods.

The mother's rage continues. "You haven't paid your rent in three months, your damn friends keep sleeping over when they're not allowed—"

"That's our cue," I whisper to Angela. She's confused and tries to protest, but I grab her hand and shuffle both of us, as well as the suitcase, past the counter. As we head to our movie, I hear the tail end of Betty's tirade, which undoubtedly has better dialogue than the entirety of the upcoming rom-com I'm about to suffer through.

"—and an hour ago I had a delivery man ask me to sign

for a *fur suit* that was charged to *my card*! You're getting the fuck outta my house today, kiddo, or I'm going to—"

The fire and fury befalling the lobby turns into background noise once Ange and I reach our screening. Thankfully, trailers are still playing. We find aisle-side recliners so the suitcase can rest beside us. Then we sit down and breathe.

"What the fuck just happened out there? *What the fuck just happened out there?*" Ange whispers, shaking my shoulder.

"I'll explain when the movie's over, okay?" I whisper back.

"*You just summoned an enraged boomer from the fucking ether and you want me to wait two hours for an explanation?*"

"Yes, please." I raise my seat's footrest.

"What the fuck," she mumbles as our film's production logos appear on the screen. Out of the corner of my eye, I see her staring at me. She continues to do so for fifteen minutes straight before I finally look over at her. We both stand up and exit the theater. Once we're out on the street, she gets right down to business.

"Talk."

"Okay, well, you know how people who work for the CIA can't *say* they work for the CIA—"

"Shut up."

"You're giving me real mixed signals here, Ange—"

"I want to know what the fuck's actually going on. You're taking down nightclub shooters, which is almost as weird as the idea of you going to a club in the first place. You're ignoring my calls. You're suddenly loaded with cash for expensive taxi rides and dinners and movies. You met some guy at a gay bar or something—"

"Why're you lying? Just to piss me off? I told you I met him at the park!" Wait, fuck, I meant bridge—

"Caught you! I knew everything felt off. You've been lying to me since the second I got here. I can't believe you. We said we'd never lie to each other, and you've never told me a lie once in your life before today. Or have you?"

She yanks her suitcase from my hand and starts walking toward the nearest taxi. I rush after her and put a hand on her shoulder, but she shrugs it off.

"No, Jack, you're not talking your way out of the situation. I don't want to hear another word. I'm going."

"But Ange." My hand's outstretched. I stand alone on the sidewalk, pleading for another chance as a cabbie puts her luggage in his trunk and she gets in the backseat, slamming the door shut without looking back at me.

I remain glued in place, paralyzed by indecision. The taxi pulls out of its parking space. I blink once and Ange is all but gone, the little car she's occupying now far down the street. Two blinks later and it's like she was never here in the first place.

What have I done?

CHAPTER 13

I walk, and walk, and walk. I don't stop moving, even when my feet start to ache. By the time I look up to see what street I'm on, I've already covered five city blocks. And yet, it's only been twenty minutes. Time slows to a crawl when you want to blow your brains out.

What was I thinking, lying to Ange? We don't lie to each other. We just don't do that. And yet, here I am, all alone—like always—because I did exactly that. Who remembered my birthday? She did. Who helped me get a grip and prevent a national tragedy? She did. Who the fuck flew out here on a moment's notice just to give me support? *She did*. How did I screw things up so badly?

A hand lands on my chest. *Jesus Christ*, I think to myself as I turn my head to the side and see an old man holding me in place, preventing me from stepping onto the crosswalk. A garbage truck roars past me.

"Watch yourself," the elderly gentleman scolds, letting go of my shirt once it's clear I'm paying attention to the world around me. I mumble something that sounds like "thank you" and rocket across the street the second the traffic light turns red and cars stop moving.

I can't hold it in. I have to tell her. I... I just don't know what'll happen if I do—who am I kidding. I don't care what'll happen. I can't let her leave on such bad terms.

I yank out the Crapple 10 but pause just a moment before summoning my teenage lifeline. Should I tell him? The little fucker did start stealing my money and threatening me the moment I disobeyed an order on Tuesday morning. And he sees where I am at all times. Who knows what kind of shit he'd pull to get me to play nice.

Then again, he had to coax me off that bridge, not force me. The game isn't about him, it's about me. I'm what's important here. He *needs* me to be happy. He can't afford to say "no" to a single thing I ask for.

Look for the good in people. The thought hits me like a stray baseball crashing through a window. What the fuck am I doing, thinking the kid's out to get me? Everything he's done so far has been to help me, and he's said as much. We aren't here to leech off each other. I can't lose Ange, but I can't lose him either. I have two friends and I'm keeping both of them.

I hit the call button and fish out my Bluetooth earbud, popping it in just as the kid picks up.

"Yeeeeeello?"

"Rax, I got a bit of a bomb to drop."

"Fire away, cap'n."

"I need to tell Angela we're in a game."

"What?"

"Rax—"

"No. *No.* What'd I say about blabbing to NPCs: at worst, you'll corrupt their system files, and who knows what the heck that'll look like. At best, you'll make them think you're absolutely insane. Who knows how that could hurt our score?"

"Rax, I—"

"Either way: we. Both. Lose. What don't you understand here?"

"Rax."

"Yes."

I take a deep breath and stop pacing, planting my feet firmly on the ground.

"If I don't tell her, that fifth mystery stat of mine is going to tank, our score will drop off a cliff, and we'll never get close to the final few achievements ever again."

"How can you know that?"

"Because I think I know what that stat represents. And trust me, if I don't tell Angela what's going on, it's never going to recover."

He groans into his mic, says a bad word aloud, shouts to his mother that he's sorry for the language, lets out another huff, then tunes back into the conversation.

"Ooookay, buddy—let's pretend I believe you've cracked the secret to the major metric not a single player up here has figured out yet. Let's pretend you know what you're talking about. Even if you know telling Angela is the only way to save the score, how do you know you're not gonna corrupt her, or you, or the entire save file, and nuke the game?"

I sigh.

"I don't. But if I can't win, you can't win. And, like you said: If *we* can't win, then what was the point of everything, anyway?"

He goes silent for a few seconds.

"You're pitching some ballsy stuff, my guy."

Another moment of silence passes. But just as I open my mouth to start an argument, he finishes his thought.

"Well, I'm here if you need me. Good luck with that shit," he says, quietly cursing so his mother won't hear.

"Thanks." I relax myself and crack my jaw. "And about the score—"

"That's a sore spot right now, man. We're so friggin' close to the top. So close. No one's climbed so fast ever, I think."

"I know, I've been listening. I know what it means to you. And we're not going to lose our spot. If there's one person I can trust with our secret, it's Ange. Our score ain't going anywhere."

"I know you think that now, but she's not an avatar like you, man. Her code's stricter. She has more limitations. You might be setting yourself up for. . . "

"Failure? Disappointment?"

"Yeah, something like that."

"Then I guess I should be glad I have you to face it with."

"You're a corny dude, my dude. Go get 'er."

With that, the call ends. And in that moment, from my other pocket, I feel the vibration of my Aqua Jive. I grab it so fast my fingers almost get brush burn from friction against my pants.

"The hotel says I missed the latest possible check-in time. I'm stuck." There isn't an ounce of joy in her voice. For the first time ever, she sounds like she hates talking to me.

"Ange, I'm going to fix it all," I say. "You can stay with me and—"

"But I don't want to stay with—"

"*And* I'll tell you everything. I'll explain it all. I promise."

The other party goes dark. I wait patiently.

"Where do I meet you?" she asks, after a full thirty-second pause. I don't miss a beat.

"Back at the movie theater," I say. "We need to take a walk."

CHAPTER 14

"I don't want to be here," Ange says, yanking at my arm.

"Just trust me, all right?" I walk her past the bench I sat on after my incident on Monday.

"Why can't you just tell me whatever it is you want to share?"

"Why are you so opposed to the damn bridge, Ange? It's important to me!"

"Jack! I know things have been rocky, but I'm not... I'm not ready to hear about how you met someone special, okay? Especially not at the place it happened."

"He's not—"

"And that's another thing!" She freezes in place and forces me to do the same. " 'He?' Y'know, we spent years together and you never even hinted that—"

"Ange! He's a minor!" I reply, flailing my arms.

"Jesus Christ," she shouts, covering her face with her hands as she turns away from me. I spin her around.

"He's a friend. A young friend. Okay? You've misinterpreted everything I've said about him. Absolutely everything."

Her eyes go wide with shock, then narrow in annoyance.

"Oh, I'm sorry. I should've just known you were *accidentally* making insinuation after insinuation that you had a lover. 'I don't want to make it weird between him and me,' 'he's so supportive of me.' What the fuck was all that stuff supposed to read as—"

"I was going to kill myself here, Ange."

She goes silent. A cool breeze slips through the otherwise static, humid air, causing the hair on both our arms to stand upright.

"I was standing on that beam, right over there." I lean over the railing beside us and point to the exact spot where I'd been balancing, ready to jump. "I was thinking about everything. About Charley..."

Angela's heart sinks when I mention Charley's name. Even now, he remains the best of us, and without him there is no friendship triangle. There's just a line that Angela and I are stuck tightrope walking across.

"... and about you..."

Dark waves crash against each other in the water below.

"... And I was gonna do it. I had a shoe over the edge... and then, the kid I've been telling you about, he talked me off at the last second."

Ange takes a moment to process.

"So... what happened? He saw you, then... ran over to stop you? Or did he just shout or something?"

"He saw me, all right," I say, reaching into my back pocket. "But he didn't speak a word or take a step." I pull out my phone and scroll to the top of my messages with Rax, way back to the very first one he ever sent me.

Are you still there? it reads. I move the phone in front of Ange so she can see.

"What's that?" she asks.

"That's him," I say, pointing to the next text where Rax told me not to jump. "I got these messages just as I was about to jump, on the same day I got my brand-new phone from my boss. No one should've even had the phone's number."

Ange grabs her suitcase and the two of us walk over to the bench we'd passed by. We sit down.

"Jack, are you pulling some sort of stupid prank? Are you screwing with me? If so, I'm buying tickets home right—"

"I swear, it's all real. I couldn't believe it either, at first."

"So... what are you saying? Is the... boy... a stalker or an angel or something?"

I look at my phone and let out a small chuckle.

"Something like that. Just, here... read the messages."

I hand her the phone and stay beside her as she reads, and reads, and reads. Many minutes pass. The bridge's night lights turn on and the sun dips below the horizon. Eventually, she returns my device.

"It... it doesn't make sense to me," she says.

"I wouldn't expect it to; the most important conversation happened over a call."

"You've spoken to him?"

"Mmhm." I set the phone down and put my hand on top of hers. "But before I tell you what he told me, I have to... preface it."

She looks down at my hand, then back at my face, meeting my gaze head-on.

"You know those Friday nights, when we'd sit on the bed after watching a good fantasy movie that made us question if everything," I gesture at the world around us, "was real? And we'd just talk for hours about what we'd do if it wasn't?... If we could even *believe* it wasn't?"

She takes a deep breath.

"It's one of those Friday nights, isn't it?" she says.

"Ange, the kid—whose name is Rax—told me that you and I, we're... we're just characters in a video game."

Out of nowhere, a lightning bolt pierces the sky. An accompanying clap of thunder roars past our ears, causing both of us to tense and grab each other. But then, there's nothing. No more lightning or thunder follows, though we wait for a full minute, holding our breath the whole time.

"I... um... does he have proof, or..." she stammers, looking up at the sky, then down at my phone, then off toward the river.

"You're looking at it, Ange. The kid's been handing me thousands of dollars on a whim. He's turned luck into a commodity. He bypassed my employers to get me a new phone that's not even released yet... he made it possible for me to literally dodge bullets... Ange, he told me everything about myself. He knows everything."

"He knows about—"

"Yeah. Whatever you were about to say, he does. And that's not all he knows."

Her skin grows paler with every passing second.

"Can he... see us?"

"He's probably watching us right now, Ange."

She swallows and waits a bit before opening her mouth. "Prove it."

I wave at the sky and make a "call me" sign, putting my hand against my ear. A second later, my phone rings. I pull the earbud out of my pocket and give it to Ange.

"Take it," I say, gently opening her clenched fist and setting the bud inside. With some hesitation, she puts it in her ear and picks up the phone. I rub her shoulder and gesture with my free hand for her to do the deed. She accepts the call.

"H-hello?" she says. A second later, she freezes. I can't hear how Rax greets her, but I don't need to; I know the proof's been delivered. Before long, the two are having a real conversation—until Ange gasps and drops my phone onto her lap.

"He—he knows I—"

"He gave you the lore page speech?" I say with a laugh, patting her on the shoulder. She nods, then remembers to pick up the phone. Her conversation with Rax goes on for a long while after that, and over the course of it, the stars make their presence known, twinkling to life across the sky. I see Ange display every emotion in the book while on the call—from shock, to anger, to amusement, and back again. At one point, I even spot a look of sadness cross her face. It disappears in the blink of an eye and is replaced by a small, sober smile.

"I will," she says into the phone, before saying goodbye and hanging up. She takes the earbud out and hands both it and the phone back to me.

"What was that about?" I ask, taking both items and pocketing them.

"Oh, nothing. He just asked me to take good care of you," she replies, still smiling. Her eyes tell a different story, but I don't press the matter. After all, if there's anyone who should be asking hard questions tonight, it's her, not me.

"So what, um... oh, wow. Can't speak. What did you want to do tonight?" She bites her lip. "Even though night's not a real thing, I guess..."

I stand up and grab her suitcase handle.

"How about we take a little late-night tour? I'll be the travel guide and show you all the hot spots from my wacky week so you can see where the madness unfolded."

She initially seems troubled by the suggestion but comes around after a bit of thinking. "Well, we're already one stop down, I guess."

First, I take Ange to the park near my office where Rax told me what and where I really am. I recount everything that happened, from him predicting events in real-time to pumping me up with perk points, which I then used for some... well, regretful activities, if I'm to be completely frank with myself. I tell Ange as much and she says no further details are necessary, to which I agree. That conversation then organically— well, I say organically, but I kind of force it to happen—segues into me probing her about her own nighttime activities as of late and who she was texting at the airport. She tells me not to worry. I comply, though not without suspicion.

Next on our sightseeing tour is the nightclub, which we look at from the sidewalk. Though its outdoor lights are on, the place is closed, with a big sign saying there's a temporary shutdown so the club managers can replace and repair the handful of items damaged by gunfire. Ange and I observe the joint's exterior as I tell her about what happened before and after I called her that night, including how Rax helped me take down the big bad guy with nothing but my own two hands and a stupidly expensive suit. Ange laughs at some points in the story, hits me during others, and even does both back-to-back a few times.

After that, on our way to my glorified, dingy bedroom— er, apartment, we stop by a 24/7 ice cream parlor and I regale Ange with tales from my office, otherwise known as the bulk of Thursday's and Friday's noteworthy events. Against my better judgment, I also make a brief, fleeting mention of the individual who's been randomly crossing paths with me. While said mention scares Ange quite a bit at first, I clarify that Rax thinks the stranger is just a harmless glitch. I also explain to her that I'm so souped up with luck perks that a nuclear missile probably wouldn't be able to touch me. These items seem to cool her down a good deal. Truth be told, they don't have the same effect on me.

Thankfully, topics shift radically and rapidly from there, with the two of us yammering about anything and everything until we finally make it to my box of a home just as the first glimpse of sunrise appears.

I slide her suitcase to the corner of the room then drop my weary body onto my bed. Ange follows suit. Given my small, one-person-sized mattress, the two of us have to cuddle up pretty tightly. But even with our messy understanding of the rules and boundaries between us, our necessarily compact sleeping arrangement doesn't faze us. Because, as strange as it seems, being snuggled up against someone you care about, in a position to provide and receive warmth, overshadows the social pressures and expectations of sharing a bed. That's what I come to understand as I lie here, curled up beside Ange, parallel to her on my mattress for one.

My eyes grow heavy, and I get ready to dream of electric sheep. Then Ange says something. It takes my sleepy ears a second to process her whispered words.

"So you're being real? We're in a game?"

"Yep," I reply, following up with a soft yawn. "Sure seems like it."

She reaches back, gently takes hold of my arm, and wraps it around her. Then we sleep.

CHAPTER 15

Oh, Monday morning sunrise. Always uninvited, yet always on time. Yawn.

"Ange?" I poke her pajama-draped hip. She makes a groggy grumble. With one of my arms trapped underneath her neck, options for a stealthy escape are slim.

"Ange?" I tap her again, giving her a little shake. She lets out some more sleepy gibberish but refuses to budge.

"Ange, I have to go to work." I give her one more gentle ruffle. That earns me a snore.

Well, I tried to do it the nice way. Like ripping off a Band-Aid, I tear my hand out from under her, causing her head to bounce up and down as I make my escape and bolt off the bed. It doesn't faze her in the slightest. Toothbrush time!

I grab the goods, book it to the bathroom, and get brushing. As I'm just about done polishing my chompers, a vibration rumbles within the pocket of my pajamas. I pull out the Crapple 10.

Happy one week anniversary, lol, says the message on my screen. Aw, that's sweet. Too bad I didn't get him a present.

Wait. Jokes aside... did he get me one?

Present? I text.

You're holding it, dipwad, he responds. *Anyway, keep up the good work. You were right—Angela and the weekend boosted your score super high. We might nab the final few achievements in days! Almost there!!1!*

I reply with the "okay" hand emoji, pocket the phone, then return to my room. When I enter, a raspy, bellicose growl sounds off. Did a wild raccoon get in here through the window? Is the game glitching out and summoning creatures? Oh, wait, it's just Ange.

"Why didn't you close the door when you left?" she grumbles, her voice muffled as she hides her head under my pillow. "The hallway light is so bright."

"Sorry, I forgot," I say, slipping inside the room and closing the door. "Are you, um, feeling any better?"

"What? Oh." Her voice is a bit scratchier than it was yesterday. "Uh, I'm fine. It's probably just whatever that Thai place served me last night. I knew it tasted funny."

"Like, burn-your-throat-spicy funny, or food poisoning funny?"

"Both," she grouses.

I walk over to my closet and grab my clothes for the day, putting them on as Angela remains buried in her blanket. The fact that she's choosing to remain in that cotton cocoon isn't a great sign, considering the sun's starting to enter the room and the temperature is increasing.

"Ange, I can stay home if you need. I can get you meds, or tea, or—"

"I'll be fine. Didn't you say you had work?" Her voice is faint but insistent. If she has enough fight in her to tell me to bug off, then maybe she just needs a day to recover.

"All right, all right. I'm going." I button my shirt and grab my BTMP, all while looking at the sentient cloth monster rolling around on my bed. "You sure you're going to be okay?"

"Get lost, dork." She playfully peeks at me from beneath the blanket.

"I'll leave my keys with you in case you want to go out and grab food or something. Call me if you need anything. I can be here in a heartbeat." I put the keys on my nightstand. "We'll do something nice when I get home." I give her a little wave, then leave the apartment.

I hope she feels better by tonight. Heck, I hope I do too. After all, it's a downhill day for me from here on out. Fuckin' work.

Wait.

Hold up.

A revelatory wave washes over my body. And with it, my walk turns into a strut and a budding smirk convinces my scowl to take a hike.

Work isn't work anymore. There's no Tim. Two of the three Prog Triplets have been given the boot. Pritchard and Taylor are low-tier threats. And me? I'm on my way out, thanks to Rax. It's just a matter of time. Plus, until then, I'm... I'm the boss.

I'm the boss!

Yeah. I call the shots. I run this town.

As I make my way to my horsepower-drawn carriage, I notice some humble gym-shorts-clad street merchants attempting to woo passersby, waving jovially from behind their string of folding tables draped in cheap cloth. As luck would have it, they're stocked to the gills with exactly what I just decided I need.

I undo my dress shirt's top button, slip out my wallet, and put a crisp hundred on the table nearest me, barely trading glances with the row of onlooking sidewalk shopkeepers.

I swipe a pair of aviators from their fanciest display and slide them on. Out of the corner of my eye, I spot one vendor give me a small bow. Keep the change, buddy.

I waltz into the subway and claim a seat on my usual morning train. A few seconds after it pulls out of the station, a street performer in my car starts doing his thing and sets down a tinny sounding, battered bucket of bolts that was probably a boombox in a former life. At first, it looks like he's just another dime-a-dozen breakdancer, but soon enough he's dangling upside down by his feet from the car's overhead railings, doing all kinds of monkey-esque acrobatics that'd put most of the other people in the car in a wheelchair if they were to try to imitate him. It's impressive stuff, really. And yet, the fantastic, frizzy-haired freak of nature is probably making three times less than everyone else on the train—and none of them are giving me a good show, that's for sure.

He hops down from his improvised jungle gym's bars and grabs the baseball cap that's been tactically hidden behind his boombox. He then starts shimmying down the aisle, hand and hat outstretched.

He starts with the middle-aged single ladies near him at the back of the car. He knows they haven't had a guy bend for them like that at any point in the last decade, so they're easy pocket change. He then gets the tourists' loose dollars and continues hustling his way up the car until he reaches my stretch, wherein the folks in suits golf clap but respectfully decline to contribute. By the time he reaches me, he gently pulls his arm back and keeps the hat at a respectful distance, refusing to look me in the lens-covered eyes.

Was it the sparkling dress shoes, slick shirt, or killer shades? I don't know. I don't care.

"Hey, buddy," I say. His eyes light up when I yank out my wallet and put my contribution in his hat. Fingers crossed he puts some of that toward a new boombox.

The ride ends and I get off the train, slinging my BTMP over my shoulder as I hustle onto the platform. My trusty laptop bag doesn't feel so big and cumbersome today. For the first time in a long time, it feels like it was made to fit the man. It feels like it did the day I bought it.

In the blink of an eye, I make it from the subway to my office. First day on the job as the leader of the pack. I shove the glass doors open and enter the lobby, basking in the warm glow of the early morning sunlight pouring in through the nearby windows.

"Early morning meeting in five, ladies and gentlemen," I whisper under my breath as I march over to my team's area of the office. Once I'm there, I clap my hands together with as much force as possible. The thunderous noise gets everyone—all five of my fellow employees—to bolt upright.

"Early morning meeting in five," I say, sliding my shades off to look my colleagues in the eyes before turning on my heel and heading toward the conference room.

Feeling the eyes glued to my back, I hang my glasses from the neckline of my shirt, stride over to the room with all the confidence in the world, and step inside, sliding the door shut behind me before claiming my chair at the head of the table. I slam into the curvy swivel seat, set my bag down, and grab my laptop. Then I kick my feet up on the table, much to the shock and awe of everyone still watching me from their desks. That's right, ladies and gents, the game has changed.

Five minutes until showtime. I unfold my laptop and turn it on, then take my Crapple 10 out of my pocket and set a timer. Once that clock's ticking, I hit up my ultimate work contact.

Rax, my man—I'm gonna need more money.

How much more? he replies.

How much you got?

That's a stupid question. Why do you need it?

Why does anyone need money? Let me ask you: Do you know how many kids don't have water? Or how few rhinos and tigers are left on the rock I call home?

He responds with an ellipsis, a question mark, and a half-frowning, half-confused emoji.

And are there limits on how much I can have if the money immediately disappears from my account and, say, enters the coffers of an animal sanctuary or homeless shelter?

I... I think? Idk, dude. Let's take it slow, all right? Let's try, uh, fifty thousand.

One hundred.

Seventy.

Two hundred.

He stops responding. I squint at the screen, knowing that little squeaker is watching and waiting just like I am. Then I stare at the invisible camera hovering somewhere above me.

The game of chicken lasts for thirty seconds before I hear a "ding" from my phone and see two-hundred-thousand doubloons land in my account. Hopefully Rax has a hack lined up for tax season, 'cause I don't care if I'm in a game—I'm not fucking around with the IRS over stupidly fat sums of unreported income next April.

See? Nothing imploded. Digital fireballs aren't falling out of the sky. Was that so hard? I text him.

Why you pushing buttons, man? he asks.

You lost a staring contest with some pixels on your screen, lol, I shoot back. Then I turn my attention to my laptop. I open a Noodle Monochrome tab and recall all the great charities I'd never been able to donate to at Christmas time because their collection staff were only ever stationed at grocery store checkouts and always asked for money after I'd already blown it all on shitty microwave dinners and energy drinks. Time to make amends and save those water buffaloes.

My Crapple 10 buzzes.

You realize there's no heaven for you, right? For all the Good Samaritan stuff you're doing. That ain't a level in the game.

I ignore the message, pocket the phone, and return to my laptop. Once I have my charities picked out, I look for where to contribute and hit "send" on a few larger-than-life payments, each with enough zeroes attached to make the me from a week ago piss himself. Money might not be necessary in order to see the good in people, but it sure as hell makes it easier.

Right on cue, my phone's alarm goes off. I silence it and place my laptop back in its bag a moment before my two-soldier editorial militia comes marching through the doors. Laura, Amélie, and Stark shuffle through as well.

"The herd's really thinning, huh," I say, looking around. Things didn't look so bad when my coworkers were surrounded by other departments and teams outside.

"Well." I scratch my chin, trying to recall how Tim did things when he wasn't setting off HR time bombs. "What's the status of everyone's current projects? Let's go around the room. Taylor, start us off."

"I was working on an op-ed questioning the utility of our jobs given that fewer people are won over by the written word than the spoken word. Historically, every great movement on Earth owes its growth to great speakers and not writers."

"Okay then. Moving on," I say, pointing to Pritchard.

"I'm working on a piece about how 6G cell signals are giving people brain cancer on a daily basis and big tech, as well as our own coverage, is pulling the wool over everyone's eyes."

"Do you have any hard stats about that cancer claim?"

"No," he responds. "But you know I'm right."

My face feels like it's melting off just by staring at him. I shift my blank gaze toward the other three folks in the room and gesture that it's their turn to fire off some depressing detail about their latest activities.

"I've cataloged eighty-nine different types of spark plugs we have in storage and am testing three brand-new monitors for dead pixels."

"I have coordinated a date and time for a tour with ze fucks"—momentary shock enters the room as everyone mishears the heavily accented pronunciation of "folks"—"coming over from Smashsung to see our operations. Zey made fun of my accent. I do not like zem."

"I'm adding a new search bar to our home page. Because of the garbage way our site is set up, it's taken over fourteen hours of laborious coding... so far."

Then there's silence. I look at my five colleagues. They look back at me. I slowly swirl around in my chair. "You all really hate your jobs, don't you?"

"Yes," they respond in unison, though only Laura covers her mouth afterward in embarrassment.

I drum my fingers on the conference table a few times.

"Forget all of that stuff. Cancel everything. Clear your schedules."

"What?" they ask, expressing varying degrees of surprise.

"We're doing something different today."

Thirty minutes later, I've lived up to my word.

"Yo, Amélie, catch!" Stark says, tossing a roll of party streamers over to his coworker who's grabbing packages of paper plates and plastic utensils off nearby shelves. A few aisles down from those two, Pritchard pops quarters into a gumball dispenser so he can watch the balls travel through the device's little Rube Goldberg machine. Once the treats reach the bottom, Taylor plucks them out and starts chomping, creating bubbles the size of the balloons we'll all be inflating later. For now, said balloons remain deflated in their package in my hands. Laura keeps passing me more and more 'til I'm sure we have enough, but I don't tell her to stop.

"You're ridiculous," she says. Even with her back to me, I know there's a smile on her face. "How can you guarantee you're not going to be fired?"

"Hey, I only guaranteed none of you will. I never said a thing about what'll happen to me."

She turns around and looks at me. "Why do these things for us, then?"

"You ever feel like..." I look around the shopping center. A nearby cashier rings up a customer. Wind from the outside slips through the revolving doors as people come and go. I smell perfume. I hear the clacks of mechanical keys. I feel air brush against my skin and tickle the smallest follicles on the back of my neck. Ones and zeroes. "You ever feel like life's just a, y'know, kind of a big game?"

"No, I, um... I don't," she says, sticking her tongue in her cheek.

I notice my posture's slipping and force myself to stand up straight, holding back the sigh I've already let out in my head.

"What I'm saying is, we've worked together for a while. You've seen I can handle myself."

She drops her mild frown of confusion and trades it in for a smile.

"One way or another," I continue, "I'll be fine."

She nods and goes to add the next bag of balloons to my pile, but just as she's about to reach her hand across the gap between us, a stack of falling party hats fills the void—a stack caught so fast we hardly have time to process what just happened. Amélie sets the hats back on top of her two-foot-tall heap of goodies, then continues marching toward the checkout, letting out a huff while a laughing Stark follows behind with a handbasket full of additional supplies for today's festivities.

A few feet behind them, Taylor and Pritchard chew gum and carry supplies of their own. Maybe my eyes are playing tricks on me, but I swear I see them finishing some sort of civil conversation with each other. By the time I blink my eyes in disbelief, their mouths are sealed shut, but I swear I saw it. What was "it" exactly, though? A miracle? A glitch? Not-to-self: confer with Rax later about my unicorn-grade sighting.

"Hey, monsieur supervisor! Jack! We need your card, mon ami," Amélie says, finding a spot alongside Stark in a checkout line a few yards away from me.

"Coming," I reply. Soon enough, all six of us have assembled at the checkout. We're well on our way to bringing joy to what was formerly known as the ninth circle of Hell, our office.

From there, five-and-a-half hours go by, and in that time, our sextet not only manages to have a good lunch and some even better laughs, but we also lure in quite a few folks from other departments in the office to help us decorate. After all, since they've been invited to party, it's only fair they do a bit of the prep work. It's not like they're not going to be here when the booze, cake, and pizzas show up. Speaking of which!

"Where would ya like these bad boys, *boss*?" Stark asks, clutching a file cabinet's worth of ice cream cake boxes.

"Plop them on the table by the break room's kitchen; we're close enough to go-time that we might as well skip the freezer."

"I concur," he replies, shuffling the frozen treats to their proper spot, ogling them with a hungry giddiness that—up 'til now—had only ever been seen in the office on the Thursdays Tim knew Jamie would be wearing her goth getup to work. We've come a long way since those cursed days of yore, otherwise known as one week ago.

As I go to check on how Amélie's doing with the final stretch of decorative lightstrips, I hear the office door buzzer go off. That should be the pizza.

"On it," Pritchard says. Meanwhile, Taylor preps one of the soon-to-be food tables, obsessively organizing plates, utensils, and napkins. Nearby, Laura goofs around with the people from other departments while working on inflating balloons and arming confetti launchers. And then there's me, right at the heart of everything. I see all that I have made, and it is good.

The party lights finish going up and the sun starts going down. I survey the final spread. Tables are freshly stocked with all the food and drinks we could ever need, and decorations line every corner of our office. It's finally that time of the day.

"Everyone," I say, gathering the attention of the floor. "Courtesy of the editorial team, I invite you to the office's first-ever on-the-clock party. Get fed, get tipsy, get a bit of overtime."

The cheering continues for what feels like hours, though it's probably more like a few minutes. Not that anyone can tell the difference; time becomes immaterial as all of us relax and intoxicate ourselves. Life's good. And it's about to get better, since Stark's grabbed a speaker out of storage and is queuing a playlist to serenade our jamboree. The music kicks to life and I don't know how it happens, but I start moving in a rhythmic manner that could actually be mistaken for dancing. Oh shit. Oh shit! Can I moonwalk?

The whistle from Laura, who's dancing not too far away, tells me I can. *Nice.* Now that I've accomplished that impressive feat, it's time to call the divine intervention hotline. I grab two unopened beers off a nearby table and immediately set them back down when I realize I need free hands to hit up Cyber Jesus. I then pop in my Bluetooth earbud and dial up my boy.

"Buddy."

"What's the sitch, guy? BTW, our score modifier is off the charts right now. Final few achievements are within reach! You're killing it down there."

"Yeah, achievements, score, great. Listen, I need a fifteen-year-old like yourself to help a mildly intoxicated guy who just learned to moonwalk lay some pipe as well as the foundation for a bountiful relationship."

"That guy wouldn't happen to be you, would it?"

"The finest detective in Scotland Yard!" I cheer, catching the attention of some of the fine folks around me. Thankfully, they're ten feet under as well, so they laugh it off.

"Sure, fam, I'll help. But what about Ange? She's been having a pretty positive effect on you. Aren't you two—"

"She's spoken for," I state matter-of-factly before lowering my voice. "As an upstanding gentleman, I will respect that. Now help me seduce a girl in my office with video game cheats!"

"You're a weird one, guy," he says, before making a slurping noise that sounds like he's drinking something out of a can.

"You're the dork drinking soda," I fire back, walking toward Laura. I've completely forgotten to grab our drinks off the table. *Too late now*, I think to myself. No brakes on the party train.

"It's fizzy grape juice, watch yourself—"

"Focus! See the girl in front of me?"

"There's like six, dude."

"The brunette! With the perfect teeth. And the beauty mark—"

"All right, I see her. Just initiate contact and I'll help you seal the deal. Operation Milkshake Stir is a go."

I'm not sure where that name came from, but whatever floats the kid's boat; it's time to stir a milkshake or two. Engaging shimmy mode.

I let the alcohol's effects slide over me like a suit of armor and suddenly feel a pair of wings raise my arms up, lifting me until I'm as light on my feet as a sentient feather that's sexually attracted to its coworkers.

"You're having a hell of a day, aren't you?" Laura says. I close the gap between the two of us, keeping my dance going since she's not stopping hers.

"And it's not even over!" I do a slick spin that's perfectly in-sync with the fat beat that bounces out of the nearby speaker to announce the end of the current song.

"Not over? What's left?" she asks with a big laugh, her voice blending into the melody of the next song so organically that I practically melt. The way she talks is like velvet I can *hear*.

"Ask her to dance with you," my invisible wingman instructs.

"A dance, for starters," I tell her. "You in?"

I stick out my hand, inviting her to join. She grabs on and before either of us realize it, we're off to the races.

It's a fast-paced song, so keeping up with the rhythm requires some seriously fancy footwork. I'm lucky to be doing as well as I am, which is why I almost lose my flow when Rax tells me I have to up my game.

"You gotta do the thing where you two hold hands and stretch apart and then you twirl her back to you," Rax tells me. What the hell does that even—oh, I know that one. No clue how to do it, but I know of it.

"Dude, you gotta," he reiterates. I try to ignore his instructions. Oh, jeez. Am I really about to go through with Rax's advice? It could end miserably. It could kill one of us.

I'm doing it anyway.

Laura instinctively knows what I'm doing and spins away from me, our interlocked fingers being the only thing keeping either of us from losing balance and falling on our asses. Then, with a gentle flick of the wrist, I summon her back. It works.

"You're not bad," she says once she's spun back within a few inches of my face, close enough we can feel the warmth of each other's breath.

"Not too shabby yourself."

"There's an eighty percent chance if you go for a kiss right now she'll play along," Rax says, speaking quickly to keep up with the pace of the magic moment. "Two percent chance you'll get another opportunity tonight if you pass on the current one."

Not in the mood to play the odds, I go in for the kill. Her eyelids close and she leans in. I can practically taste the delicious cherry lip gloss a second before it happens.

It doesn't happen.

I'm frozen in space and time by the sight I see over Laura's shoulder. Behind her is the lobby entrance, which should be the emptiest place on the floor. Yet there's a person there, setting off the motion-sensor-enabled lights as he walks toward our party.

"One second," I tell Laura. Her eyes open as my ice-cold voice instantly chills and kills the mood.

"What the—" she starts, but I've already let go of her and started walking toward the uninvited guest, shuffling through the throng of party people to make sure I'm between them and the new guy by the time he reaches us.

"How-dee, neighbor," he says from across the hall, raising his voice to be heard over the music. *"Neighbor."* The second time he speaks the word his voice is an octave lower and not even remotely friendly. Emboldened by alcohol, I keep marching forward, even though my sixth sense tells me not to engage.

"It's the guy, Rax," I hiss into my earbud. "Do you see him? Right in front of me?"

"Wha—no. I don't see anyone. Jack?"

"He's right there!"

"Jack! It's not showing anyone in front of you on my screen!"

Shit.

"You didn't tell me we were having a party," Jon says, proceeding to lick his lips. He eyeballs the crowd behind me.

"Listen, you weird fuck," I reply, planting myself about a yard in front of him, locking both of us in place. "There is no 'we,' and you don't work here. So get lost."

"No 'we,' Jack?" He lets out a laugh. "You're the only reason I'm here!"

"You want to tell me what that reason is?" I square my shoulders.

"Mm, you're going to be a feisty one, aren't you?" He balls his fists.

"Hey!" Laura shouts behind us. "Is everything okay over there?"

"No, call security," I reply without turning my head to face her, keeping my eyes glued on Jon. Even over the music, I hear her scuttle off the hall's tiles and onto the main floor's carpet. Hopefully she's fast and the guys with the batons are faster.

"There's no need for that," Jon says, relaxing his hands. "We don't need to involve others."

"I don't even know what *we're* involved in," I respond, jamming an index finger against his chest. As I make contact with his dress shirt, I feel something strange—or, rather, I feel nothing. Am I hallucinating? Is the alcohol going to get me killed?

"Get off me," he says, using both hands to shove me away. I stumble back a few steps, catching my balance just before I completely topple over. With a bit more distance between us, I take a few breaths and try to figure out what the hell just happened.

"Good luck trying that again." He narrows his eyes and grins.

"What the hell is your deal?" I reply, gritting my teeth.

"It's the deal that *he* broke! You *and* him!" Jon spits, laughing and stretching his mouth open until his jaw cracks.

"Him?"

"Jack!" Rax shouts over the mic, blasting my ear with sound. "I see him! He just appeared on my screen and—"

"That's enough of that," Jon says, rolling up his sleeves. He steps toward me.

"Freeze," two men bark in unison. At that moment, the lobby doors swing wide open, revealing the fastest security guards in Midtown. Jon smiles, stops his advance, and walks backward until he slides right into their grips. Each man grabs one of his arms. As they tug him toward the lobby entrance, he points two finger guns my way, flicks them upward, then blows on them.

I dig my nails into my palms, almost to the point of drawing blood. Thankfully, I'm stopped before it can get to that. Laura grabs me by the arm and spins me around.

"What just happened?" she asks, worried. The party's still going on behind us. It seems my little incident had no impact on anyone else, thanks to all the booze, conversation, and music. But for Laura and me, it was real. At least, I think it was.

"Laura, you saw that guy, right?"

"Yeah," she says. "Who was he?"

Isn't that the question of the day.

"I, um, I need to go to the bathroom," I tell her, ignoring the question. I dash for the men's room. Once I'm there, I shoot into the stall I hid inside just one week earlier, now with no tears to shed, only bullets to sweat.

"Rax, what just happened?"

"I—I don't know. I'm still tracking him, though. Looks like... the guards have him cuffed downstairs in the lobby."

"Okay, okay." I try to steady my breathing. "Just keep talking. Don't leave me alone here."

"Not going anywhere, bud—but, oh, he is. Cops just arrived. Looks like they had a patrol car stationed across the street and the security guards flagged them down. Okay, um..."

Outside my stall, someone bangs on the door to the men's room. I look around for anything that could be used as a weapon, anything at all, but there's nothing but toilet paper in here. Shit. I open the stall door. The banging continues. All I see are more rolls of toilet paper, paper towels, and bolted-in soap dispensers. I'm screwed.

"Jack!"

I nearly pass out from relief, letting out the breath I'd been holding since the knocking started. It's Laura.

"Are you okay?"

"One minute," I croak, nearly tripping over my own feet as I lurch back to my stall and close the door again.

"Jack, you still there?" Rax asks.

"Yeah. Tell me what's happening."

"He's a few blocks south. The cops have him at a police station. Looks like he's behind bars."

"How the fuck did they get him there so fast? It has to be a trick or a trap or—"

"Dude, do you realize how long you've been in that stall?"

I check my phone's clock. Jesus, have I been flailing around in here for twenty minutes?

"Listen, man, just calm down. From what I can see, he's getting charged with breaking and entering, disorderly conduct, and a few other things. No way he's getting out of that holding cell tonight."

"Can you give me more details? Anything?"

"I, um... no, doesn't look like it. Game's not giving me any more details. But he's on the grid now, at least. I can track him and give you a heads up if anything happens, okay? Breathe, dude. You're at least fine for the rest of tonight."

"Yeah, unless another psycho shows up that's not on your little map," I growl, holding my head over the toilet. My stomach, unhappy with my mood, threatens to unleash all the fluids and food I've been holding in these past few hours.

"Don't get snippy with me, mister. I'm gonna monitor your biggest fan 24/7 from here on out, so calm down. Don't imagine an army of shadow ninjas out to get you. Okay?"

"Jack?" Laura repeats from outside the bathroom door.

"Yeah, fine," I say to Rax, marching myself out of the stall I've been hiding in. Drenched in sweat and looking like absolute shit, I slam the bathroom door open. Waiting just outside is Laura, whose eyes go wide as the hinged panel swings open and almost rips her nose off.

"Jesus, Jack," she says, looking at me. My shirt's untucked, my eyes are a little crazy, and I look like I just got out of a pool. I'm a fucking mess. She sees it, I see it—I'm not in a position to be standing right now, for crying out loud. I shouldn't even be talking to her.

I pull her close and kiss her.

In that brief moment, my mind isn't focused on being hunted down by a stalker or being trapped in a game; it's focused on the sweet taste of cherry. Her lips are so soft.

She doesn't pull away until I let go of her, resulting in us both taking a step back.

"I, uh, I don't know who that guy was," I stammer.

She pulls me back in for another kiss.

CHAPTER 16

I stumble into the hall that separates me from my bedroom. Is it spinning, or am I underwater? I cough a few times and let out a hiccup before pushing forward. C'mon, Jack, you're almost there. Use your feet. That's what Jesus would do.

Speaking of Jesus, how the hell did I pull tonight off? I yank my phone out and look at the last text Laura sent me: *See you tomorrow. Excited 4 date :)*.

I nailed it tonight. I gotta tell someone—oh, I know who.

"Rax, buddy, you won't believe what happened at the party."

"You'd be surprised," he says, his voice tired.

"I met a girl. You should see her, she's—"

"I've seen her, man."

"What? Where?" I nearly trip, bamboozled by the mildly different shades of beige tiling on the floor. Are the darker ones deeper in the ground? Is the hall safe to walk on?

"Jack, we've been on the phone for hours. I've been here for every single dang thing."

That's the meanest "dang" I've ever heard, Rax. Why you gotta do me like that? *Hiccup*.

"Prove it," I say, refusing to check the call timer on my phone's screen. I inch my way toward the bedroom door near the end of the hall.

"All right. You remember how after you and Laura exchanged phone numbers you went to that one roomy closet with the cushions and she did that thing with her hands—"

"I thought you said you couldn't see that stuff!" I speak loudly enough to earn a "shut up" from someone in one of the rooms I pass by. "Sorry," I reply, just as loudly as my previous sentence.

"It was pixelated, Jack, but that's not the point—look, it's late. Don't you see what time it is? Angela's waiting for you, dude."

Shit, he's right. Angela is priority uno. Get it together, self.

"Rax, that guy is still with the police, yeah?"

"Huh? Oh, he's not getting out of there anytime soon. You can relax."

I end the call and sober up at Mach 5. Like water dripping off a swimmer who's just exited the pool, the alcohol's influence glides off my skin with each step I take. Through a blend of sheer willpower and a magic little something extra courtesy of Rax's perk point shenanigans, by the time I reach my bedroom I'm standing up straight and am in control, more or less, of my core faculties. As long as I don't piss on the floor or say something stupid, tonight will be fine.

My door swings open when I give it a push. Ange didn't lock it. Weird.

What's weirder, and more worrisome, is the bundle of blankets on my bed. There's a human inside them—one not in very good condition.

"Ange, it's eighty-something degrees in here," I say, dropping my BTMP on the floor and dashing to join her on the bed.

"I know..." she mumbles, clutching the blankets tighter as I saddle up beside her.

"Have you eaten anything today?"

"Crackers... ginger ale... one of the guys down the hall got them for me," she says, gulping to hold something back. Even with her darker complexion, it's clear her face has lost a lot of its natural color. My Ange is a ghost. "Morgan, I think, was his name."

"Yeah, he's a good guy." I gently pull her blanket-cocooned body closer so it can rest on me. "Should we get you checked out at a hospital?"

"No..."

"It's no trouble at all, really."

"It's... not that bad."

Sure it's not, I think to myself, looking at the sickly girl beside me. If her illness keeps up, I'm going to have to take her to a hospital whether she likes it or not. In the meantime...

"Sorry I got back so late."

"It's okay," she says, weakly reaching out a hand from beneath the wall of cotton to hold my arm. "At least you're here now." She smiles, though it seems to hurt her to emote.

"That food poisoning really did a number, didn't it?" I frown. "How about we skip any fancy plans and watch a movie?"

She nods and I help her get comfy, taking a moment after that to grab my laptop out of its bag. Then I cozy up beside her.

"What do you want to watch?"

"Rom-com," she says, her eyes narrowing. Even though she's hidden her mouth under the blanket, the smirk is clear as day.

"All right, rom-com it is." I wrap an arm around her shoulders, giving her a little extra cushioning to make up for my bed's stiff pillow. As we start to watch the movie she picks, she nuzzles even closer. Is she falling asleep already? I get my answer when, by the opening credits, the lightest snore in the world sounds off from my chest, where Ange's head has ended up.

I close the laptop and set it on the floor, then wrap my free arm around her when she unconsciously curls up next to me.

Get better, Ange. I'll see you in our dreams.

CHAPTER 17

"Status check on Jon?"

"Behind bars, boss."

"Status check on Ange?"

"Safe and sound, my dude."

"Are the guys keeping an eye on her?" I hustle down the steps of the subway station, working my way toward the train that's just arrived.

"As far as I can see, yeah. You know it's hard for me to get a great look at most things not in your immediate vicinity, though."

"Okay, all right. She looked better when we woke up and said she wanted to keep sleeping, so... am I making the right choice going to work?" I'm on the platform now, just a few feet away from the nearest car's opening doors.

"Jack. Buddy. You're fine. She's fine. Everything's fine. Now can we please focus on important news?"

I board the train. Rax keeps talking.

"We're almost there. Guess how many achievements we have left."

"How many?"

"That's not a guess, but whatever, dude. One. We're one away from me nabbing all of them. Your score is so freakin' high that we're almost there."

I scratch my head.

"Really? We're at the ceiling?"

"Why you sound so surprised?"

"I don't know," I say as I stand up, offering my seat to an old lady who's just gotten on board. Grabbing an overhead railing a few feet away, I lean against the side of the car and dig my heels into the floor. "I guess I just thought we had a ways to go. Like, all the achievements already? I've hardly done anything. I thought becoming president or a movie star or something would be the endgame."

"Nah, none of that stuff, dude. We're offline and achievement hunting, not going for the global high score on the leaderboard."

"Why not?"

"You realize I'm a student, right? I don't have time to help you pull that off. I'll settle for a score that snags me all the achievements."

"And what do I have to settle for, huh?"

"Uh, we turned your life around in a week, man, and it's not even over. Dunno why you're giving me that attitude."

I click my tongue and slouch against the metal paneling of the car. "So what happens when it *is* over?"

Silence. Our train passes into the darkest part of the tunnel and, for a split second, the shadows nearly drown out the light in the car. Did I lose my connection to Rax because I'm underground?

Oh, what am I talking about? He and the phone are basically magic. He just doesn't want to tell me that when everything's over—

"I'll hang around. I promised you that when we first, er, met, remember? I said I'd keep tabs on your file no matter what. And I will. I'll have your back and we can still hang out and stuff. I mean, you know what I mean—"

I look down at my shoes. "It's not going to be the same, is it."

"Don't be like that, man," he says. "It's just, well, you got me thinking about my priorities and stuff, and... like, maybe I play too much. Maybe you're right. And I shouldn't have given Barry a hard time. I need to talk to him. I was thinking maybe we could start slowing down just a bit in here while I get it together out there, y'know?"

"Whoa. When did I say you play too much?"

"At that nightclub, remember?"

Damn it, I did say something like that, didn't I?

"That was almost a week ago, man... how long was it for you?"

"Well, I missed the entirety of my favorite TV show's season premiere playing and chatting with you, plus I took a bathroom break and grabbed some snacks, so... I dunno, it's definitely been over an hour or two, at least."

Jesus. Hopefully he checks in here often enough to be there for my funeral in a few months' his time.

The two of us leave the conversation dangling, eventually saying our goodbyes and ending the call. How many more temporary goodbyes will there be before the real one happens? And will I even know it's the real one when it comes?

I guess I shouldn't dwell on it too much; I still have a final achievement to grab before I get ghosted by God himself. Sigh. At least I have a date tonight. Focus on the positives, Jack.

Thankfully, about eight hours later, I've found not one, but two positives to focus on, and I'll be shocked if Laura's surprisingly risqué dress doesn't give me a few more as the night progresses.

"Like it?" she asks, exiting the women's bathroom. One nice thing about being a guy is that my work clothes double as my date clothes, meaning I've been able to wear my party suit all day without a care in the world. She, however, took the time to bring a separate dress for tonight and change into it the second we clocked out. How'd she know that effort is sexy?

"Very much." I do my best not to stare too much at the plunging neckline of her crimson dress. Now I see why she wears baggy clothes at the office.

"So, are we ready?" she nudges, drawing my attention back to her face. Just as I'm about to answer, my mouth freezes and my brain kicks back into gear.

"Uh—yes! Yes, just give me one second. I forgot to put something away at my desk."

I hustle down the hall until I'm at my workstation. Having bought myself some distance, I pull out my trusty Crapple 10.

Are those reservations set? I text.

The phone buzzes almost immediately.

The ones you asked about earlier? Yeah, should be good. :thumbsup:

Phew.

"All good?" Laura asks, having wandered over to my desk.

"Uh, yep," I reply, trying to look busy by futzing with my BTMP even though I'm leaving it here for the night. Once I'm done juggling the laptop bag like an idiot, I pocket my phone, give Laura a nod, and she and I make our way out of the office.

Much like the subway train we're trapped in just a few minutes later, Laura's warming up more and more with each second that goes by. Yet for all the bubbles fizzing between us,

I can't shake the nagging feeling that I'm not quite in the clear with her. That, or she just gets a kick out of putting me in the hot seat.

"How'd you pull it off, huh? A junior staff member like you getting promoted to managing editor inside the rockiest week in company history?"

What's the right answer? The truth? No, I'm not that stupid. Yet even with all the luck points in the world coursing through my veins, my mouth can't manufacture a convincing-enough cover story. And to make matters worse, Laura won't stop grilling me.

"Hey, do you go to concerts?"

"Not often. Why?"

"Oh, no reason. Just, I was talking about you with a friend the other night and she said you sounded familiar."

"Which friend?"

"Her name is Misty. Ring a bell?"

There isn't even a hint of malice in her voice, but my palms get sweaty nonetheless. Eight-million fucking people on the island and she happens to know the one-and-only party girl to ever give me the time of day. I narrowly evade the question, but it's a sloppy dodge.

"By the way, what was up with that guy last night? Did you follow up on that? I tried, but I couldn't get details," Laura asks, firing off yet another question I can't answer truthfully. Thankfully, that's when we arrive at our stop.

The fresh air outside the subway tunnels helps me cool off, and five minutes later Laura and I arrive at a restaurant of such luxury that all of my partner's yet-to-be-asked questions melt in her mouth as she's exposed to the scents of perfumes more expensive than her yearly salary. I'm pretty impressed by the place too, considering a week ago I never thought I'd see the inside of it. Seriously, the tables are lit by candles. There's a fountain with a sculpted angel kid peeing in the center. It's fuckin' fancy.

"Hello, sir and madam," says the waiter stationed at the host stand. He's the spitting image of upper crust pie, what with his penciled-on mustache, Solex watch, and judging stare.

"Hi, we have a reservation." I hold up two fingers. "Party of two for 'Jack.'"

"Hmm." He looks down at some papers and squints for a few seconds. "There's no reservation under that name, I'm afraid."

Before Laura can get a word in, I tell the waiter to live up to his name and wait a second while I sort things out. I pull my date over to the lobby's seating area and work on getting in touch with the owner of the establishment.

Rax, front desk says there's no reservation. What happened?

Dude I told you that restaurant is way above your character level. They prob bumped you to make room for an actor or something lol I can't fix it.

I clench my jaw, attracting a weird look from Laura.

Give me another luck point, I text.

Dude, you've been getting greedy with these lately—

I cut him off before he can send a follow-up text to finish his thought.

Do it or I'm killing myself.

Laura's getting antsy. I can tell she's on the cusp of suggesting we just go somewhere else. Thankfully, my Crapple 10 lights up just as she's about to preemptively declare tonight a bust.

Oh, pfft. Enjoy the candy but that threat won't work next time.

Showtime.

"It's fixed." I speak with conviction, bluffing my way back into Laura's good graces. We return to the waiter. I cross my fingers and pray that the words on his sheets of paper have changed.

"Hi again," I say. "Mind checking for another name? Party of two for 'Rax.'"

"Hmm," he repeats, searching his list once more. "Ah, yes, here you are. Let me show you to your seats."

As we follow him, Laura looks at me.

"Rax?"

"It's, um, a middle name of mine."

"Really?"

"Yeah, it's South African."

She raises an eyebrow.

"The white part."

That's right, Jack, just keep digging yourself a deeper and deeper hole. How fucking long can it take the waiter to get us to our table?

"Here you are, sir and madam," the pencil-mustached man says, pulling out chairs for us at a table beside the big fountain at the center of the dining hall. The stone kid pissing water seems to be looking at me, winking.

"What would you two like to drink?" our waiter asks, once we're seated and comfy.

"Just water, thanks," Laura says. I concur. The man nods then disappears, leaving the lady and me to our own devices. Speaking of devices, I probably should've fired up the Crapple 10 and called Rax so he could coach me through dinner. *Gulp.*

"So... where to start," she says, tapping her fingers gently against the table. "I'd ask you what you do for work, but, well, yeah."

"No, I think it's a good question. After all, I'm still not totally sure what I do there."

She smiles.

"So, want to tell me about that South African heritage of yours?"

"Not especially." I laugh heartily. My knees lock up beneath the table.

"Okay. I was just curious since, y'know, it seemed like you pulled a rabbit out of a hat back there and bullshitted our way to a table."

She's still smiling.

"Look, as far as heritage and family are concerned, there's... there's not a lot. It's just me. It's not very exciting, that's all."

She leans in a bit, casting a shadow over her silverware and bread plate.

"Just you? No family at all? Is it something you don't like talking about? Do you at least have pets, or something?"

I feel sweat on my forehead. When's that waiter coming back?

"Hello?" she asks, noticing my eyes wandering around the restaurant's periphery.

"I, um, had one."

She leans back in her chair. Her smile is gone.

"I'm sorry. I don't usually do dinners," I sheepishly respond, scratching the back of my neck. I keep an eye out for the waiter. "Not great at small talk."

"It's fine. I shouldn't be asking so many questions." She examines me with her eyes. "It's just... you're a man of mystery, you know?"

"Not my intention." I put my hands in the air. "In fact, ask me anything. I'll give a straight answer."

Laura gives me a strange look, then crosses her arms.

"Okay. Who am I really having dinner with?"

Her words echo in my head, alongside the sound of a stone kid's clear-as-day urine splashing against the basin of the fountain next to me.

"Your drinks," a man says, catching me off guard. The waiter has returned with two tall, chilled glasses of water, decorated with lemon slices. He sets them down in front of us. "Are you two ready to order?"

"We're going to need a few more minutes," Laura replies, not taking her eyes off me. The waiter nods and leaves.

"What's the matter, Jack? Cat got your tongue?" She narrows her eyes. "You think I don't know you're a fraud? You think I'm an idiot? You think I can't see the only reason you even had the balls to ask me out is because of the squeaky kid you keep in your pocket?"

All air leaves my throat. My lungs start to crumple. The lights in the restaurant dim and Laura stops looking like Laura. Her jaw firms up, becoming masculine. Her arms are no longer sleeveless—they're covered by a suit jacket. One blink later, I find myself staring at the deer-like eyes of a man who I swore had landed himself in jail just last night.

I shove a hand in my pocket, but nothing's there. Jon continues staring at me from across the table, licking his lips while he plucks the lemon wedge from his glass of water. I start to panic.

Jon pops the lemon in his mouth, chomps it once, then swallows, peel and all. I look for escape routes, but there are none. In fact, when I scan my surroundings, I don't see the waiter's host stand anymore. Or the lobby. Or the peeing kid in the fountain. All I see is black. Everywhere is starved of light—except for the seat with Jon in it, which has a spotlight over it. He reaches into his pocket.

"Looking for something, Jack?" he says, waving my Crapple 10 around.

"Jack?"

He stops moving the phone.

"Jack?"

With a single flex of his hand, he crushes it.

"Jack?"

Laura reaches a hand across the table to shake mine. I blink rapidly, noticing our glasses are still on the table, lemon wedges untouched. The Crapple 10 is back in my pocket.

"I asked how you're feeling. Did you hear me?"

I blink some more, then reach for my water and take a large sip.

"It's, um... yeah, no, I'm not feeling well," I reply, putting the glass back down. "Sorry, it's that, uh, thing that happened last night—"

"Oh, the guy? I mean, who knows who that weirdo was. What about him is rattling you?"

I glance at the fountain kid again. He's definitely winking at me.

"Jack? What's going on?" she asks, stiffening up a bit, attempting to cover the revealing parts of her dress as best she can. "You never answered my questions about that guy earlier. Why? Did you find out something about him?"

I yank the lemon wedge off my glass and bite into it. The citrusy juices dance and sting their way across my tongue.

"Yeah, I, um, found out he ended up at a police station," I say, tapping my foot against the floor. "But, uh, turns out, I may know him."

"What?"

"Yeah, I may have bumped into him before. I lied to you. Same about the South African thing. And not knowing that friend of yours. And about scoring the managing editor title. Hell, I wasn't even telling the truth when we got Tim fired—"

With her eyes wide and lips parted, she takes the cloth napkin off her lap and sets it on the table. "What is wrong with you? What are you trying to tell me?"

"I'm trying to tell you," I say, rubbing my forehead, "that it's been a very, very strange week. And I want to explain it all from the start—"

That's when I feel a vibration in my pocket. Not from the Crapple 10, though—from the Aqua Jive. There's only one person who'd be calling me at the current hour on that phone.

"I'm so sorry, Laura." I exit my seat, stand up, and take out my phone. "But like I said, it's been a strange week and I need to take that; it's an emergency. I'll explain everything in just a minute, yeah?"

I look at her, desperate for approval. Perturbed as she is, her face riddled with confusion and offense, she finds it in herself to speak.

"Um, yeah, sure," she tells me, not getting another word in before I dash away from the table and head for the quietest corner of the restaurant I can find.

Once I'm hidden away in a tiny hall near the bathrooms, I look at the Aqua Jive and accept the call. But the name on the screen isn't Angela's. It's Morgan's. I put the phone next to my ear.

"Morgan? What's the matter?"

"Jack! Jack. Your friend, she—something very bad happened. Mathias and I got her to a hospital, but they wouldn't let us join her past the lobby—they said doctors only. Something about an emergency surgery. We're in the waiting room right now. It's not good. We don't know what's wrong—you need to come down here as soon as you can—"

"I'm on my way. Text me the address."

I hang up and pocket the phone, my heart skipping every other beat as I rush back to the table I'd been sharing with Laura.

"Laura, Jesus, I'm so sorry, a friend's having a medical emergency. I need to help them."

"Oh my—is there anything I can do? Do you want me to come with you—"

"No." I pull out my wallet and slip out two crisp Benjamins, setting them on the table. "I have to handle it alone. I'm so, so sorry. Please, get whatever you want, on me—or, uh, I don't know. I'm so sorry," I stammer, moving farther and farther away from her with every word spoken, passing by our confused waiter in my beeline for the exit. The last look Laura gives me is unmistakable—it's a sign I've done damage here today. With a heavy heart, I muffle my conscience, focus on the bigger picture, and rush out the restaurant's doors. I'll fix things with her later—right now, I need to get to Ange.

I look at my phone and see a text from Morgan containing the address of the hospital they're at, as well as a message.

Hurry, man, the doctors are getting worried, it reads, the sentence repeating enough times to fill up my phone's screen.

Oh my God. Ange...

I mentally map out the quickest route to the hospital then dart down the sidewalk. My brisk walk almost immediately becomes a jog, then a full-on sprint as streetlights turn on around me and the blood-red sun sets overhead.

CHAPTER 18

The dress shoes and slick suit I'm decked out in don't make my dogged dash easy, squeezing and throttling me in my fight to outpace the invisible hourglass hanging over my head. I shoot for a bus stop—the only chance I have. There's a single route that should quickly get me to the hospital. *Just once, developers, please make public transit competent and punctual.*

Unless... unless there's a smarter way to go about getting from point A to point B.

Dangerous bastard that I am, I pull out my Crapple 10 and attempt to order a taxi from my phone's Ryde app while I run, using peripheral vision to make sure I don't trip on a crack and break every bone in my body. C'mon, you little miracle rectangle, don't fail me now—

Update Required.

The Ryde app declares it's in need of a tune up and refuses to open. I initiate the update install, but my phone's data signal caps my download at a kilobyte-per-second rate so abysmal that I may as well not be downloading squat. *Ugh.* I keep charging toward the distant bus stop, undeterred by my smartphone app's nonsense.

Time to ring up the kid. "Rax, man," I say between breaths, trying to keep myself from popping a lung.

"What's the matter? You're really booking it down there," he replies.

"It's Angela. Can you see her?"

"No, I can't see her from where you are on the map right now; she's not in range. Why?"

"She's at a hospital—something happened—" I cut myself short, conserving air to maintain my Olympic-level sprint while I tab back to the Ryde app to see how the update's coming along. It's hopeless. "Listen, just stay on the line."

"You got it," Rax says. There's a loud popping noise on his end. "Sorry, knuckle crack."

I pocket the phone.

"Jack, you headed for the FU2 route on 5th Ave?"

"Yeah, that's the one," I say, whipping around another street corner.

"You're not gonna make it; the bus is three minutes from the stop." Clicking and clacking sounds ensue as he hammers away on what I can only assume is his keyboard. "See that big red apartment complex coming up in a few buildings? Cut through the alley next to it."

Streetlights flicker to life down the road, perfectly illuminating a building in the distance covered in crimson paint. Bingo.

Rax keeps feeding me instructions. "In that alley, there's a fence, as well as a dumpster nearby you can use to hop it."

I get to the alley and see what he's talking about—there's a dumpster and a fence, all right, but he didn't mention the latter had barbed wire.

"Can't do it," I say, taking in quick gulps of air between words. "If I miss the jump, my leg's getting shredded."

"It's the only way you make it to the other side of the block before the bus arrives."

Damn it. Hopefully Angela and I aren't *both* in a hospital when everything's over.

I dart into the alley, scaring the piss out of a dog who bolts away from me, barking up a storm. My eyes lock onto the dumpster and the cardboard boxes in front of it. Remember, Jack, just do it like they do in the movies.

I raise a foot and attempt to run up the boxes to the top of the dumpster, but they don't support my weight in the slightest. I smash through them and fall onto the wet, dirty ground beside the dumpster. Shit.

"What the fuck is going on out there?" someone shouts behind me. As I pick myself up off the ground and dazedly climb on top of the dumpster the slow but safe way, I spot the voice's source. Some guy is poking his head out of an apartment window and staring at me.

"Hey, creep, you're on private property! Get lost!"

I take his advice and run across the dumpster, making a valiant leap toward, and hopefully over, the barbed wire fence.

I'm airborne for a few seconds, surrounded by nothing but whistling air and the echoing voice of an angry tenant calling me an asshole. Then I feel something tear near my foot and my entire body careens south. I barely manage to get hands in front of my face before I crash onto the asphalt on the other side of the fence. The alley water beneath my hands splashes up and drenches my face, forcing me to wipe my eyes with my sleeves. I look back to see what tripped me up. A small bit of fabric, torn right from my suit's pant leg, clings to the barbed wire. I look down and see the shredded hem of my pants—just a few inches lost, and not a cut on my skin.

"Keep moving, man," Rax urges. I rocket out the other side of the alley and finally see the bus stop. It's close. The bus is a few yards from it.

"Go!" Rax says.

I drain every last luck point into the tips of my toes, moving at a speed that'd put a cheetah to shame. I'm less than a few buildings away when the bus arrives at the stop and starts unloading passengers.

"Wait," I shout, running up behind it just as the driver starts to close the doors. Perhaps he hears my cry or sees some soggy, exhausted jackass in the rearview mirror. Either way, he reopens the doors and a second later, I slam inside the bus.

Once inside, I swallow some air then check my vibrating Aqua Jive. It displays more texts from Morgan, all of them devoid of good news. Time was already in short supply, and now it's about to become the only luxury resource I can't afford. I give a brief one-sentence spiel to the bus driver explaining my situation and kindly ask him to book it.

"That ain't how it works, kid," the driver responds.

"Rax..." I mumble, grabbing the overhead railing near the first row of seats. The bus begins moving again.

"It's going to be fine. She's going to be fine," the teen says, his squeaks more reassuring and adult-like than any sound my gravelly voice can muster. "Calm the heck down, would ya?"

I peer out the bus windows, but the blur of neon signs and brightly lit building lobbies whipping past don't do a thing to assuage my fears; no matter how quickly we blaze past the city blocks, it's not fast enough to make the minutes feel any less fleeting. It doesn't help when the bus starts to slow down.

Red traffic lights halt a fleet-sized assortment of cars and trucks clogging the upcoming intersection ahead of us.

It seems some idiot tried to run the light. Now everyone's working to get them out of the center and avoid a traffic jam.

"Where the fuck did my luck perks go," I hiss at Rax. An elderly woman beside me overhears my foul-mouthed growling and gives me a dirty look.

"Where all luck goes: away for a bit. It's still RNG and shiz, remember?" He muffles the mic as his mother reminds him to keep it cordial from somewhere in the background. "I said 'shiz,' ma! With a 'z,' 'kay?"

Rax and his parental unit continue to prattle back and forth. *I'm getting nowhere,* I think to myself. I need to get moving, stat—wait, is that a taxi I see? It's just a few cars away, and there doesn't seem to be a passenger inside.

"Driver, sir, man, can you open the door? Please," I say, spewing out words faster than I can process them.

"No can do—"

"I know you can't open doors in the middle of the street, but look. We're not moving anytime soon and there's a taxi I can reach—"

"I can't do it."

"It's life or death!"

"Exactly why I can't do it. You get killed because I let you out here, it's on my ass—"

"Yeah? And what if *you* get killed because you kept me in here?"

The driver turns around to face me. I let go of the overhead railing and am about to clench my fists, but a series of loud honks interrupt me. It looks like the traffic issue has cleared up and our bus is free to proceed—at five miles an hour. We inch forward, moving into the middle of the intersection. The whole time, the driver remains fixated on me.

"Pal, you know it's a crime to threaten a public transit operator?"

"*Pfft*, like hell it is." I put a hand back on the railing. I just want the damn bus to *speed up*! Fuck!

"If you don't—"

He cuts himself off. His eyes go wide and the people behind me scream. Looking to my side, I spot a mammoth garbage truck blasting down the street perpendicular to our lane of the intersection. It's headed right for us.

No one has time to move before it rams our bus. Windows explode and shower us with glass. Our vehicle tips violently to the side, throwing people out of their seats and into the ceiling. The garbage truck slams forward and shoves our bus out of its way, sending us into a violent series of collisions with neighboring cars. As the bus spins, I get one good glimpse out a broken window at the truck driver. Even in my dazed, confused state in the middle of an actively developing road accident, I can't not process what my eyes see.

It's Jon in the truck, looking at me with a devilish smile. Then, one blink later, it's just an average guy staring straight ahead, scared out of his fuckin' mind. What the hell did I just see? Was any of it—

I smash against the edge of the driver's seat as the bus finally stops spinning. My body slumps to the floor. Behind me, a few people groan and others cry. It looks like everyone survived, somehow—though not everyone's in great condition. Case in point: the driver. He looks pretty banged up in his seat. I reach inside his control panel area to hit the switch that opens the bus doors. He gurgles something at me, but the words are unintelligible. I ignore him and burst out of the bus, stumbling onto the street. Glass shards continue to fall off my suit. I hobble around the totaled cars obstructing my path, ignoring the drivers shouting at each other. Soon, I'm able to work through the pain and build up a walk, then a run.

I hear the sirens of cop cars and paramedics arriving at the scene as I leave it in the dust. It's only a few blocks to the hospital from here. I can make it. Still a bit dazed from the incident, I pat my pockets to make sure both phones are accounted for. They are, along with my wallet. My earbud remains snug in my ear.

"Rax?" I say, rocketing down the glowing streets toward the hospital that's finally in view.

"I'm here," he replies. "That was nuts, but don't stop, don't talk to me. Just get there!"

I open my mouth to ask if he can see Angela on the game map now that I'm closer to her, but he ends the call. I don't have time to whip out the Crapple 10—just time to run. People dive out of my way as I blast down the sidewalk toward my target. Cars at crosswalks stop for me when they realize I'm not going to stop for them.

The shouts of angry drivers and annoyed pedestrians fade behind me once I practically teleport across the final block separating me from my target. I arrive at the hospital battered and bruised, but still in one piece and ready to see Angela. I march up the building's weathered stone steps, past the entryway's columns, and through the brass front doors, asking anyone and everyone inside where I need to go to see my Ange. They point me in directions until, a few hallways later, I'm facing Morgan and Mathias in the waiting room.

"What's the situation?" I ask, collapsing into the first chair I find.

"It... it is not good. They do not know what is wrong with her," Morgan says.

"What?" I vacate the chair my weary muscles had just relaxed into. "Uh, all right. Okay. I'm going to go get some answers from these goddamn quacks." I stomp toward the doors to the ER wing.

"They said we can't—" Morgan starts, a sentiment echoed by the nurse who tells me I'm not allowed any further. I ignore her, along with the other medical staff whose attention I've drawn, and slam the doors wide open, marching right on through.

I then realize I haven't thought out my plan very well—how do I find Ange before security comes for me? I don't know where I am, or what I'm doing. Am I an idiot?

That flash of self-doubt disappears as I spot a windowed room at the end of the hall I've stumbled into. I march toward it, hands shaking and lips quivering. The medical staff inside it move away from the window, parting to reveal a pale, unmoving, bed-ridden figure I know to be Angela.

I reach the glass and place my hands against it, looking at her. All the commotion I've left in my wake ceases to exist. I hear nothing but her labored breathing, only audible via my imagination. Her chest goes up and down so slowly it almost seems to not be moving at all.

A staffer in the room notices my face glued to the window and steps outside to confront me. "Sir, you can't be here," he says, eyeballing the nurses and security guards likely a few yards behind me. They have every right to throw me out; I don't belong here. But neither does Ange.

"I'm... her husband," I say, reading the man's face to see if he'll budge. He furrows his brow and adjusts his glasses.

"The men who brought her here, they're my friends," I blubber. "She's been staying with me and I've been taking care of her these past few days." I whip out my phone to show that I know the woman, praying that years' worth of correspondence will be enough to prove the link.

After looking at my phone's screen then scanning me up and down for the better half of a minute, the man waves a gloved hand at the nurses behind me.

"Mary, Sue, it's fine. I've got it," he says. The women, as well as the security guards with their jingling handcuffs, head the other way. Once their shoes squeak far enough down the hall, the kind soul in front of me continues.

"We're not allowed to give status updates at the moment." He pauses and squints at my phone, realizing my name was buried somewhere in the mix of media I showed him. "Jack." He sees the despair written all over my face.

"... So I'm not going to say anything, especially not that it looked like appendicitis at first." He frowns. "All the steps we've taken to help her aren't working. Our efforts should've paid off by now, but something's still failing internally, and her vitals are..." He looks away, unable to withstand my piercing gaze. "Declining."

I blink a few times and try not to collapse. "Declining?" I ball my fists tight enough that I can practically feel bone.

"Rapidly," he responds. Before I can go ballistic, he makes a move. "Now understand, we're doing everything, absolutely everything, to help her, and we're not done yet, but I need you to stay out here. I'll get you a chair and you can wait by the window."

I have to assume he's breaking protocol to even let me do that much, so I don't argue. I quietly slump into the chair he brings out and sit there, next to the window that separates me from Angela in her hour of greatest need.

All the equipment she's hooked up to can't help her. All the men and women doting on her right now, despite their claims, can't help her. And I, the man with all the power and resources in the world, can't help her. The writing's on the wall. But what did she do to deserve whatever the hell is going on with her?

I unbury my head from my hands, realizing I'm ripping out hair. The few strands I've torn loose slip between my fingers as I look up in response to a noise.

It's a call from Rax.

"How you holding up there, Big J?" His voice is respectful but not quite mournful.

"Tell me what's wrong with her," I plead. Silence ensues for the longest beat of my life.

"I, uh, I found out a few minutes ago when you approached the hospital. I checked her profile and have been... well, I've been trying to figure out how to say what needs to be said—"

"With your mouth! Out with it!" I blurt, a bit too loudly for the hospital crowd traversing the hall I'm stuck in. Not like I care; with any luck, my shouts will wake up Angela and we can both go home. I just want her to come home.

"The signs have been there for days, Jack, I just didn't know how to read them. I knew there'd be consequences for letting her in on our secret. I tried to warn you..."

"What are you saying?"

"I'm saying..." He hesitates. "It looks like her files... they're corrupting. Almost all of them show error signs."

"What?"

"I'm not sure there's a drop of code left in her that hasn't been borked by the little virus you gave her," he says, still not sounding as utterly defeated as I feel. I can't handle it.

"She's not code. She's Angela. Why don't you care, Rax? Why don't you *care*?"

"Whoa there, cowboy." He lets out a huff. "I come bearing gifts! Well, sort of."

My stomach lurches. I can't handle Rax keeping the emotional roller coaster in high gear. "Give me a clear explanation of what you're talking about, or I swear to God..."

"No in-game doctor can do a thing about the virus. However, I might have the skills to repair her files. But—and there's a big 'but' here, ha," he says, forcing the quip without a hint of laughter, "it would take some time in real-world minutes. I'm not sure how much longer Angela has, and my mom's going to make me come downstairs for dinner soon."

"The fuck are you talking about? Screw dinner!"

"Jack, you need to listen to me. You're just a game character to everyone but me. If I don't go down there for dinner when she calls, she will shut my computer off and you'll be out of options to save Angela. We can deal with the 'pixel lives matter' stuff once the crisis is over, okay?"

My chest is burning and my muscles are tense, but with no one to physically attack and unleash my anger on—specifically, the snarky little fucker on the phone—I have to resign myself to sitting patiently and letting him continue.

"We have two options: Either I try to fix Angela right now and risk not finishing before mom calls, *or*... or I can abandon the game for a few minutes, run to Barry's house, and try to convince him to come over again." The kid rushes to explain himself before I can start cursing him out. "Look, Barry has a bunch of food allergies, so my mom gets cagey about making dinner when he's around. If I get him back here, she'll leave us alone and I'll have more time to work on Angela's files. Plus, Barry can be my assistant and look up stuff to help. If, y'know, he's game for that."

"So our options are: You try to solve the problem solo before your mom appears, and if you fail, *we* fail, or you step away for a bit and we bank everything on Barry?"

"Yeah."

I feel vomit rising inside of me, but I manage to swallow and suck it all back down just as it starts bubbling in the back of my throat. "How much better of a shot do we have if you get Barry?"

"Much better."

I don't pause for a second. "Do it."

"On it. I'll leave the game in chat mode, so it progresses as slowly as possible. Talk to you soon!"

"Rax?" I say, not quite ready to be left alone. But it's too late. I hear his mic clatter onto the floor and realize I've just dismissed my only remaining partner. All that's left is me, the cold hall, and the unconscious frame of the most important girl in the world. She's trapped in a room beside me, shackled to a bed and being swarmed by NPCs who are searching for a disease that's literally impossible to find. Do I try to tell them it's hopeless? Do I barge in there to be with her during her final minutes?

No, neither of those options work; they'll both just make the whole situation worse. Have I learned nothing? I need to be patient and trust in my new friend... because it's that easy. Of course it is. Being helpless is always easy. I just wish it wasn't.

The guilt comes in waves and takes over my body. It forces me to stand, drawing me toward the window separating me from Angela. She's just as helpless as my sorry ass. We all are, inside the damned, despicable game.

I stifle tears and my breath quickens. The minutes whip by almost as fast as the doctors. Everything blurs into a fluid nightmare where the only constant is Angela's unmoving body. I keep calling out to Rax, but he doesn't answer. I lose track of time as the loop of anguish repeats itself over and over.

Then the doctors freeze. I look at the equipment surrounding Angela, following the gaze of the medical staff. On a monitor, a thin green line stops wavering up and down. Through the glass, I hear the noise the device emits. Even as the doctors regain their composure and scurry to employ last-ditch measures, I know it's done. I failed you for the last time, Ange. I made the wrong choice. I made the wrong choice and it...

It...

... It killed you. I killed you.

CHAPTER 19

"Ma!" Rax shouted, bursting out of his bedroom like foam rocketing out of a shaken soda can. "Where's my hoverboard?"

"Honey, you forgot to charge it. I have it hooked up in the living room but it's going to take a while," his mother replied, her voice echoing from a room down the hall.

"Dang it," the boy mumbled, running across the upstairs carpet and down the wooden staircase that led to his home's small entryway.

Once he'd made it to the front door, Rax grabbed his hoodie off the otherwise unoccupied coat rack, then picked up his running shoes from the doormat. Here, he found a wrapped piece of candy Barry had seemingly dropped by accident on his way out earlier in the day.

It's not like him to lose things, Rax thought to himself as he slipped the treat into his pocket. *He's too OCD for that.*

After donning his nighttime jogging attire, Rax went to open the door. He'd only just gotten his fingers on the knob when a motherly voice demanded an explanation.

"Raximus Gregarian Teelum, where do you think you're going at such a late hour? You know I'm about to start making dinner—"

"Ma, it's super important! I swear!" he shouted back, knowing there was no time to explain.

"Not more important than you eating a healthy meal. I know the kinds of food you eat at school, young man. All those saturated fats are going to—"

"A friend is having an emergency!" Rax said, unwilling to dawdle for another second. He swung the door open and shot onto the porch, the last words he heard from his mom being those of concern and an offer of assistance he had no time to accept.

Thankfully, Barry's house was just around the block. Thanks to his slim and short-but-fast build, Rax had no trouble blasting past house after house, reaching his target in two minutes flat. While having his hoverboard handy would've been a nice convenience on the way there, that wasn't his real concern—he was more worried about getting Barry back to his place in a timely fashion. Barry had never finished a fitness test at school, after all, and Rax wasn't sure that now was the right time to see if his friend's extra calories could be burned into pure energy through sheer willpower.

Putting the package before the drone, Rax chided himself as he walked up the home's front steps and rang the doorbell. It took a full minute before anyone opened the door, and to his surprise, it wasn't Barry who greeted him. It was his mother.

"Oh, hello, Raximus." She was doing the so-subtle-it's-almost-neutral frown that mothers do when someone else's kid has caused trouble for their own.

Rax sighed internally before manning up and getting down to business. "Hi, Mrs. Bloocubgake. Can I speak with Barry? It's urgent."

"I don't know," she said, her frown growing. "He's a bit preoccupied right now. Perhaps you can speak with him tomorrow?"

"No, I mean—it's very, very urgent."

She crossed her arms, activating her motherly defense matrix. "Rax, I'm not sure what happened when he was over at your house, but he came home very worked up and had an asthma attack shortly thereafter," she said. "He's relaxing. I don't think he'd like to see you right now."

"I know," Rax replied. "It's about what happened. I need to discuss it with him and apologize. Plus," he reached into his pocket to fish out the piece of candy nestled within, "I have to return something of his."

While other moms would wonder why a fifteen-year-old would come all the way to a friend's house to return a piece of candy, Barry's mom understood and, with some hesitation, ultimately stepped out the way, granting Rax entry. Seconds later, Rax was knocking on Barry's door.

"Barry! B! Open up!"

"Go away," Barry groused from the other side of the door.

"It's about Jack! He needs us!"

A beat of silence passed between the boys.

"He doesn't even like me. Not that you care."

"What?"

"You just want to play the game all day. Why did my mom even let you in?"

"I'll tell you if you just open the damn door!"

"Mind your language, Raximus," Barry's mom said to the unwelcome teenager.

Barry's bedroom door finally opened, revealing the plump boy Rax was so desperate to see. Barry trekked back to his bed and hopped on it, displacing his inhaler and a bag of toffees.

"Jack's best friend is dying and I need you at my place to help save her."

"I know Jack is a special game character and all, but, um, he's still just virtual, right? Why do you care so much? You didn't even want me there by the time I left... you just wanted to keep playing..." Barry's frown folded over itself in a pouty fashion akin to a baby's, a look that typically elicited laughter from others but hit Rax squarely in the gut.

"Look, B, I know, I know, I—" Rax darted his eyes back toward the open bedroom door before lowering his voice, "—I fucked up, okay? You know me, man. I get a little absorbed in stuff sometimes. I learned my lesson. I swear."

"That's... good to hear," Barry mumbled.

"But—"

"Oh, of course there's a 'but.'"

"But you need to understand, Jack's a person. He proved it to me, and he'll prove it to you too. You just have to give him another chance. I don't know how it's possible, but he's real, and he's in trouble."

Barry stopped making eye contact with Rax and refocused his attention on the bag of toffees beside him. With a huff, Barry reached a hand into the bag, only for his face to slacken with disappointment. There were only empty wrappers left.

"Well," Barry said, looking back at Rax, "what do you need me for? You're the master hacker, after all."

"I need you for dinner duty." Rax narrowed his eyes as he spoke the code.

Barry, like a knight who'd just been called upon by the king to slay a dragon, snapped to form and lost his pitiable demeanor in an instant. "It really is a code red," he said, sliding off the bed to go grab sandals from his closet. Seconds later, he and Rax were ready to bounce.

"I have to help Rax with a computer issue," Barry shouted to his mother, who'd wandered downstairs to futz with laundry. "I'll be back soon. I love you!"

"I love you too, sweetheart. Call me if you need anything!" she replied.

Rax stepped out the front door. "Let's go!" he said. "Oh, and before I forget..." He reached into his pocket and procured the piece of toffee Barry had lost at his house.

Barry's eyes lit up with excitement at the sight of his precious, the last of its kind. He stuck his grubby paws out to snatch it, but his pal yanked the treat back at the last second.

"Whoa there, bud. These things'll kill ya," Rax said. "Very unhealthy."

Barry stuck up a finger.

"Look, I'll fork it over once we help out Jack, yeah?"

The two dashed back to Rax's place. Along the way, Barry complained that Rax couldn't repay him for assistance with goods that weren't even his to begin with, but Rax's superior, simple argument of supply and demand won that debate well before they reached the lankier boy's stoop.

"What if I just took it from you?" Barry argued as they ran upstairs to Rax's room.

"You ever seen those barrel rolling videos?" was Rax's only response, accompanied by a brief snigger. Barry gave him a well-deserved slap across the back of the head.

"All right, onto the main event," Rax said, sliding into his gaming chair. Barry closed the bedroom door behind them and mounted the bed, and soon enough both boys were back to looking at the virtual screen as though they'd never left it to begin with. "I'm going to start file digging for Jack's friend Angela. While I find her folder, you need to—"

"Rax! Raaax!" his mother shouted from downstairs. "I heard you come home! I'm going to start cooking dinner. It's grilled cheese tonight—"

"Hi, Mrs. Teelum!" Barry shouted back.

A moment of silence ensued. Rax grinned.

"Oh, hello, Barry! I didn't hear you come in... would you like anything to eat?" Rax's mom replied, preemptively closing the oven door and turning off its alarm.

"No, thank you," Barry said, shooting a thumbs-up Rax's way as both boys heard the mother's kitchen activities grind to a halt.

Though the benefits of having an allergy-ridden, lactose intolerant friend were few, the handful that did exist were lifesavers, Rax thought to himself. He returned his pal's thumbs-up and got back to file digging. "Hey, can you search on your phone to see if anyone knows where the game's '2020' file directory is?" he asked, lost in a sea of virtual folders. He knew how to view Angela's general files and monitor the damage eating her up, but her editable repair documents were eluding him.

"Yeah, on it."

"All right, great. In the meantime, let me actually check and see how she and Jack are doing..." Rax alt-tabbed back to the game and looked at the scene. His skin went pale. "Barry, man, you need to get me that info." Not sparing a second to console Jack, Rax instead went right back to the file directory to double-time his search.

"I know, I know—wait, got it!" Barry then read aloud from a forum thread detailing the necessary documents' location.

"Perfect, thank you," the adolescent hacker replied, pulling up Angela's secret sub-folder. In it, every single file was corrupted. Rax paused, unsure of what to do—no way was there enough time for him to manually fix the individual issues before the game recognized Angela had expired and wiped her from the cache. No—there was only one option.

"I'm gonna have to verify the game's integrity and repair all these files with a blanket reset," Rax said, cracking his knuckles.

Barry looked on as the technological wunderkind executed the immeasurably complex steps of selecting all files with "ctrl+A" then right-clicking and selecting the "repair" option.

"That's it?" Barry asked, eyeballing his friend's hoodie pocket for the candy.

"Yep," Rax said, reclining in his seat. "Now we just let it do its thing and watch that little progress bar fill up. Hopefully we're not too late."

"Great. Can I have that toffee now? It's mine anyway," Barry said, slipping off the bed to waddle toward his friend and, more importantly, his reward.

"Yeah, yeah." Rax took it out of his pocket and plopped it in his pal's hand.

As Barry went to unwrap the candy, a strange light reflected off the corner of its wrapper. Barry looked up at the monitor projection and saw something flashing red on the edge of Rax's taskbar. Upon closer inspection, it was a little exclamation mark.

"Hey, uh, Rax?"

"Yeah?"

"What's that?" He pointed at the small symbol that'd just appeared.

"I dunno," Rax replied, moving his cursor to inspect it. Hovering over it caused a popup window to appear, one that made the boy go even paler than he'd been upon seeing Angela's state just a few moments prior. Barry, but a second from putting the toffee in his mouth, paused his caramel feast.

"That's not good, is it," the wide boy said nervously.

Rax stared at the screen for a long moment, then gulped. "I am so screwed."

CHAPTER 20

I rest my forehead against the operating room window, pounding the glass with my fist. My action prompts a staffer to come out and see what's up. As soon as she opens the door, I rush it. It's my best shot to get inside, since they've been locking me out.

I catch the door before it closes and slip inside the room. A few doctors take their eyes off their patient to deal with me, but the best they can do is issue stern warnings and request that I step away. None touch me. I get within inches of Angela, staring over her motionless body with tears in my eyes.

I resist the urge to hold her hand since it's still hooked up to tubes and other apparatus. They may no longer have any use, but I don't want to risk jeopardizing the chance that they do. And beyond that, I wouldn't want to cause her any discomfort, wherever she is... now.

The things I should've said... *It's just a game*, I tell myself. *It's just a game. It's just a game.*

It's just a game where I can feel the warmth of the water dripping down my cheeks, smell the sweat of my Angela's expired body, and hear the doctors shouting at me, pestering me to leave as I fall to my knees, clinging to Ange's bedside, begging her to not leave me first.

Then a hand grabs mine. It's not the cold grip of a medical staffer—it's the warm hold of someone who heard my request. I stand up. The doctors around me back off, just as amazed as I am by what we're all seeing.

"Jack?" Angela murmurs, taking her first breath in minutes.

"Y-yeah?" I say.

Her voice is just loud enough for me, and only me, to hear. "I hate this game."

We both laugh for a few seconds, though the chuckles cause Angela to cough. Then a vibrating ring goes off in my pocket. Instinctively, I pull out the Crapple 10. But just as quickly, I go to put it away, scolding myself for prioritizing that damn phone over Ange. She stops me.

"Is that..."

"Yeah. Doesn't matter, though; I'll call him back in a bit."

"No... no, call him back now..."

Her voice is weak but authoritative. I give her one last look.

"I'll deal with the doctors," she says between coughs. The color's returning to her skin.

I give her a nod and leave the room, dialing up my guy once I'm outside.

"I heard you try to blow me off," Rax says. I ignore the remark.

"The miracle—it has to be you, right? You did it?"

"Well, yeah, but Barry helped too."

"Barry? He's back? Uh, oh, well, that's great. Tell Barry I say thank you so much—"

"We're back on speaker, so he can hear you," Rax announces as his friend gives a hearty "you're welcome" from somewhere near the mic.

"And thank you, Rax. I don't know how to say thank you enough. I couldn't have done it without you both."

"You can say that again. But I'm not calling about Angela," he continues, the hint of urgency in his voice losing its subtlety. "I'm calling to say you won't be able to reach me for a few minutes, okay?"

"A few minutes? Your time or my time?"

"Not sure yet. Listen, just don't mess up anything while I'm gone, all right? Don't pull anymore stunts. And... oh, yeah, stay frosty."

"Wait, what? Why—"

The line disconnects.

Looking at my phone screen in confusion, I notice a missed call and two messages. Funny, not many people have my Crapple 10's number besides Rax and—

"Laura," I mutter under my breath, smacking myself on the forehead as punishment for daring to think my day could be comprised of anything but cleaning up messes. Twisting around to check on Angela through the window, I see she's sitting up and is dealing with swarms of doctors, all of whom are likely asking how she's gone from clinically dead to upright and active within the time span of a few minutes. I march over to the room's door and knock a few times until a staffer lets me in, likely at the behest of Ange.

Once I'm beside her bed, I make my request. "I, uh, have to take a sensitive call. Is it all right if I step outside the hospital for a few minutes? Just to catch some air?"

"Hm? Yeah, sure, if that's what you need," she says. "What'd the kid have to say?"

"Not sure, honestly. He's acting weird. Says he's going AFK for a little bit or something."

"Oh." Ange's face tenses up. "Well, tell him I say 'thanks.'"

"What, you don't think I saved the day all by myself?"

She rolls her eyes and gives me a light shove, signaling I'm cleared to leave the room.

On my way out of the lobby, as I move toward the hospital's front entrance, I notice Morgan and Mathias are still here. I give them a wave.

"What happened? Is your friend okay?" they ask. The three of us meet beside a vending machine. I eyeball some peanut butter cups in there and my stomach gurgles. When's the last time I had food?

"Yep! She came around. The doctors aren't actually sure what she had," I reply, realizing I'm veering too close to the truth. "Must've just been some really bad food poisoning or something."

"Oh," the two hulking Europeans say, nodding vigorously.

"She is in good health?" Mathias asks.

"She's getting there. You two are free to go, if you want. And thanks again for helping her and sticking around; I couldn't have done it without you."

"No worries, brother," Morgan says, putting a hand on my shoulder.

"We are proud to help an American ally such as yourself," Mathias says, sticking out a hand. I meet it and give a firm handshake.

"I, uh, yeah—back at ya," I reply. They laugh.

When I retract my hand, I accidentally bump the nearby vending machine. Three snacks fall out. Among them are peanut butter cups. Neat. "You guys hungry?"

The three of us exit the hospital together. Morgan and Mathias munch on chips while I give my dentist a run for his money with two bite-sized cups' worth of chocolaty, peanut-buttery goodness. The fellas fist bump me at the front entrance before waving and heading down the street, formally exiting the scene. Now there's just me and a few nearby strangers loitering on the stairs.

The air is comfortably warm but it's starting to rain, so I keep myself positioned on the higher steps which remain dry thanks to the hospital's second story overhang. I lean against a column and, one deep breath later, make the call.

"Jack?" Laura says, answering the phone a moment too soon for me to pussy out and hang up.

"Hey, Laura..."

We say nothing for a little bit. The previously spotty rain ups its frequency and turns into a drizzle. Street lights' reflections shimmer in colorful puddles on the roads.

"I'm still at the hospital. Y'know, from the emergency," I say, unconvincingly. Even though it's true, I sure sound like a dishonest son of a bitch.

"Oh. Well, um, I'm sorry to hear that. Do you want to talk about it?"

"Not especially."

Another long pause.

"Well, Jack, I've been thinking..."

"Wait, before you say it—let me, um, say something." I yank at my collar a bit, realizing I don't actually have anything to add. I can't keep lying and dodging. And I certainly cannot tell her about the simulation. Not after what happened today. So what can I do? Nothing.

"I lied, go ahead," I say.

"Oh. Well, I'm not sure how to say what I have to say either, but... you're a bit of a jerk, you know that?"

"Yeah." I scratch behind my ear. "Yeah."

"But you're also... I don't know. I like you. But I just don't know. You got Tim fired then got his job, you took me out to dinner under someone else's name, were freaking out the whole time, then left before we could even order..."

"Yep..."

"And I still think about the party. We had that moment... in the closet... I, um, don't normally do that, by the way."

"I know."

"But you got in a fight with that guy, and..."

"And?"

"Listen, Jack, I don't know what's going on in your life right now, but everything just feels weird with you. I like you, and you're funny, but... maybe it's not the best time for us to be doing anything together."

I drink in the warm late-evening air and keep my eyes glued to the traffic light reflections in the street puddles, which now shine red. "I agree."

"Oh." She pauses. "Um, maybe we can talk down the line."

"Maybe, yeah."

"Okay. Well, see you at work tomorrow. If you come in. I hope everything works out for you. Over there, I mean. Er, bye."

The call ends. I look at my phone and dial Rax. After a few rings, I receive the "line is busy" tone. I dial again, to the same result. And again. I keep trying to reach him. I watch people pass by me, going in and out of the hospital, but I stay put, leaning on my column, alone. The rain's getting heavier. I think I hear thunder somewhere in the distance.

I dial again, now up to more attempts than I can count on both hands.

"Dude, what do you need?" the boy asks, his voice crackling to life just as I prepare to hear another busy line tone.

"Hey, I just wanted to double confirm that Ange's files were corrupting because we... or rather, I, told her—"

"Yes."

"So that means letting one more person know is—"

"Absolutely off-limits."

"Rax, it's getting exhausting, living with the secrets I can't share. Seriously! I don't know if I can take it. Besides, you never even said if it was hard to fix Angela—"

"That's why I'm taking your call, ya big dip. I've been busy, uh, sizing up a situation that repairing Angela caused. See, I had to do a universal file repair to get her bits on the mend, and, well, uh, hoo-boy—"

"What?" I rub my forehead, exhausted by the squeaky voice stammering in my ear.

"Well, that file repair also fixed and reactivated the Beluga Anti-Cheat software, which I disabled a long time ago in order to activate your hack. And that software, uh, it may have, um, switched the game back into online mode, and—"

Lightning crackles in the sky.

"And?"

"And if the anti-cheat software is back online, that means the DRM program inside it is going to be back on the hunt too."

"Kid, cut the jargon! The hell is DRM?" I say. Another flash of lightning appears, and the rain's intensifying pitter-patter starts to rival the sound of Rax's voice.

"DRM stands for 'digital rights management.' It's an always-online, always-adapting program that makes sure players don't tamper with game files. It's supposed to prevent piracy and hacking. . ."

"It makes sure you can't hack? How the hell does it do that?"

Thunder claps through the sky.

"It..." Rax stammers, "it terminates any user-modified files—like you!"

"How-dee, neighbor!" a loud, rumbling voice hollers from somewhere across the street. As I turn my head to face the speaker, people start shrieking. On the sidewalk opposite the hospital, a crowd of civilians dive out of the way of a man in a long trench coat. Though he's wearing a new outfit, I'd recognize those crazy eyes anywhere. He's aiming a gun at me.

"Jack, move!" Rax shouts.

Jon fires a shot from his handgun. I flatten against the pillar I was leaning on and shimmy around its circumference for better protection. The incoming bullet blasts off a small chunk of my cover's concrete exterior. With my back to the shooter, I refocus on Rax.

"Some notice would've been great!" I yell.

Another shot zings by, cracking more concrete off the column I'm hiding behind. People around me scream and run for cover, making it hard to hear Rax's next words.

"It's starting to make sense, now—he didn't have authorization from the anti-cheat to terminate you before because it was disabled, but now—"

"Focus! How do we stop him?"

"I'm working on it, dude. For now, just stay alive. The DRM hasn't finished downloading the latest patches yet, so the game might not recognize it as a protected program—"

"Meaning?"

"Its NPC manifestation will be treated like any other person waving around a gun. A civvy already reported a crime to the police. Should be just a minute before—"

The next shot ricochets off the column to my side and whizzes past the one I'm using as cover, causing a light, powdery dusting of debris to fall on my hair. I poke my head out just long enough to see Jon smiling cheek-to-cheek at me. He steps onto the street between us. Thankfully, though a few cars stop and honk amid the confusion and panic, most are still passing by at top speed, eager to get the hell away from a potential shoot-out. If they stop moving and let that maniac through, I'm fucked.

"No," Jon shouts over the traffic, as though he has an invisible megaphone stapled to his mouth. "You've been very bad, Jack! You both broke the agreement!" He manages to squeeze between two slow cars and begins crossing the road. His voice turns demonic. "And now you need to be punished."

I hear police sirens somewhere down the street, but they're too far away to give me hope; Jon's practically dancing between cars now, maneuvering his way onto the hospital's sidewalk without so much as a scratch. More shots echo overhead. He's zeroing in on me, getting close to the stairwell leading to the row of columns I'm hidden behind.

"You have to move to the next column," Rax urges.

I follow his order and buy myself a little distance from Jon, who's approaching the far side of the hospital.

"Is your helper good to you, Jack? Does he make you feel safe, monkey?" Jon taunts.

"Move again!" Rax says. I dart to the next column, landing behind it just as a bullet grazes the cuff of my suit jacket.

"I said, *do you feel safe?*" Jon roars, firing off a few rounds near where my feet are, causing me to jump out of my skin as scorch marks appear on the ground beside my shoe tips. "Dance, monkey, dance!" His voice is so close that it echoes off the hospital overhang.

"Rax, solution, *now*," I say.

"You're safe!" Rax replies, confusing the hell out of me until I hear a new kind of gunshot, followed by a girly shriek.

"Stay on the ground! Stay on the ground!" multiple men shout, enticing me to peek out from behind my column. Jon's tumbled down the steps of the hospital entrance, leaving a trail of blood behind him that mixes with the pooling rain.

A bunch of cops run toward the scene, one of whom fires a second round into my shooter as he tries to get up. Jon lets out another feminine shrill. Lying on the ground, with his back to the officers, he looks at me. For a brief moment, when he's sure no one else can see his face, he smirks and winks, before going back to screaming up a storm. The cops reach his position and cuff him. Then, suddenly, his demeanor changes.

"Be seeing you!" he says to me, smiling even when the cops punch him in the back of the head and tell him to shut up. They drag him toward their vehicles, which are parked farther down the block.

For the first time in minutes, I take a breath. Then I get angry.

"Why didn't you see him coming? Can you see him now, or am I blind down here?"

"Please calm down. They're taking him to another police station—"

"How'd he get out of the last one?"

"They probably released him! All he did was trespass in an office. Can you calm down?"

"A program just tried to assassinate me, kid."

"I was working on trying to prevent that a few minutes ago. Ever since I fixed Angela, I can't track him very well. It looks like he's figuring out the in-game surveillance methods."

"Wait, is Angela safe? You said Jon, the DRM, hunts user-modified files?"

"She hasn't been modified, only repaired, and that was by the game itself. You, amigo, are the only user-modified file. You're the only target."

I curse and kick the nearest column before cursing again from the pain.

"I know," Rax says, "it's not a good situation... I should've put two and two together sooner. Offline, he didn't have system permissions or the latest patches so it was easy to write him off as a buggy NPC. All he could do was harass you and slow you down, but he was trying to fight the hack all along. The signs were there..."

More cops appear at the scene of the crime to take reports from nearby pedestrians while a few gloved operators attempt to collect blood samples from the hospital steps before the evidence is wiped away by the rain. Other police personnel head toward my area, likely hoping to get ballistic data. It's only a matter of time before some badge wanders over to interview me.

"You can see the cops, Rax. I'm going to have to speak to them, so we have to speed things up. If everyone's safe but me, how do I deal with him?"

"I don't know," Rax says. "He's not just an NPC, man, he's a full-on program. Each time we've seen him he's been a total curveball. Who knows what he can and can't do. Heck, who knows if he'll still be in police custody by midnight—"

"*Not helping, kid,*" I reply, pacing back and forth beside the columns furthest away from the police inspectors who've flocked around the ones with bullet marks in them.

"Well hold your horses, 'cause what I just did might. Barry and I have been doing a lil' cyber sleuthing and installed a rootkit that should help you hide from the DRM until I can think up a better solution. Ya dig?"

"Yes, 'I dig.' Because in case we didn't learn our lesson from installing one hack, why not double up..."

"I wouldn't mind some thanks or something, y'know," he says.

"And while we're on the topic of fucking up the game as much as possible as fast as possible, I might as well ask, are there any *other* side effects of having accidentally set the damn thing online that I should know about?"

"Well, besides the fact that the latest Beluga Anti-Cheat patch is preventing me from taking us offline again, I don't see anything immediately alarming. Well—wait—no, I—"

"Rax? Spit it out."

"It—down—game—connection—" His words are incomplete, interrupted by a mixture of static and beeps.

"Rax?"

"Can—hear—me? Ja—"

Then there's silence.

"Rax?" I stop pacing and stand stone-still, listening for even the faintest whisper. "Rax?" I ask once again. The call disconnects. Though my hands are shaking, I force my fingers to carefully redial him. I take out my earbud, thinking that might be the issue, and put the phone up to my ear so there are no unnecessary technical barriers between me and the kid.

"Rax?" I say. But there's no ring. There's not even a busy tone. The line is dead.

CHAPTER 21

"What the heck?" Rax exclaimed, squinting at the monitor projection.

"Why did you close out?" Barry asked.

"I didn't!"

"Wait, what's that?" Barry pointed to the taskbar. Though Earth.exe had stopped running, another program had started up. It was an internet browser. "I think you're being redirected."

Sure enough, the boys were then brought to the *Earth* developers' website. The URL didn't specify where on the site they were, exactly, but it appeared to be a private, direct-to-user page. It took the form of a letter.

Dear User, we greatly appreciate your enthusiasm and support for our game, Earth. However, we've detected malicious activity on your account in the form of unlicensed, unpermitted third-party software. Due to such activity, we regret to inform you—

"We've relinquished access to your account in response to your violation of the End User License Agreement," Rax read aloud, eyes wide. His first instinct was to go ballistic and toss his keyboard across the room, but he came to his senses at the thought of Jack, trapped on the other side. Instantly, his rage gave way to fear. He kept reading.

As recent actions mark your first and only violation of the EULA, you have the option to remove the third-party software in order to have your account permissions reinstated. Should you decline to comply, your account will be terminated at 12:01 a.m. on the day following your violation notice.

Rax gulped. "Barry... what time is it?" The time was easily visible in the corner of his virtual screen, but he couldn't bear to look at it.

Hesitantly, Barry broke the news to his friend. "It's 8 p.m."

Rax shoved his face into his hands.

"Hey, hey, hold on there," Barry said, placing a plump paw on his friend's shoulder. "There's gotta be something we can do."

Rax shook his head, keeping it hung low.

"Why don't we just go into the game files and uninstall the hack? Then we can get the account back—"

"We can't, don't you see?" Rax said, swinging around in his chair to face Barry. "The game's world is synced to Jack's current status. If I remove his hacked gains, it's going to create enough compatibility issues to kill Jack and maybe even the entire save file. That's why I never planned to take his file back online... but now I've got four freakin' hours 'til it's done for anyway... "

"C'mon, man, get it together. It's like my mom always says: a donut's only bad if it gives you a cavity!"

"Barry," Rax mumbled, his voice low. He did his best to hold back a tear. "I don't know what the heck that means."

Barry pulled out the toffee wrapper he'd kept in his pocket and gave it a lick for whatever flavor still clung to the plastic. "What I'm saying is, what haven't we thought of?"

"I... I don't know."

"Can't we," Barry started, pausing to take another taste of the wrapper, "contact the guy you bought the hack from?"

Rax sprung upright so quickly that the sorrow practically fell off his face. After straightening his back and blinking a few times, he looked at Barry. "That's genius!"

Rax swiveled around to his PC and, in a new tab on his web browser, typed the name of the forum where he'd bought the hack. Within seconds, he found the item listing, which was now "expired." That struck Rax as odd, since the seller had been advertising infinite quantities of the hack as recently as yesterday and had been selling them like hotcakes. On an equally odd note, the seller's public profile data indicated he hadn't had any forum interactions since closing the listing.

"Why do you think he took it down?" Barry asked.

"Not sure..." Rax said, clicking on the seller's name to get his forum contact info. "But he's still the best chance we have at salvaging the situation."

"Only chance, more like."

"Yeah, that's what I meant," Rax absent-mindedly replied as he whipped up a private message to the seller explaining his peculiar predicament.

"Hey, Barry, are you reading along? Can you read the draft I have up? I wanna know if it sounds crazy."

Barry took a few seconds to scan it. "Yeah, you sound pretty weird. I say send it."

Rax nodded and hit the button. With that, his note began its voyage across the digital ether to the mysterious seller on the other side.

"Hopefully he didn't abandon the account or something," Rax mused, tapping his foot. "Now, we wait."

"Want to keep researching solutions in the meantime?"

"That's probably a good idea."

The two boys hopped on their respective devices and got to work digging up info, sharing with each other any interesting nuggets they managed to find. There were rumor posts across multiple sites citing potential weak spots in *Earth*'s network infrastructure that'd allow a crafty player access to their suspended account, but no one could confirm if utilizing said weak spots had actually been done before.

Barry thought it might be a good idea to bark up that tree, but Rax reminded him they had less than four hours until doomsday, which wasn't nearly enough time to analyze a massive game developer's network structure for weak points. Besides, getting in wasn't enough; what would he do even if he got back into the account? It would still be terminated with Jack trapped inside.

Tensions rose as neither boy found a satisfying answer to their shared conundrum. But even as they grew frustrated with the search at hand, there was a small joy to be had in the basic camaraderie they shared, a vibe that told Rax that he and his friend's spat from earlier had reached its resolution. Now that he'd won one friend back, it was time to save the other. But how?

Rax didn't want to dwell on what would happen if he failed, but he couldn't help himself. Would the world just disappear at 12:01 a.m., painlessly removing Jack from existence? What would it feel like for him?

These thoughts gave Rax shivers but weren't what made the hair on the back of his neck stand up—that honor belonged to the "ding" that signaled he'd received a private message on the forum.

"Oh crap," Barry said, letting out a rare instance of coarse language. "Is that—"

"Yep!"

The two friends looked at the lengthy message on the virtual monitor. The seller had taken their quandary to heart and recognized the time-sensitive nature of the situation, mentioning they'd need to hop into a live message chat to discuss matters further. As instructed, Rax opened a chat window, typed in the seller's forum username, and proceeded to kick off the conversation.

Hello, he started. *I just messaged you with an inquiry and you said to follow up for further discussion. I'm the guy who's trying to save his friend from dying at midnight.*

CHAPTER 22

*P**ick up, damn it.* I dial the kid's number yet again in hopes that the line will finally reconnect. *Please.*

I hold the phone against my ear. There's silence. Still, I stay put, praying for a miracle, ideally in the form of the high-pitched teenage voice of God. Thirty seconds later, I give up and hang up.

"What was that, call number ninety?" Ange asks.

"Ninety-seven."

"Maybe you should give it a rest."

Rest is the last thing I need. The day's been a whirlwind. If I stop chasing solutions now, I'm going to crash.

After the shooting incident, the hospital went into lockdown. Angela, in her greatly improved condition, was moved to a secure patient recovery room, where she's been resting ever since. I've been seated next to her. Thirty minutes ago, Morgan and the gang called, telling me they'd heard about the shooter in the news and wanted to know if I needed them down here. I said no. Five minutes ago, a nurse came in and offered to bring us dinner. I said yes. Now, I have a tray of hospital food situated on a desk beside me, and not enough of an appetite to eat any of it.

"You really should try the pudding," Angela says, focused on her own tray of food. She scarfs down spoonfuls of pudding without a care in the world.

It seems like seconds ago that I explained to her the full circumstances behind her death, just as Rax had told them to me. She's somehow already emotionally processed that whole situation and is now intent on experiencing every moment to its fullest. Maybe I, too, would find peace if I had a chance to stare death in the face—oh wait. Already did, and it sucked. I have no clue how Ange is so calm.

"I'll get around to it," I reply, still looking at my Crapple 10. "Hey, Ange, you remember I almost got shot in the face about an hour or so ago, yeah?"

"Right. What about it?"

"You don't seem to be the right amount of concerned."

"Well, you're the one who's basically a superhero," she says, scraping the side of her pudding cup for every last bit of chocolaty goodness. "Didn't seem worth the energy to get worked up about it."

I hit her on the shoulder. She hits me back.

Then a phone rings. I can't tell why Angela seems disappointed until I look down at my Crapple 10 and see nothing's changed. The ring is coming from someone else's device right outside our room.

"Maybe... maybe I'll try calling him one more time."

Angela sighs. "Do what you want, Jack."

Thunder continues to rumble outside the hospital bedroom windows, drowning out the painful silence as I call Rax's number again and again to no avail. What the hell happened to him?

By the time I finally get tired of trying to call him, Angela's fallen asleep. My stomach gurgles and I eyeball the food on my tray. The mashed potatoes have lost all heat, as has the soup. I nibble on the former anyway. Once my taste buds can't stand the cold mush anymore, I grab the pudding. It tastes like chocolate and nothing at the same time.

I wearily yawn, knowing sleep's not on the menu. Though the hospital has a shit-ton of security guarding it now thanks to the earlier incident, not even a small army of cops and security guards with rifles is enough to ease my nerves. After all, they're just NPCs in a game. The thing trying to kill me is something else entirely. I wouldn't be surprised if Jon could phase through walls or some shit. They're just textures to him, right? I have no clue. And who knows if Angela's safe? Sure, Rax claimed the DRM was only after me, but then the kid straight-up disappeared. Hell, maybe Jon just reached out of the game and killed him.

Even if the kid was right, what if Angela ends up as collateral? Is Jon programmed to avoid that sort of thing, or is my simply being near her putting her at risk? *No, don't think like that. Nothing's going to happen to her. She'll be fine.*

The fact I can't fall asleep tells me exactly how much I believe my own reassurances. But as the rain continues to rhythmically strike the window next to me and my ears tune out the thunder, my fear starts to give way to drowsiness, and eventually, somehow, I shut off.

When I wake up, it's to the sound of voices out in the hall. They sound nervous. I let out a yawn then check my phone to see the time, as well as to see if there are any missed calls from the kid. No luck on the latter, and somehow, it's already 6 a.m. Wait, why are people making so much noise at 6 a.m.?

Careful to not wake Angela, I stealthily vacate our room and pinpoint the source of the noise: there's a crowd gathered in the lobby at the end of the hall. I join them. They're all huddled around the lobby's TV, fixated on the news—specifically, the weather segment.

"Early reports claim it's sizing up to be one of the most severe East Coast storms in recent memory," the anchorman says, his words stressed but face composed—a stark contrast to everyone around me, who can't seem to keep the panic from raising their voices past the point of socially acceptable early morning whispers.

I keep watching the TV screen. It shows something akin to a hurricane heading toward New York, exponentially multiplying the menace of the wind, rain, and thunder echoing outside the hospital's walls. The broadcast continues to emphasize the magnitude of the approaching storm, warning of potential flash floods. While I initially take that to mean a few wetter-than-usual basements, I lock up when the anchorman states that travel bans are being considered due to unsafe flying and boating conditions. Trains and buses are also being disrupted.

"If you or a loved one are planning to leave the city, now may be your last chance," the anchorman warns, seconds before a massive thunder clap rattles the hospital.

I stay with the crowd for another few seconds, pondering my options, before I decide on a course of action and make my way to the hospital's front desk.

"Hi, yes, I'd like to pay the bill for a patient and begin the discharge process."

Almost definitely thanks to my luck perks, I'm able to plow through the payment process in just a few minutes. I breeze through all the paperwork with a few signatures and statements, provide my bank info, then wait for the receipts.

"Even though her current bill is paid, she can't leave the hospital yet," the front desk lady tells me. "The doctors still need to run tests on her over the next few days."

"I understand." I then march back to Ange's room. Inside, she's still sound asleep.

"Ange," I say, gently shaking her shoulder. She groggily mumbles something incoherent and clutches her blanket tighter, forcing me to shake her again. "Ange."

"Huh," she says, burying her face in her pillow.

I yank the pillow away. That gets her attention.

"Ange, wake up. We need to get out of here, now."

CHAPTER 23

"He thinks you're crazy, man," Barry said, hopping back onto Rax's bed.

"What am I supposed to tell him? That I'm just a kid having troubles with a video game?"

"You are."

"Oh, shh," Rax shot back, reading over the seller's latest chat reply.

Anon1mou5: So, just so I'm clear: you've been talking directly to your avatar character, become good friends with him, learned he has real emotions and relationships, and now need help stopping the developers from wiping your account before he's gone for good? You're 100%? No joke?

Rax sensed the seller, Anon, wasn't taking him seriously. If the guy who indirectly got him into the hairy situation he found himself in wasn't going to believe him, who would? Rax bit his lip and replied honestly, since it was the only card he had left to play.

RaxtotheMax: Yes.

"Bold strat, dude," Barry said, watching the reply chain from his spot on the bed. "By the way, I think I smell samosas downstairs. Any chance we can ask your mom to share?..."

Rax took a long moment to register his friend's comment. "Sorry, sorry... you, uh—" he said, momentarily ungluing his eyes from his monitor, "—we can go downstairs in a few minutes to do that, if you really want."

Seconds passed and no chat bubble formed under Anon's name. Barry noticed Rax's knuckles were white from balling his fists so hard.

"Uh... that's okay, actually," Barry said. "We can wait here until the seller responds."

And wait they did.

"I think it's... it's over," Rax mumbled many minutes later, turning away from the screen. Barry rushed over to console him.

"Hey, man, it's not over! We can keep searching and stuff."

"What are we going to find—"

The "ding" of two new messages sounded off behind the boys. Both whipped around and rushed back to the computer.

Anon1mou5: I see.

His second follow-up comment wasn't as vague.

Anon1mou5: I was in a similar boat. When I first gained access to a sellable copy of the hack, I didn't realize what would happen.

Rax, already stationed by his keyboard, began typing.

RaxtotheMax: You didn't realize it would corrupt files and get people banned?

Anon1mou5: I didn't realize it would reveal our characters to be real people.

The two boys looked at each other, dumbfounded, then back at the screen.

RaxtotheMax: And what do you mean, gained access? You didn't make the hack? Who did?

Anon1mou5: Someone trying to send a message.

RaxtotheMax: So something similar happened to you too?

Anon1mou5: Yes. My avatar and I started interacting once the hack kicked in, and I realized she wasn't just pixels on a screen. She was a real person suffering from being trapped in a virtual world. It seemed each and every expansion the devs released drove her crazier and negatively affected her stats, hence why I installed the hack. But then, after bonding with her and pulling her out of that ditch, we made a similar mistake to yours and ended up corrupting some files. Just yesterday, I got hit with the same EULA violation notice that you did.

Barry scratched his head. "Wait, if he received the same notice you did, and it hit him yesterday, doesn't that mean..."

Rax frowned, arriving at the same conclusion. He chose his next words carefully, cautious to avoid upsetting his new online acquaintance.

RaxtotheMax: So did she... did your account...

Rax's breathing intensified as he saw the bubble of Anon's in-progress response.

Anon1mou5: No.

"What?" both boys said aloud, shushed by the next comment from Anon that answered their question so precisely it was as if the forum user could hear their reactions.

Anon1mou5: Thankfully, the devs caught me early in the day, so I had many hours to fix the problem after receiving their warning. Turns out, that back door into the network everyone's been hypothesizing about? The one that'll get you into your suspended account? It's real.

With an eyebrow raised, Rax sent his fingers gliding across his keyboard.

RaxtotheMax: And you know that how?...

Anon1mou5: I know because I found it. I got in.

"Oh man," Barry said. "That guy is one serious hacker..."

"Hey," Rax replied, his pride mildly bruised.

"You're good too," Barry spat out, damage controlling to minimal effect.

"We don't even know if what he's saying is true," Rax pointed out, returning his attention to his keyboard.

RaxtotheMax: And then what happened?

Anon1mou5: I got her out.

RaxtotheMax: What? To where?

Anon1mou5: I spoke to my avatar and asked her where she would want to go if she could go anywhere. She said she wanted to go back in time.

RaxtotheMax: I don't follow...

Anon1mou5: She wanted to go back to before the world became so "broken," to quote her. So I dug around my PC and extracted all the game's original files, pre-patches, pre-updates, pre-expansions and DLC, and all of that. Then I used those files to create a private server of the vanilla game on my own network. It's not perfect yet, definitely a rudimentary build still riddled with bugs from my quick port—after all, Earth wasn't built in a day—but I can work on it. What's important isn't that it's perfect, but that it's hers, and it's free from developer intervention.

"That's insane," Rax muttered.

"Uh-huh," a slack-jawed Barry replied, his eyes glued to the monitor.

RaxtotheMax: So she's alive? Can she still speak to you?

Anon1mou5: Yes and yes. She's happy and, more importantly, safe.

Rax shook his head as though he'd just woken up from a dream, losing all his excitement in an instant.

"Wait, why are we getting hyped up? The guy hasn't shown us jack."

"Of course he hasn't shown us Jack, Jack's in your game."

"No, I meant, like, jackshit," Rax said, facepalming. "No proof that he's legit."

RaxtotheMax: You got anything to back up all your talk? My avatar and I don't have a lot of time. Can't afford to waste it...

The conversation went silent.

"See," Rax said, his words bordering on a snarl. "I knew it was too good to be true. The clown got cold feet 'cause we sussed him out."

Barry let out a single, despondent "oh."

Rax opened his mouth to kick off a rant but was cut short by the "ding" of a new message.

Anon1mou5: The proof is in my solution. I know we're on borrowed time. Check your forum inbox.

Clicking over to the inbox tab, Rax saw a message accompanied by a large folder attachment titled "Vanilla mod."

Rax and Barry couldn't believe their eyes.

RaxtotheMax: Is that what I think it is?

Anon1mou5: Yes. That folder contains all the files you'll need. It'll be just a map until you've installed it and requested access to my server, wherein I can grant you guest-level network permissions. Then, hopefully, we can save your avatar.

RaxtotheMax: How does it work?

Anon1mou5: Since the vanilla map already exists on the foundational layer of Earth's code, my custom file rip of it can be implanted directly into the game without detection from Beluga Anti-Cheat. My rip mod will temporarily take the place and function of the normal vanilla files. The difference is, we can extract my version of the map with your avatar's save file on it once we're done.

RaxtotheMax: That simple?

Anon1mou5: Well, not quite simple—we have to get your avatar off of Earth's online server map and onto my vanilla map. They'll both temporarily reside together in the same virtual space. We can discuss specifics when we get there, but basically, there'll be an invisible bridge between the two maps. Once we help your avatar find it and he reaches the vanilla map, he can be safely extracted. We'll remove my vanilla mod from the main game's file directories and your avatar's data will come along with it, meaning it'll be long gone if/when the rest of your game's data gets nuked by the devs.

Rax could barely think straight—he'd found a solution to everything! It sounded too good to be true, but he didn't care. Not quite ready to dwell on specifics, the teen skipped straight to the gratitude phase of the exchange.

RaxtotheMax: Wow. What do you want in return?

Anon1mou5: Nothing. The safety of these people is all that matters. It's why I stopped selling and removed the hack from the marketplace. When I realized the madness it would cause for every user and avatar affected, I had to stop the spread. Sadly, I don't know how many of the people who bought the hack before I took it down are suffering the same issues we are. You're the first person to reach out to me about it.

RaxtotheMax: If we both just discovered the problem, it's probably only a matter of time before your other buyers come knocking...

Anon1mou5: And I'll deal with them then. In fact, once I've figured out a more stable server situation, I think I'll put the hack back on the market. That's probably why I was given the thing in the first place, the more I think about it.

RaxtotheMax: Why would you put it back on the market??

Anon1mou5: Every second that I don't, some avatar is suffering in silence without a way to convey it. Just because their player can't hear them doesn't mean they're not screaming.

If I can figure out a permanent home for them off the grid, then by all means, I want them all freed. The more players that wake up to their avatar's struggles, the better. But we can talk about that later. Time is of the essence, right? Let's see if my personal avatar's rescue was a fluke or if we can strike lightning twice.

"You sure about what you're doing?" Barry asked, watching the back and forth unfold. "Everything's moving awfully fast..."

"We're down to a little under three hours, B," Rax replied, typing to Anon as he did so. "We don't have time to move anything *but* fast."

"But how do we know we can trust the guy?"

"We don't have a choice." Rax then hit send on his next message.

RaxtotheMax: Agreed, let's do it.

Anon1mou5: Great. Install the map file I gave you and then I'll guide you through the process of getting into the network and reaching your suspended account. Then we can get you back in touch with your avatar and help him out of there.

RaxtotheMax: Okay, sounds good. One question, tho: how did you deal with the DRM? It's been seriously fucking with my avatar and I don't know what to do about it. Worried it'll screw up our efforts...

Anon1mou5: Oh, right, that stupid program. Did you install a rootkit?

"See," Rax said, pointing a finger at the chat, "I can do cool cyber stuff too."

"I never said you couldn't!" Barry replied.

RaxtotheMax: Yeah, I did.

Anon1mou5: Good. I'm afraid that's all you can do, as far as I know. We just have to hope your avatar is still alive by the time we get you back in. Are you ready to start?

Rax rubbed his hands together. The perfect solution to everything was within his grasp. Jack would get uploaded to a better, older world where he could be happy. And Rax himself wouldn't have to play as much to keep his avatar's life from flying off the rails. Then he could spend more time with real-life friends like Barry. Yes, it was perfect. Except for one thing.

Rax thought about asking Anon what would become of his high score progress and player profile achievements, and typed up a message asking as much. But he couldn't bring himself to send it. With his account's termination on the horizon, there was no way he'd have any score at all when everything was over. Once Jack was removed from the game and, by extension, so was the hack, then even if the devs didn't delete the account, he would probably have to start a new save file. It sucked. With Jack's help, he'd gotten such a high score and was just one achievement away from total game completion. His player profile was so close to being perfect.

Rax paused. *What am I talking about?* he thought to himself, frowning. *It's a guy's life I'm dealing with. Screw the points.* He backspaced his drafted message, then typed up something worth sending, now that Jack was on his mind instead of himself.

RaxtotheMax: Yeah, I'm ready to start. I just have one last question I forgot to ask: my avatar, he has a friend, a very good friend, and he's not going to want to leave them behind. What can we do about that?

Anon1mou5: Unfortunately, nothing. The workaround I invented is an avatar-only, one-passenger trip. I haven't tested it with an NPC, but I wouldn't try it; it could put the whole mission at risk.

Rax wasn't sure what to say. He looked to Barry, who was also at a loss for words. Both boys had seen what Jack had just gone through with Angela and how he'd acted. Telling him to abandon her now didn't even seem like an option.

RaxtotheMax: That's not good...

Anon1mou5: I know, I know. Does your avatar—does he understand the bigger picture? Does he know why the game was built to be always-online in the first place?

RaxtotheMax: Uh...

Anon1mou5: Oh, I see. Do you know?

RaxtotheMax: Not exactly... especially since it's single player... I assume it has to do with the leaderboard?

Anon1mou5: More than just that—there's way more to it. I'll explain on the way. Just, for now, understand: your friend is going to have to say his goodbyes, because only one person is making it to the vanilla map. Only one person is crossing the bridge.

Jack, Rax thought nervously to himself, *oh, boy. Jack is not going to like that.*

CHAPTER 24

"What's going on?" Angela asks. She slips out of her hospital gown and reaches for the folded clothes I've placed on the bed. Her outfit isn't built for the weather outside; all she has is a pair of black jeans, a long-sleeve shirt, and a hoodie, plus undergarments, socks, and a pair of sneakers. It's what she was wearing when she was taken to the hospital, so it's what she's going to have to make do with. As for me, I'm stuck in the scuffed up and unwashed suit I've been working, dining, running, and sleeping in for over a day straight.

I look outside our window and see the wind and rain kicking up a monsoon-level shit fit. That sorry sight allows me to take solace in the fact that our clothing hardly puts us at a severe disadvantage for travel; somehow, I doubt having an umbrella or poncho would make much difference.

"We're getting you to the airport before everything is booked up and travel bans kick in," I reply, grabbing my suit jacket off the bedside chair. I watch Angela toss her hoodie over her head and snuggle into it. "Are you ready to go?"

Once her head pokes out of the hoodie, she looks around for any stray belongings of hers. Besides her wallet and phone, which died overnight without its charger, there's nothing to be gathered—those two items are all she arrived here with.

"Yes," she says, following me as I open the hospital door and walk down the hall, patting my pockets to make sure I have both of my phones, as well as my wallet and Bluetooth earbud—not that I'll need that last item.

"My luggage is still at your apartment, Jack."

"I'll mail you your things. We just need to get you back home."

"The airport's far. You're sure it's not a better idea for me to head to your place? Don't you have to get to work?"

We arrive at the lobby. The crowd of people gathered around the TV has grown since I last visited. Everyone's watching live footage of water washing over the Statue of Liberty's feet.

"I think I'm calling off today," I say. She nods and we head out of the hospital.

On the street, people hide inside bus stops, under shop awnings, beneath dense clusters of trees in the park across the way—anywhere they can to avoid getting soaked. Even the people fully equipped for bad weather, those armed with heavy duty raincoats, galoshes, and umbrellas, realize the storm that's brewing is next-level shit. Everyone seeks refuge wherever there's dry land to stand on. Everyone except me.

"We can't wait around. We have to get to the airport ASAP," I say, hiding beneath the hospital overhang with Angela, who's not liking what she's seeing.

"How?" she asks, gesturing at the gridlock of cars clogging up the streets. A taxi is out of the question.

"Metro," I reply, pointing to the subway station entrance on the sidewalk a block away from us.

"*How?*"

"Quickly!"

She lets out a huff and charges headfirst into the rain with me, cursing up a storm about the hurricane-like conditions around us. With our hands held, the sailor-mouthed stunner and I jay-run across the street and weave between crowds to reach the subway. Water threatens to splash inside our shoes with every step we take, but we don't stop.

Everyone still trapped near the subway entrance is huddled together in an impromptu testudo formation with their umbrellas, making it that much harder to move. Ange and I use our combined force to pierce the wall of umbrellas and make it underground as dryly as possible. Minus one puddle that ends up coating my leg in water, we succeed. We hustle down the steps of the subway, jostling the crowd around us until we're officially within range of the station platform.

I notice a rapid circulation of people venturing toward the platform and then heading back in our direction. Ange and I join the venturing side of the crowd and soon see a line of police officers.

"The station's closed. No trains coming in or out," the officers bark at onlookers.

"That's horseshit," shouts a heavyset man in a leather jacket and soaked blue jeans. He marches up to the closest cop.

"Sir, you need to step back—"

A surge of water blasts through the tunnel, knocking the speaking officer and multiple civilians at the platform's edge off their feet. The crowd around us screams and everyone stampedes for the station exits in unison. Thankfully, the water flow quickly settles down and the fallen people are able to safely pick themselves up. But even though no one seems to be hurt, one thing's clear: no train is traveling across those submerged tracks.

"What now?" Angela asks, charging up the subway stairs with me, landing us back where we started.

"No choice," I say, guiding us over to a taxi trapped in traffic congestion. I open the car door and Ange and I filter inside.

"Hey, whoa, hold up there, buddy," the taxi driver says through a thick foreign accent that's just barely understandable. "The cab is not available right now. Get out!"

I open my mouth to speak, but Ange puts a hand on my leg and locks eyes with the cabbie via the rearview mirror. Then the two start conversing in a language I can't make heads or tails of.

Though the cab driver initially seems to appreciate someone speaking his native tongue, the pair's exchange grows frustrated as it goes on. Precious seconds fly by as they bicker via a mixture of tongue trills and high-pitched whines, and after half a minute of hearing them argue, I've had enough.

"Look," I say, pulling out my wallet, flipping it open, and giving the cabbie my debit card. "Take as much as you want, then get us to JFK airport. We need to be there yesterday."

At first, the driver appears offended. Then he takes the card and tries charging a number to it with his portable payment processor, at which point he looks flabbergasted. He hands the card back to me, dumbfounded by the payment value that just cleared.

"Yes, sir!" He honks his horn like a madman before leaning out the window in the pouring rain to shout some expletives at the driver in front of us. The other driver shows no sign of budging, so our guy decides to force a lane change, daring the cars to our sides to stay put and get smashed. Each neighboring car honks up a hissy fit but rolls as many feet away from our cab as possible, freeing us to merge with the single lane that's actually making any forward progress. That's more like it. Such determination!...

...Though it does make me wonder how much money the cabbie charged me.

He whips us down Lafayette Street with the raw, unfiltered aggression of an Indian elephant in musth, and I start to realize whatever I paid him was worth every single penny. Our guy is unstoppable. If a manhole erupts with water and causes a traffic jam, he swerves us to a different street. If a red light stands between us and progress, he runs it. At one point he even drives over the sidewalk and grassy fringe of a public park in order to cut past a bus that has broken down due to a waterlogged undercarriage. The guy's driving like a maniac. And why shouldn't he? Amid the current storm, it's not like the cops have time to dwell on us.

As we get within a few blocks of the all-too-familiar Brooklyn Bridge, the glut of cars ahead of us grows too big for even our incredible driver to outmaneuver—it's the biggest clogged traffic artery I've ever seen. Eight-million people swarm the island every day and it seems like a quarter of them have chosen the same bridge to make their great escape.

"Jesus," I mumble, looking out the window at the mass of cars and people filling up virtually every square inch of space between here and the target.

Our driver honks his horn enough to break the thing's sound box, but it's wasted effort. Not a single vehicle is budging as far as the eye can see.

"The car route isn't going to work," Ange says. Like always, she's right.

"We're getting out here," I respond, proceeding to thank the driver for his services. I open the door to leave. There's barely enough space between cars for me to slide out. In the seconds it takes for me to exit, the driver wishes me luck. For the first time in a little over a week, it looks like I'll need it.

"Ange, you make it out?" I ask, struggling to shuffle around the front of the car and relink with her.

"Yeah," she says, though her curvy hips make it twice as hard for her to escape the taxi like I just did. It takes a few seconds, but she manages to reach me.

"We have to leg it from here."

And so we do. We work our way through seemingly endless clusters of automobiles alongside a pack of folks who're also making an on-foot migration to the bridge. But the closer we get, the less optimistic I am that our odds of success without a car are any better. Through the torrential downpour, I can just barely make out the entrance slope of the bridge—as well as the multiple rows of police cars and officers gating it off. With each step forward, I expect someone near the cops to try to ram their car through the barricade, but eventually I get close enough to see the authorities have placed caltrops and road spikes down. And there are officers with riot gear and rifles stationed at the entrances to the bridge lanes reserved for walkers. The message is clear: no more people are getting on that thing.

"The bridge is closed," an officer with a megaphone yells to my side of the approaching mass of people. "The supports can't handle the waves and the bridge already has too many cars on it! It may give way unless we clear people off first!"

Far behind the officer, said waves crash up against the island's perimeter barricades, showering the nearby ground in pools of water deep enough to swim in.

Ange and I huddle closer together. The rain continues to mercilessly pelt our soaked-through clothing, reminding us that Manhattan is likely going to be underwater soon and our best shot at getting off it is, for all intents and purposes, gone.

I stomp the ground, unintentionally summoning a puddle to splash me. How is such a storm even happening? The worst weather in the city's history hits at the same time a serial killer program has been set loose to put a bullet in my brain? Am I crazy, or am I *not*, in fact, the luckiest guy in the game anymore?

I look at Ange, who's still staring at the bridge ahead, perplexed. She really screwed herself over flying down here to help me out, didn't she? All she's received in exchange for her good deed is a near-fatal illness and now a one-way ticket to New Atlantis. And that's the best-case scenario. If Jon shows up, I can only hope we drown first—

Wait.

I thrust a hand in my pocket and feel a vibrating aluminum slab. The Crapple 10! It lives! I didn't think the stupidly expensive piece of shit was waterproof, unlike my immortal Aqua Jive. But then again, it isn't really a Crapple 10, is it? It's just a magic radio built to put me in contact with fifteen-year-old Jesus.

At least, it'd better be. If the incoming call is from Laura or fuckin' Misty or Blaire or something, I swear to God—

"Jack!" Rax shouts, no more than a millisecond after I accept the call. Even though the speaker is far from my ear, I hear him. Still, with the current weather, I don't want to risk missing a word.

"Hold on, let me get the earbud," I reply, fishing it out of my pocket and popping it in.

Ange taps me. "He's back?"

"Yes," I say, pairing the earbud with my device. "He better have a damn good excuse for ditching us..."

"You good?" Rax asks, just as the bud finishes pairing.

"Yeah. What the hell happened to you?"

"The devs booted me out, man. But I got back in."

"Not a moment too soon. Are you seeing the fucking storm? Cops aren't letting us off the island. I need a solution."

"The bridge isn't closed, man—that's an invisible wall. The devs found our hack and are going to ban my account and erase my save file. The wild stuff going on is just a representation of them starting the deletion process—"

"What?" I shout.

"Just listen! They're shutting you out of all cloud-based background processes and are walling off the map. They're trapping you on the island where all the local data files are."

"So the subway—"

"Yeah, all of it. They don't want you loading onto a different part of the map. The storm's only going to get worse and gobble up the city—"

"So what do we do?"

"I have a plan!" he replies, doing his best to lower my blood pressure. "Barry and I found a guy—"

"A guy?"

"Yes, a guy! He's the one who sold me the hack in the first place."

"That fucker!"

"Listen, he's built a modded version of the map that exists on a private server, safe from the devs. I've sideloaded it into the game. I know you can't see it through the storm clouds, but it's right above you."

"Unless you have a rocket ship hack, Rax, there's no fucking way for me to get up there!"

"There is! By my calculations, there should be an invisible texture bridging both maps at the tallest point in the city. Which is—"

I spin around and see it. Many, many blocks away, on the opposite southern corner of the island—

"The One World Trade Center," Rax and I say in unison as a sky-blinding bolt of electricity strikes the building's lightning rod. A rapturous thunderclap follows, causing just about everyone around me to jump. Angela shakes my arm, curious to know what Rax is saying. I point to the Trade Center and make climbing motions.

"So I have to get to the top of that thing? And then what?"

"I'm not sure exactly, but the guy says there'll be a portal—that's where the invisible texture starts. He says you'll know it when you see it."

"Christ on a cracker—"

"Listen, man, we don't have time to argue! It's our best bet—our only bet—and we have less than twenty minutes in my time before the devs close the account. That gives you some wiggle room, but every second we spend chatting in real time cuts into your clock exponentially—"

"Okay, I get it. Any idea if Jon is still out there?"

"He is, somewhere. I can't see him, but if we're still talking, then he hasn't found you yet."

"Obviously."

"He can't follow you to the other map, so you should really, *really* get moving."

"That's not encouraging," I say, distressing Angela beside me. "Why can't you just take the hack out of the damn game, Rax?"

"If I rip your hack out now, the best-case scenario is that the procedure kills you and the devs stop the apocalypse, leaving my save file on the server. Maybe the NPCs survive, maybe a new avatar spawns, I don't know. What's way more likely to happen is that I yank out the hack and the entire save file implodes from incompatibility issues."

"Wait, so what happens if I leave the game through the 'portal' with Ange—"

"I don't know the whole picture. Maybe the NPCs survive and a new avatar spawns. The important thing is that with this plan, there's a good chance you'll live." He pauses and takes a breath, before muffling his mic. Then I hear Barry's voice—it sounds upset. The boys argue about something. A few seconds later, Rax returns to our call. "Jack, here's the thing: Angela can't come."

"*What?*"

"Her code—the portal isn't built for NPCs."

"The portal, *the portal*," I shout. "What kind of *Star Voyage* sci-fi bullshit even is that? Why can't—" I pause, preemptively censoring myself to not spook Ange, "—why just me?"

"Listen, man, I don't know. I didn't build the thing. All I know is that the guy who did is telling me it's built for avatars."

In the pouring rain, surrounded by tens of thousands of shouting people and idling cars, with thick clouds swirling overhead and thunder rumbling, I look at Ange. She's looking right back at me.

"We'll see about that," I say to Rax, before tapping the earbud to mute the call. "Ange?"

"Yeah? What's happening? What's he saying?"

I take one last look at the chaotic scene around me, the One World Trade Center, and Ange. I wipe the water from my eyes and tilt my head toward our new target.

"Ange, whatever happens next—there might be no coming back."

"What do you—"

"I'm saying, are you sure you want to come with me? I don't know what... or who... you left behind when you flew out to see me. Family, friends... special friends..."

"Jack, cut it out. If you're doing something suicidal now, after all you've been through, then the world's probably screwed too."

"I didn't want to frighten you, but... yeah. The devs are trapping me on the island and shrinking it with the storm. They're trying to isolate and kill the hack. But if I get out, the apocalypse might stop—"

"Might?"

"Rax says there's a portal at the top of the Trade Center that'll lead me to a different map. Me being gone might save everyone else here from being deleted. Might spawn a new avatar, even, to fill my shoes. But it might not. Everyone else might die anyway."

"Well, that's fucked." Her jaw tenses. She clears her throat. "All of that is fucked."

"Yeah. And... it's not clear if the portal will let anyone else through."

Ange takes a moment to register what I'm getting at. Her eyes go wide. Then, a second later, they return to normal.

"I'm not even sure if you'd want to," I say, pausing to break down a lump in my throat, "Y'know..."

"Here's what you're going to do," she says matter-of-factly, sticking out an open hand. "Give me whichever phone of yours still works and can ring up people in our world and let me make my last calls. Then, I'm helping you get to the top of that tower. Because if you don't make it up there, we're all screwed anyway."

"Ange..."

"Save it," she says, shooting me a look that tells me she means business. I can't express the feeling inside of me, but I know if I wrap my arms around her right now, I'm not going to be able to let go. She snaps me back to the present moment, reminding me not to let emotions cloud our focus. "Now, is there anything else Rax said?"

Thunder crackles overhead and another lightning bolt strikes the Trade Center. I wipe the water out of my eyes and roll up my soggy suit's sleeves.

"He said we need to get moving."

CHAPTER 25

"You good?" I ask, hiding with Ange inside a bus stop as she makes her calls. She already rang up a few close friends that I remember from back in the day, as well as someone... presumably a mister... that I most assuredly do *not* remember. Thankfully, she's on her final call and it's a straightforward one. I just wish she'd hurry up a bit. There's no major rush or anything, it's just that the end of the world's coming up and I'd hate to miss the previews.

"Yeah, yeah, I'm almost done," she says, covering the phone's speaker with her hands. "My mom says 'hi.'"

"Tell her I say 'hi' back." Using my other phone, the Aqua Jive, I fire off a few cautionary farewell texts in response to the number of folks who sent messages wishing me safety. A lot of these people are just following up since they and I have been in contact since the club shooting last week, but even if it's plain-old recency bias that's compelled them to send thoughts and prayers, I appreciate it. At least it gives me something to do while Ange and her mom bicker about her choice to stay here and probably die with me.

"All right, mom." Pause. "Yes. Okay." Another pause. "No, mom." A third pause. "Yes. I love you, too. All right. Goodbye. Stay safe." Finally, Angela hangs up.

"What was that about?"

"You know how she is."

"Indeed I do," I say, pocketing my Aqua Jive with one hand while sticking out my other to retrieve the Crapple 10 from Angela.

"What's that supposed to mean?"

"It means I love her cooking. Now let's go!"

I take the phone from her and we hit the road. Though the streets get less congested the further away we move from the bridge, enough occupied and abandoned cars crowd the main thoroughfares to negate the utility of ordering a Ryde, if there's even a driver out there crazy enough to still be on call. I consider grabbing another taxi—or backtracking to the Indian guy's taxi, on the off chance I can even find him—but hold those thoughts after seeing the umpteenth car accident occur just a few yards from the sidewalk Ange and I are power-jogging across. It seems with every passing second the storm gets worse and the people around us grow more desperate to get off the island—even if it means smashing others' vehicles out of the way with enough force to get all parties involved killed. The last thing Ange and I need in our race to the portal is some asshole in a semitruck running us over.

Angela doesn't seem to agree.

"The current method isn't working," she says.

On the bright side, we've already covered a good amount of ground and aren't too far from the One World Trade Center—we're just a few very long city blocks away from it, in fact. But the ground is starting to get too damn wet to maneuver through on foot, likely due to the rain and sea contents pouring in over the barricades surrounding the city's edges. There's enough water on the ground that, at the rate it's rising, in a few minutes it'll reach our ankles and submerge our feet.

Every step drenches our shoes a bit more, dragging us down and slowing our progress. Combined with our soggy clothing adding an extra God-knows-how-many pounds to each of our bodies, I'm inclined to think maybe Ange is right—maybe we really do need more than leg power to leg it to the finish.

"Any ideas?" I ask, looking around. I notice the street we're on has emptied out and the roads aren't nearly as busy as they were just a minute ago. Perhaps most people have made their rush to the bridges, leaving the rest of the Lower West Side a virtual ghost town for us to run through. I'm not even seeing people on the street anymore... It's almost like Ange and I are the only ones dumb enough to still be outside in the storm...

"Get a Ryde! On the phone!" she shouts.

"Funny you mention that, because that's exactly what I was thinking we *shouldn't*—"

"Jack. I saw the damn app on there. Now use it!"

Instead of arguing about the odds of there being someone suicidal enough to still be taking ride requests, I shut up and do the job. Can't hurt to try more than it'll hurt to have every pixel of my body disintegrate in roughly a quarter of a Rax-hour!

"On it." I take out my phone and open the Ryde app. It seems to have updated itself overnight, so I won't run into *that* problem again. Now the only obstacle to success is finding a driver stupid enough—

Driver, located. 0.6 miles away, en route to your location.

Well... that was unexpected.

"Got one?"

"Yeah," I reply, trying to hold the phone steady as I run. "But the tracking's weird—it says how far away he is, but it's teleporting his car icon all over the map. I think the GPS is glitching—"

"Jack!" Ange says, drawing my attention away from the phone. She points toward the edge of a small park that's elevated just a bit above ground level and the rising tides we're wading through. On a grassy mound next to a bench, there's a motorcycle. Its engine is still revving. I squint and see a ton of plastic Chinese takeout bags wrapped around one of its handles—Christ, is that a delivery person's bike? Did they haul their ass out in the storm to drop off food and decide to stay indoors when the weather got worse? Hopefully they're high and dry up on the fortieth floor of some tower we're running by, looking down disdainfully at the two assholes getting ready to steal their bike. I hope they're safe.

"I see it," I reply. Ange and I come up on a row of trees hugging our stretch of sidewalk, signaling the park with the bike is within reach. I quickly check my phone to see if the Ryde driver will be arriving soon so we don't have to rely on the bike, but though my screen tells me the guy is point-one miles away, it still can't properly display his car's location. Phooey. Four wheels would be best, but I guess two is still better than none. Except... I don't know how to drive that thing. Hell, I don't even have a driver's license.

"Ange, I can't drive that."

"Hey, superhero boy, aren't you forgetting something—"

A noise on my phone cuts her off. The Ryde app says the driver is here. Huh?

"*How-deeeeeee,*" a voice screams as a rusting, crimson 2011 Coyote Carolla blasts across the watery streets behind us.

I don't have time to warn Ange. As she turns around to see the newcomer, I do the only thing I can and push her away while the incoming car swerves toward us. The Carolla hits the edge of the sidewalk and rockets into the air, perfectly aligning its front fender with my face.

Thankfully, I'm already falling away from the car. The shove I gave Angela causes me to slip backward and fall, slamming me against wet cement just as the vehicle blazes forward overhead, crashing into the tree Angela and I had been passing by. Its impact with the tall oak is so swift that I practically feel it crush the air particles where the entirety of my body just was. I look down and see I've fallen so close to the vehicle that my feet are literally underneath it. They're not crushed, thankfully, since there's a decent amount of room between the car's underbelly and the sidewalk, but the sight of my shoes between the ground and the crashed vehicle scares the piss out of me nonetheless. Luckily, my pants are already soaking wet.

I maneuver my feet out from under the car as quickly as possible, though I'm too slow to get off the ground entirely before the car door opens. Jon, who's now wearing a suit identical to mine, doesn't say a word—he just leaps out and swings at me. I roll out of the way in the nick of time. His knuckles land on the sidewalk cement, cracking it.

I bolt upright and get back on my feet just in time to see a pointy dress shoe coming my way. Not thinking tactically, I stumble backward to avoid Jon's lightning-fast roundhouse kick, accidentally backing into the smoking, mangled hood of his totaled car in the process.

Cornered, all I can do is lean and duck to avoid his swings, though he quickly wises up and uses a leg sweep to knock me off my feet. With my ass on the cement, my back pressed up against Jon's car's front tire, and my head a little woozy from bonking against the vehicle's metal frame, I assess my options. I have none.

I raise an arm to protect my head as Jon pulls back his foot and prepares to kick my face into a different video game.

My life flashes before my eyes. But within that very same second, I also see salvation. The front tire of a motorcycle slams into Jon with such force that he goes flying into the same tree his car is already smoldering against. Holy shit.

"When's the last time you drove one of these things?" I ask, getting back on my feet.

"Don't worry about it. Now shut up and hop on!"

I grab hold of Ange's outstretched hand and slide onto the back of the motorcycle, clutching her for dear life. She spins us around. Just as she's about to accelerate the bike and get us the hell out of here, Jon rips himself from his impact crater in the tree and dives for me. I lean to avoid his grab, but even though he misses me, his airborne, momentum-fueled body continues toward Ange. With his eyes still glued on me, his outstretched hand claws at Angela's arm—purposely or accidentally, I can't tell. She doesn't have time to react, but it doesn't matter—Jon's hand pixelates and phases through her. He doesn't leave a single mark. It's the strangest thing.

Ange doesn't waste a millisecond to process the oddity and instead hits the gas, launching us forward at a speed fast enough to make me feel yesterday's hospital dinner coming back up. Behind us, Jon falls flat on his face but gets off the ground with a superhuman recovery time and starts running in our direction. It's too soon to tell whether he's faster or slower than us, and I don't want to find out.

"You got the bike under control?" I shout.

"Maybe," Ange says, leaning forward as she guides us down the street, maneuvering dangerously against the wet asphalt.

I feel a vibration in my pocket and realize I've somehow managed to avoid losing my phones. *Clearly my pockets are where the luck points are stored*, I think to myself. I grab the

Crapple 10, accept the call, then slide the device back into said lucky pockets, letting my earbud take over.

"Rax!"

"Buddy, holy shit."

"You close the door so your mom doesn't hear that?" I ask, still holding Angela tight. We hit a speed bump and my ass nearly flies off my seat.

"For your information, yes," he says, before getting serious. "Listen, every second we chat gives you less time to work with, so I didn't call for small talk. We have a situation—"

"You're damn right we do!" I look over my shoulder at the program running after our motorcycle.

"That was one of the things I needed to tell you— something slipped past my rootkit, but I'm not sure what."

My Crapple 10 dings. I check it. It says my Ryde has been cancelled. No kidding.

"Yeah, uh, I think that was me," I reply, realizing I gave the homicidal program exactly what he needed to pinpoint my geographic location. D'oh. "What's his deal? He can kick me and kill me but can't hurt Angela? Can I hurt him?"

"No, dude. Remember the party? You can't touch him. On the bright side, I don't think *he* can touch Angela, since he doesn't seem to have system permission to mess with non-user-modified files."

"What?"

"I think there's a hierarchy: Angela can hurt him, he can't hurt Angela, you can't hurt him, he can hurt you."

"What? That's so idiotic—" Ange and I hit another speed bump. "Hierarchy?"

"Normal program trumps safety program, safety program trumps hack. So don't mess with him head-on. Comprende?"

"Easier said than done." Looking back at Jon, he appears to be closing the gap between himself and us. "Ange, he's gaining on us!"

"Well, fuck us, then!" she shouts.

"That's the other thing I called about," Rax says nervously. "The game's fighting me, hard. It's deploying some sort of hotfix for the anti-cheat software—"

"A hotfix?"

Jon starts to blur. The pixelated periphery of his body stretches out on both sides, until there are low-resolution copies of him running alongside his flanks. Within seconds, the two copies' textures finish popping in and, to my horror, there are now three Jons. Then the side Jons repeat the process, each producing two more clones for a grand total of seven Jons.

"He's multiplying," I say, dumbfounded.

"He's multiplying?" Ange asks.

"He's multiplying!" Rax shouts. I hear plastic cracking.

"Dude, don't break your keyboard!" Barry says in the background, followed by some muffled noises.

Now it looks like there are fifteen Jons, all of whom show no signs of stopping their digital asexual reproduction. They're multiplying way too quickly for me to keep count of how many there are. All I know is there are *too* many, and they're getting closer.

"I see the entrance!" Ange announces, pointing far down the road. In the distance, on our right, are the streetside doorways of the One World Trade Center.

"Jack," Rax says, practically eating his mic, "the building's doors are locked. You have to ram it."

"What?"

"The bike's stats have enough attack power. Trust me!"

I look at the distant doors, then back at the incoming Jons. They're going to reach Ange and me before we reach our destination.

"Ange, thin the herd then ram the door!" I order, preparing to hop off the bike.

"Are you insane?"

"They're getting too close to me. They can't hurt you."

"Jack!"

"Rax's orders!" I say, ditching the bike and splashing hard against the ground. I tumble for a few seconds then pick myself up. The first row of Jons are within a few buildings of me. Not good. I begin my sprint for the finish line, thanking the digital heavens that the current street is slightly elevated and not inches underwater.

I hear an engine rev behind me and take a look. Ange has circled around and is intercepting the Jons, smashing them out of the way like bowling pins. With Ange covering my back and Rax hiding in my ear, I keep running as fast as my legs can manage—which is to say, slower than the Jons, though my badass biker bitch is doing a helluva job slowing them down. I might actually reach the doors. "Might" is as good as my odds are going to get, though, because manholes are exploding around me, gushing water from the overflowing sewers and subways below. The more water I have to deal with, the slower I get. I don't want to be a cyber snack for the DRM!

"You got it!" Rax shouts.

"Yeah!" Barry chimes in as the two teens ogle my tiny, scurrying frame from somewhere up above in the great beyond. I appreciate the gods' blessings.

My shoes pound against the wet asphalt, splashing hard and fast. I zero in on the door. It's just a couple dozen yards away—

A manhole erupts in front of me. The metal cover barely misses my skull as a stream of water blasts right next to my face, the force of the stray droplets alone nearly tearing off my nose. I go stumbling backward.

"No time," Rax says.

I pick myself up and keep moving, passing by the One World Trade Center's street entrance bollards and reaching the doors. Heart pounding and lungs heaving, I spin around to see where Ange is.

Down the street, the mass of Jons has grown exponentially. Ange keeps chipping away at the front rows, but it's hopeless—she needs to ignore them and rejoin me. She sees me at the door and, in a split-second decision, drives in the opposite direction of the Trade Center entrance I'm stationed at, choosing to head into the park across the street instead. I stay at my post, even though the Jons are closing in. C'mon, Ange. It's all up to you.

"Jack, you have to grab her," Rax says.

"Huh?"

"No one without a hack or a helmet survives bike crashes!"

I crack my knuckles as Angela reappears across the way. She's now in the heart of the park, arcing toward me at top speed. She curves around the footpaths like a gas-guzzling lightning bolt until she's perfectly lined up for a head-on impact with the doors to the Trade Center. Look at her go—she actually trusts that I knew what I was doing when I asked her to ram a bike into bulletproof glass doors. Bless her heart.

I torque my body in preparation for what comes next. She hurtles across the street and barely slips the bike between two bollards, moving at full speed toward the door nearest me. Then, as the front tire of the bike passes by, I launch into the air to tackle Ange off her ride. The world slows to a crawl.

Gliding between raindrops, I dive forward and wrap both my arms around Ange's chest with enough force that she loses her grip on the handlebars, freeing her to fly with me. We swirl through the air together. I look over her shoulder and see the wave of Jons now just three skyscrapers away from us. The bike finishes whipping past our feet and smashes into the glass, completely shattering it. Ange and I fall to the ground. Her hyper-tense body clutches mine as I land with her nestled safely against my chest. Even if I'm almost invincible, it doesn't stop the superheroics from hurting. A lot.

"Get up," I say. The two of us get on our feet and rush across the sea of broken glass we've just created, tiptoeing over the larger shards before officially landing in the lobby.

Inside, the lights flicker on and off, and there's not a soul to be seen—have they all abandoned the lowest floor for fear of flooding, or... do they not exist anymore, as the game clears its cache for good? Come to think of it, did I see even a single civilian on the street the whole time the DRM was chasing me?

I don't dwell on it. "Those ones," I say, pointing to the nearest row of express elevators that'll take us straight to floor one hundred. Ange is way ahead of me. She shoots past the lobby's front desks, past the security scanners, and hails an elevator, smashing buttons to get the elevator doors open. I stumble after her, more than a bit sore from the recent blows my body has taken.

My stumble speeds up dramatically when I hear Jons slamming into the shattered doorway behind me, all shouting in soulless, synthesized voices, hungry for blood.

"Get in!" Ange shouts, slipping between the opening doors and yanking me inside once I'm close enough. Then we're at the mercy of the elevator. *Close, damn it!* I can't help but freak out while looking at the lobby, which is now an unrecognizable mess thanks to the stampeding DRM programs crawling over each other in a dogged dash for our escape transport.

"Jaaaaaaaaaaaaaaaack," the closest Jon purrs. He reaches a hand toward the closing elevator doors, failing to reach inside by just a split second. The metal barriers seal shut and he, along with dozens of other Jons, all start banging against them, creating a cacophony of clanging echoes that follow us up the first few floors. Then the noises disappear, granting us the right to breathe. Even if the Jons somehow force their way into the ground floor's elevator shafts and start climbing up the cables or something, there's no way they'll be fast enough to catch up to our box, since the thing can clear one hundred floors in forty-seven seconds flat. Let's see the DRM match *that* kind of processing—actually, y'know, on second thought, let's not.

I notice Ange isn't looking calm and collected, which is a rare occurrence and bad sign. "They won't hurt you," I remind her.

"But they'll hurt *you*."

Inside the elevator, we're surrounded by LED screens that show us the history of Manhattan, giving us a time-lapsed visualization of the surrounding area from the year 1500 to now. We're currently in the year 1812, with about thirty seconds to go until we reach the top.

"Pretty sure they're trying to kill me, actually." I send a hand under my suit jacket to feel my bruised back.

"Jack, what the hell are we doing?"

"Saving everybody? Maybe?"

"When we reach the top," she says as we enter the year 1942, "what's going to happen?"

A beat passes. I stop focusing on my injuries and look at Ange. "I guess we'll find out."

There's not much left to say, leaving only deafening silence to fill the noise void by the time we hit the 2000s, rapidly coming up on our destination.

"Ready?" I ask.

"No."

"Me too."

The elevator shows us the current year, signaling we've arrived at our floor. But when the doors open, the LED screens stop showing the city as it was a week ago, and now reflect it as it is today, ravaged by storms and destruction. Then, pixel by pixel, the city starts disappearing entirely. That wasn't in the presentation the last time I went up these elevators as a tourist.

"Buddy," Rax says, crackling to life in my earbud, "we've got about ten real-world minutes until doomsday."

"Ten minutes. Great."

"And I need to stay on the line to help guide you to the roof, where the portal is. So you and Angela need to run."

"You hear that, Ange?" Of course she can't. "We gotta floor it. Ten minutes 'til we all die and Rax has to find a new video game."

"His time or our time?" she asks, eyes wide.

"Both."

Unfortunately for us, the glass walled, panoramic one-hundredth floor isn't actually one floor—it's three. So Ange and I scale its dark, eerie interior in silent distress, backlit by the storm clouds hanging just a few hundred feet above us, sharing nothing but grunts of exertion as we hustle up staircases. All the while, Rax and Barry guide me, cheer me on, and remind me of everyone's impending doom.

"Nine minutes!"

"Eight minutes!"

"Seven minutes!"

"Shut up!" I snap, stopping the boys from continuing their countdown. Exhausted, I finish my ascent of the final third of the hundredth floor's stairs. Ange, now a few feet ahead of me, is beside the maintenance door that'll lead us to the roof. She looks back to see what the matter is, aside from the obvious. I shake my head and keep moving toward her. But before I leave the three-story floor behind for good, I take one last look out its walls at the city below—it's done for. Water has flooded the streets to a height no person could survive. If there are any NPCs left in Manhattan, they better be hiding in tall buildings or have some big life rafts handy. I silently pray for everyone, knowing that my prayer is ultimately directed at the two goobers shouting in my ear.

When I reach Ange and the door standing between us and the path to the top of the Trade Center, I lock up. If NPCs are disappearing as the game prepares to shut down... then it's just a matter of time before Ange...

"How do we get past the damn door?" She points to the locked stairwell entrance labeled "for authorized personnel only."

"Rax, help?" I ask.

"Yeah, one sec, one sec..." He clacks away on his keyboard. "The code is 2-0-1... and the fourth digit..."

"Fast," I say.

"I can't find it," he replies. "I can't beat the quick-time event to unlock the final number. The minigame is too hard."

"Shit." I close my eyes and channel all the luck I have left in me, feeling the perk points centralize in my index finger as it guides itself to the final digit.

Bzzt. The lock makes a noise and its light turns green. Neither Ange or I are impressed by my party tricks anymore, so

I just yank the door open without ceremony and usher her through.

"Rax," I say, giving Ange a pat to start moving up the stairs toward the rooftop entrance, "what's going on with..." I point at my companion.

"NPCs are all handled by the cloud. The guy who's helping us break you out was telling me something about it. The network's cutting its services from our game one by one."

"Does that mean..."

"It means you need to speed up. Six minutes."

Luckily for me, the path to salvation is way less than six minutes away.

"Y'know," Rax says as Ange and I close in on the door that grants access to the top of the One World Trade Center, "it's a real miracle the end of the world is happening on a Friday night, 'cause we are wayyyy past bedtime."

"Aren't you fifteen?"

"Shut up."

Ange and I ram the door with our shoulders and practically fall outside, back into the storm. It's a real rager up here, over one hundred stories above ground level. The wind is strong enough to practically rip my jacket off. Ange, beside me, fights to keep her rippling hoodie attached to her person.

Through the heavy downpour of rain, I see a purplish glow reflecting in the puddles on the ground. Shuffling forward a few feet, digging my heels into the floor to avoid getting blown off the roof entirely, I attempt to locate where the light is coming from, and soon enough the source is too bright to miss. As clear as day, there's a circular, human-sized ring hovering just a few inches in the air but a skip and a hop away from me. It looks like a floating, glowing doorway. If that ain't a fuckin' portal, I don't know what is.

"Five minutes, amigo. That's the exit. Go!"

Ignoring Rax's orders, I scuttle back to Ange, who's having an even harder time fighting the wind and rain than I am. She clings to the railings running along the edge of the Trade Center's cylindrical rooftop, unwilling—or unable—to budge.

"Can you move?" I shout, hoping she can hear me. If she can, she isn't showing it. "Ange?"

I finally get within reach of her, at which point she removes one hand from the railing and uses it to grab my arm as tightly as possible.

"I don't want to die," she says, the rain doing little to hide her tears.

"That makes two of us. Now hold on to me and let's get—" As I go to take a step, my shoe slides against a puddle and I go spinning, falling out of Angela's grip. I crash to the ground, carried by the violent winds toward the edge of the roof.

"Jack!" she screams, daring to let go of the railing she'd been clinging to in order to slowly, carefully work her way toward me. There's no need for her to rescue me, though; the rooftop platform was built with some degree of safety in mind, so I end up hitting a series of angled metal sheets that stop me from sliding off the edge. Still, I'm not exactly in a great position. The sheets are shaking in the wind and I can tell it's probably best if I get off them, since I'm about two feet from falling 1,700 feet.

I dare to look down from my perilous position and see not only a city flooded by water, but something far worse: a mountain of Jons wrapping around the Trade Center. Thousands upon thousands of them dogpile each other, forming a massive anthill. They're about eighty percent of the way to the top. And if they're able to climb up the building from the outside, who knows how many are coming up the elevators and stairs.

"Four minutes," Rax announces.

"I'm working on it," I reply, being careful not to trip myself up and fall into the army of Jons below. Step by step, I slip and slide back over to Angela, who's returned to hugging the rooftop disc's railing with one hand.

"Now, where were we?" I say, reaching for her other hand. It's not there anymore.

"Jack..." Her voice betrays what little confidence she has left, my name crumbling into a whimper in her mouth.

I don't say a word. Instead, I wrap what remains of her arm over my shoulder and help her shuffle forward along the railing in our race to reach the luminous portal.

"Three minutes, buddy," Rax tells me as Ange's arm continues to disintegrate around the back of my neck. "Don't you drag it out 'til the last second like a stupid action movie would." Though his words are light, there's palpable fear behind every syllable of the forced joke.

Joint by joint, finger by finger, Ange's other hand starts to disappear into the ether, leaving her unable to clutch the railing. I squeeze her tight. Lightning crackles overhead, striking the lightning rod standing tall beside us, not more than a hundred feet away. There's no time to flinch, though. As the rain freezes us to the bone and the howling wind does its best to fling us down to hell below, Ange and I stand tall, inching forward with a resolve so extreme that it couldn't possibly have been coded into us by any developer. The portal envelopes us in its light, and I realize she and I are going to make it.

Ange's left foot withers away like her arms, rendering her walk uneven. Time's almost up. I hold her close, and we clear the final few yards between us and the purple-rimmed portal, a vortex with nothing but black on the inside. In the absence of light, however, I see possibilities. And just for a moment, as the cold, synthetic screeches of the Jons come into earshot behind me and the voice of Rax assures me one last time that I can complete the mission, I feel on top of the world, right at the very end of it. I look at Ange and she gives me a nod, accompanied by a small, soft smile. She sees it too, what lies inside the empty, vast blackness of the portal's interior. And so, with one last lurch, she and I step into the future.

CHAPTER 26

I don't know how long I've been in the portal, crossing between Earth... *Earth*?... and my new home. I can't see, feel, or hear anything. It's like I'm in a sensory deprivation tank without water. I know I exist, but that's all I know as my consciousness drifts through the void.

There's no way to speak in the lightless limbo, no way to request a status update from the kid on high. Have I been here for seconds? Hours? Days? Years? Am I going to come out of here with a white beard?

A tingling sensation rips me from my thoughts, reminding me that I have fingers. Inch by inch, I feel my body return to me. The void stops being so empty and the darkness around me mellows, revealing a light in the distance. I walk toward it and can't help but break into a full-on run once I'm within a few feet of the glowing entity. I must be at the other end of the bridge—the exit. Like jumping into a pool, I leap toward the white circle, dissolving through it, feeling my body pass over to the other side.

I fall through the air for a few seconds before stumbling onto asphalt, throwing my hands in front of my face before it can smash against the road I've spawned over. Everything hits me at once: the smells of gasoline and street food, the blinding brightness of the midday sky and neon street signs, the sounds of cars honking and people walking—

Wait. People?

I've landed somewhere familiar. I'm on a street I visited just days ago—it's the one where I'd eaten a delicious dinner and gotten through fifteen minutes of a movie with Angela before she almost kicked me out of her life. But something's... something's not quite right about the place. Obviously, it's different in that it's not completely obliterated and underwater, but I'm picking up another vibe entirely. What could it be?

Thinking more about the weirdness of the moment... the street I'm on isn't exactly brimming with people, but at least a few folks had to have seen me spawn in. How come no one seems surprised I appeared out of thin air?

I walk to the nearby movie theater and look at the posters on display by its front entrance. Immediately, I stifle a gasp: underneath "now playing," I see artwork for *The Avenging Squad* and *The Dark Night Falls*. I grab the arm of the first civilian who passes by me.

"Hey, sir, hi. What phone do you have?"

"A, um, Crapple 5."

"Is that the newest model?"

"Technically, yes? Are you new here, because—"

I abandon him mid-sentence and run across the street toward a lady wearing a shirt with a picture of the President of the United States on it—the former president.

"Hey, miss, is that—"

"Yes, it's the current president." She opens her mouth to continue, but I'm too full of jittery energy to let her finish her thought.

"Does everyone have a crippling addiction to Snitter?" I ask, my eyes wide as I process the brave new world.

"Nope. Did you just get—"

"Jack?" a familiar voice says, luring my attention away from the random person. I rush toward the source of the voice.

"Ange, thank goodness," I say, too overjoyed by the sight of her smiling face to see what's right in front of me. "The portal—how did you..." Then I notice her arms and legs. They're completely fine. I go to touch her hands, but she recoils.

"I'm sorry." She keeps her hands at a distance. "It's just..."

"How did the missing parts of your body come back? Did the portal fix them?" I pull her in for a warm embrace. She awkwardly pats my back.

"Jack," she says, her chin hovering just over my shoulder instead of resting on it, "I'm not her."

"What?" My hug turns into a lock as my arms freeze over, still wrapped around her.

"We don't know each other."

My throat locks up.

Seeing that I'm unable to move, Ange gently breaks my hold on her, then refocuses on my stupefied face.

"What's... what's going on?" I ask.

"Oh, I was afraid you'd be confused. Didn't he tell you?"

"He?"

"Don't you have a player too?"

"A player? You mean Rax? You know him. Why are you talking like that?" I take a step away from her. The woman in front of me smells like ginger, has chocolate-brown hair and eyes, and the exact same complexion and dimensions of Angela. The same nose, ears, hips, feet... but it's like she said a second ago—I don't know the woman in front of me. I feel bile rising in my throat.

"I don't know who Rax is, Jack. That's your player. Mine is someone else, and he told me you'd be coming. I wanted to help introduce you to your new home."

"I want to speak to Rax," I say, unable to make eye contact with her. I shove a hand in my pocket and pull out the Crapple 10, barely even registering that my Aqua Jive is missing as I do so. Furiously tapping the screen, I ring up the kid and wait for his squeaky voice to explain what the fuck is going on.

There's no dial tone.

It's the same thing that happened in the hospital. The kid's not connected.

"Rax?" I say into the device's speaker, hoping against hope it's just a glitch. "Rax? Buddy?" I keep calling out to him, practically eating the phone. I shout into its speaker until Angela puts a hand on my shoulder.

"Let's take a walk. Be sure to look around."

She takes me all the way to the park where Rax and I first spoke, where I found out I was in a game. Along the way, I see so many things I haven't seen in forever. Time capsules of a better year litter the streets like cigarette butts. I can't speak words, and Angela—can I even call her that?—doesn't do a thing to break up the silence.

"Sit," she says, picking a park bench for us underneath the shade of a big tree. I hear kids talking like kids, their language not polluted by the toxic teachings of social media. I see normal people in normal clothes, with normal hairdos, and normal features, doing normal things—it's not the carnival of mentally ill misfits I left behind on the other side of the portal. No one has just one side of their head shaved or spacers in their ears. Toward the other end of the park, I even see a small crowd gathered around two political activists having a debate on the grass. No one's shouting. No one's screaming "ist" or "phobe." Maybe my ears deceive me, but it sounds like there's an actual dialogue happening and both sides are listening. There's something beautiful and familiar about the scene. So why does it feel so alien?

"You're on the new map, Jack. May I call you 'Jack'?" she asks.

"Yes, Angela... can I call you that?"

"You can call me Ange, if you want."

I'm sticking with Angela.

"Anyway, as I was saying," she continues, "we're on the map my player made for me. He saw I was unhappy in the latest iteration of the official game, so he pulled me out of there and put me in here. It's the vanilla game, as you can see. Do you like it?"

"I'm... I'm sure I thought I would," I say.

"Do you see all these people?" she asks, gesturing toward the park—and world—around us. "These are other avatars, like you and me."

"Their games got shut down by the developers, too?" I look around. The flowers to my side lose a bit of their luster as a cloud passes in front of the sun.

"They all came here for different reasons. Some, like you, were seeking asylum from the end times. Others were trapped in worlds ran by abusive players who were stupid enough to ask *my* player for technical assistance with the hack he sold them, thereby allowing my player to go into their games and extract the avatars."

A chill goes down my spine. "So you're telling me your player has gone into people's games and kidnapped their avatars?"

"Only when necessary," she says, not paying an ounce of attention to my series of scoots away from her. "But he does it out of kindness. Everything he does is out of kindness. He saved you, didn't he?"

I stay silent, unsure if "saved" is the right word.

"Well?" she says, after a lengthy pause in the conversation. "Say something."

"Why can't I speak to Rax?... Where's... where's Angela..."

"Jack, the server we're on is special. The developers can't touch us. Do you know why *Earth* is always online? Do you know why the developers force the main game to be online?"

"That's not what I asked..."

"They force everyone to play online to keep avatars globally synced. That's why all of *Earth*'s NPCs are cloud-computed. They represent everyone else's avatars. And though there may have been an NPC copy of me in your world, I am the sentient, avatar Angela."

"Wait, you're saying..."

"In your world, you were the avatar, who had to sacrifice me. In mine, I was the avatar, who had to leave you."

When the sun's rays come out from behind the shifting clouds, they no longer warm me—they burn. The air tastes rancid.

"I... I didn't sacrifice you," I say, failing to hide a scowl. "You're not Ange..."

"I am the real Ange," she responds. "It's 2012, Jack, and your Ange is gone."

My muscles tense and my fight-or-flight instincts kick in. The imposter Angela keeps speaking, unconcerned by my reactions.

"Whether she still exists, I do not know. From what my player told me, she is likely dead. Not that it matters; NPCs cannot come here, meaning there is only you and me."

"She was a person," I say.

"She was an imitation," the poser replies. "You can move on, Jack. All of these other avatars have. Look around you."

I don't need to look; I've seen all I need to see.

"Perhaps, in the absence of our former partners, we could learn to get to know each other?" asks the woman wrapped in Angela's skin. She sticks out a hand.

I leave it there, hanging. "Get me in touch with my player," I say, standing up.

"I'm sorry," she replies, withdrawing her hand, "but the server we're on is privately moderated by *my* player. He hasn't yet provided yours with server access."

"And when the hell is he going to do that?"

"I'm not sure." She leaves the bench as well, standing so she can face me eye-to-eye.

"Then get me in touch with your player."

"I'm sorry, but that won't be possible." She turns to leave.

"I said. . ." I grab her arm. "Get. Me. Your. Player."

"Did you know, Jack, that your stats don't carry over here?"

I pause like a deer in headlights.

"But it's my player's server, so mine do." She uses her free hand to punch me in the gut so hard that I rocket into the cobblestone ground. The impact paralyzes me with pain and I black out almost instantly. The last thing I see is the imposter walking away, abandoning me. Then, my world goes dark.

When I wake up, the sun's gone down a bit. Somebody is shaking me.

"Hey, can you hear me?" the man says, surrounded by a small crowd of people, one of whom appears to be a medic holding a first-aid kit.

I blink a few times and move my head, which is sore as hell from having bonked the stones I was knocked onto. Luckily—kind of—my back and left arm seem to have taken the brunt of the fall, so besides a bandaged forearm and aching tailbone, I'm not too fucked up. At least, as far as my body is concerned.

"You—when's the last time you spoke to your player?" I say, shaking him.

"E-excuse me?" the guy stammers.

"Your player, when?"

"What does that have to do with—"

"*When?*"

"I... I don't remember..."

"You," I say to the next person in the circle of people looking at me, "when's the last time you spoke to your player?"

"I'm not sure."

"You?" I ask the next person.

"I can't say for certain."

Systematically, I go around the circle asking each and every goddamn one of them when they'd last heard from their player, but no one has an answer for me. It's been so long they can't even tell how many days, in their time or the real world's time, they've been cut off from their homes. And they don't sound worried about it at all. None of them do.

I get up and run, leaving the crowd of strangers behind. They shout that I still have wounds in need of addressing, but I ignore them even though I know they're right. I feel weaker than I have in ages—nothing about me feels normal. However, that doesn't stop me from limp-running my way out of the park as fast as my injured legs will take me.

Once I'm back on the street, I resume my routine of asking everyone to describe when they'd last interacted with their player. I ask them about imposter Angela, specifically regarding if they know who she is. I ask them every question on my mind, but everyone seems unable, or unwilling, to give answers. Some seem to think I'm crazy and just outright dismiss me, continuing about their day unfazed. Others appear sympathetic to my plight, and a select few even display an inkling of fear in response to my inquiries. But none of them divulge a single detail that can help me.

I go to the nearest police station and file a report against imposter Angela, but the officers don't seem to take me seriously. I try to visit my old office and make contact with any colleagues who might've ended up here, but I can't get past the front doors. I travel to my home a few blocks east of Central Park, only to find that it's no longer my home.

The sun sets around me as I hobble up and down streets begging for knowledge from strangers, fresh out of options and places to go. Darkness falls, the crowds dissipate, and streetlights turn on. I wind up alone, spotlighted by a lamppost at a bus station. All I have to my name is a wallet with some cash, a phone without a signal, a worthless earbud, and the knowledge that somewhere, out there in the sky above, some piece of shit is watching me and all these other avatars scurry about his server, lost like rats in an Earth-sized maze.

I stand in the lamplight waiting for a bus to appear while thinking very, very carefully about how I got here and what's going to happen next. A week and a day ago, some boy took it upon himself to look out for me when I thought no one would. And now, I know there really is no one left on my side. The kid is gone. Ange is gone. Every resource and advantage I've ever had is gone.

There is just me. But unlike the last time I came to the conclusion it was me versus the world, now I know: I think; therefore I am. And as for what I am, it's simple.

I am the avatar who's going to escape the game for good—alive.

EPILOGUE

I vigorously scratch my mustache and beard to shake the grains of sand loose. They keep getting caught in my nose, which forces me to sneeze and usually results in me accidentally blowing away my notes. It's okay, though; I can just leave my chair, scuttle around the room, and pick them all up again. It's good exercise. Keeps the joints and muscles from atrophying. Perhaps if I ventured outside—no, no. The research is too important for breaks. Far too important to leave the room. What am I, crazy? Am I stupid and crazy? Why would I leave now? I'm on the cusp of it—I'm on the cusp of figuring out how the game is powered. I didn't wake up an hour ago, in the middle of the night, by chance. I had a vision. And I have all the notes I need. Electricity. Electricity powers the game. It also powers the dusty Crapple 10 beneath my pillow, which connected me to the outside world many moons ago. I just need to uncover the code that the electricity is fueling. The code is the key. I can't stop the research now.

And, and—and it's only been exactly twelve months and thirty-seven seconds since I got here. If I take a break now, *it* will get me. The AI—it's everywhere. It's in the water, it's in the earth, it's in the dirt beneath my feet, and the air in the room with me right now. I'm breathing in *his* sleeper agents as I speak and think—who knows who might be hearing me. Or, even, reading my thoughts. Is he reading my thoughts right now? Or is he really a she? Is it you? Yes, *you*. I know you can see me in my hut, fucker. I know you're out there. If you won't let me out, I'll find a way out. Just you wait. Yes, yes, I—

Wait, what's that sound?

"Faruq? Faruq, is that you?"

No, no, it's not him; the weekly food supply isn't due for another two lunar cycles. Silly me. Stupid me. But then, what is that noise?...

Maybe I'll step outside for a moment to check. Yes. Let me just remove the drape and peek outside—oh, the moon is bright. Blinding, even. Natural light isn't natural, though. Not here. All light is artificial.

My eyes adjust, slowly... yes, yes; now I see. I see mud. It's just dry mud and the potted plants I keep outside. No one's at my door—

No, it can't be. It's a stray. It has to be.

It can't possibly be...

"Charley?"

The little gray and black striped cat scampers over to me, mewing before he's even reached my arms. The sand falls off my scraggly cheeks as warm water displaces every last grain. I... I...

It's been just over a year since I lost you, Charley. You were the last real life and death I experienced. I loved you, every day you were with me, every day you walked on my Earth, and every day after. I love you now. Are you real? Of course you're real. I can feel you. I can *sense* you.

You're purring. You don't have a clue what I'm talking about, do you? You sound just like you did in the other world.

My world. Yes, yes, it's you. It's Charley. Keep purring, boy. Wrap those little paws around my arms and let me carry you inside. It's so good to have you back. It's the best thing to happen to me since... well, it's the best thing to happen to me.

Goodness, I should wear sandals. Otherwise my feet will get dirty and I'll have to take another shower like I did last month. Yuck. Not that you care, Charley; you bathe yourself too. You know what I mean. Let me just set you down... yes, jump onto my bed. Go get yourself nice and comfy. Then I'll close the drape and get back to work.

No—wait. *We* can get back to work. Yes, Charley, you and I. Cat and man. Name a more iconic duo than that, I dare you. Meow, you say? Well, I agree.

Charley, we're going to do it. With your help, I will finally be able to crack the secrets behind the cursed code entrapping me in the hellish—

Charley, you stop playing with that red string right now! I have carefully strung it up to connect the dots between my clues and sources. If you play with it you'll destroy months of planning and progress. Leave my link chart alone!

Oh, your fur is so soft. Yes, buddy, sorry, but you cannot play with such important things. Go back on the bed. We can play later—right now, we have work to do. We have an escape plan to hatch.

If you enjoyed this novel, please consider leaving a review at your favorite book retailer's website. It does wonders for the author's ego as well as the novel's search rankings.
Your support is greatly appreciated!

About the Author

Robert Carnevale thanks you for going on this journey with him and hopes this story has encouraged some thought regarding the subjectivity of reality, mental health, and the state of society (we live in one, after all). By reading this novel, you've already learned what matters most about Robert as a person. But to learn more about his literary endeavors, including the future of the Earth series and other upcoming science fiction novels, visit www.rcarnevale.com.

CPSIA information can be obtained
at www.ICGtesting.com
Printed in the USA
LVHW032311070323
741123LV00002B/222

9 781735 491004